LINKS

THE SAVIORS OF SOULS BOOK 1

SHIRLEY O'NEIL

This is a work of fiction. Names, characters, places, and incidents are products of the author's imagination or are used fictitiously and are not to be construed as real. Any resemblance to actual events, locations, organizations, or persons, living or dead, is entirely coincidental.

World Castle Publishing, LLC
Pensacola, Florida
Copyright © Shirley O'Neil 2018
Paperback ISBN: 9781629899534
eBook ISBN: 9781629899541
First Edition World Castle Publishing, LLC, July 23, 2018
http://www.worldcastlepublishing.com

Cover: Karen Fuller
Editor: Maxine Bringenberg

CHAPTER 1

The last time Hayley Johnson had told anyone about her abilities, the psychiatrists diagnosed her as a schizophrenic. But what did they know — or she, for that matter? By the time Hayley turned nine years old, her self-esteem had been shredded by peers as well as her parents, who had convinced her she was mentally ill. Constant tears and frustration had forced her to look for other reasons for the voices in her head. It had taken all of her life, twenty-eight years, to focus her talents and realize she wasn't ill, but gifted. Today, finally, she had told her secrets. Less than an hour ago, Hayley confessed to five strangers that she could see the past, present, future, and the dead.

She took the road into town, returning to Paranormal Search and Analysis after getting the call that she'd been hired. While driving through Sutterville, North Carolina, the town she'd grown up in, Hayley tried to remember the faces of those who had sat around the conference table at her interview. *So many names to remember. Roger Hudson's the acting boss, and Lee Franklin's the second in command. I know I have that right. Who's their third partner? Jim Newton. I didn't meet him yet. And what were those tech specialists' names? Oh yeah — Clint and John. And next to them, Kathy,*

3

the receptionist and researcher. She might be about my age.

Hayley turned the corner a few blocks beyond Main Street. Next to Henry's Hardware stood her new place of employment, formerly—ten years ago—Sam's used-car dealership. Once she turned into the driveway, she parked next to the entrance.

While taking a calming breath, she pulled the keys from the ignition. In front of her the office's burgundy drapes were drawn across the showcase window. *Good. The meeting hasn't started yet.*

As she stepped out of the car, an awareness of being watched triggered her psychic senses. She could see the observers in her mind. Two boys, with skateboards in hand, stood at the far end of the parking lot, staring.

Not detecting trouble, Hayley released the vision and again looked toward the curtained window. *But there's something about Lee.* In that instant, she felt his gravitating energy tug at her. She closed the car door harder than she meant to, annoyed with herself for constantly thinking about him since the interview. *Stop it. This is ridiculous. I don't even know him. Now focus,* she told herself. Reaching up, Hayley secured her purse strap across her shoulder and walked briskly to the office.

Through the glass door, Hayley saw Kathy stepping out from behind the reception desk. She wore a pink blouse matching her lips and fingernails, her platinum blonde hair pulled back into a braid wound into a knot.

They met at the door.

"You got the job. This is so cool! Jim's not here yet, and the guys are in the back room working on evidence from a haunting in Greensboro. How about some coffee?"

"Yes, thanks," Hayley said.

Kathy grabbed her empty mug from her desk and led Hayley to a small cubicle behind a tall, nondescript room divider before the hallway.

"Help yourself. There are muffins, too." Kathy pointed to a round pink container. Paper cups sat nearby. "The sugar's here if you need it." She poured a cup for Hayley and refilled her mug. "I hope you'll like working here. It'll be great having another girl in the office. Sometimes the testosterone gets to be a little much around here."

Only having Gramps and her dad as a reference to male behavior before they passed away, and occasionally when either of them visited after their deaths, Hayley guessed at the meaning of Kathy's comment. "Everyone seems to be really nice." She reached for the sugar, put a couple of teaspoons' worth in her coffee, and stirred it with a swizzle stick. "Anything I should know about anyone in particular, so I don't say or do anything stupid?"

Kathy lowered her voice. "Roger, Lee, and Jim started this business about nine years ago. I do what any of them ask, but Roger's the residing boss."

"What about their personalities?"

"Roger's a freak about first impressions. He wants us to be sharp and act professional when we're on a case. This type of work sometimes gives people the idea we're weird or something, so he's really serious about the way we present ourselves."

Hayley glanced down at her black, short-sleeved blouse and khaki dress pants, then brushed her hair behind her ear, revealing her silver hoop earrings. She stepped back. "Am I dressed okay?"

"You're dressed fine for the office, but if we go on a case, I'd recommend jeans, and don't wear jewelry. Sometimes we need to squeeze into some pretty dirty places, like basements or attics. Jewelry could get snagged. Oh, and don't wear any perfume or fragrant soaps. When we're investigating, we need to be aware of residual scents like cooking odors, cigarette smoke, and even perfume."

"That's good to know." Hayley diverted her gaze, casually stirring her coffee, and asked, "What about Lee? What's he like?"

"He's the quiet type, and never moody. He writes a lot of stories for a magazine."

Is he married? I can't ask her that.

"Lee's really a nice guy. You'll like him."

She's definitely right about that. "And Jim? I haven't met him yet."

"Jim's a character. Most of the time he doesn't think before he speaks. His sense of humor's a little different, so if you think he's insulting you, he's not. I hope you have tough skin. I can't tell you how many times Jim's embarrassed me. If blushing could kill, I'd be dead by now." Kathy chose a blueberry muffin and set it on a small paper plate. "But as much as he likes to joke, he's really serious about this job, and so are Roger and Lee. They've all been interested in the paranormal their whole lives, so this isn't just a hobby to them. This is their real passion."

"That's the way I feel." Hayley picked up her coffee, trying to keep the liquid in the cup, and followed Kathy across the room to the black oval conference table by the front window.

"You'll fit right in," Kathy said. "Have a seat, and I'll tell them you're here."

From where Hayley stood at the end of the table closest to the front door, she watched Kathy approach Roger, who sat at the computer, his back toward her. Hayley set her cup down, pulled out the chair, sat, and placed her purse on the floor. Her hands shook, her body tensed, but this time her stomach fluttered from missing breakfast. She glanced at the hallway, seeing Roger and Lee walking into the room. She calmed herself and smiled.

"You're here, great," Roger said, taking a place at the head of the table, a notepad and pen in front of him. "Jim should be in any minute. He's been setting up a case. I see you have coffee, but can we get you anything else?"

"I'm fine, thanks." Hayley cupped her shaky hands around her coffee cup, feeling its heat, and focused her thoughts on Roger. He seemed possibly ten years older than Lee and taller, or maybe his wavy blond hair gave that impression.

Roger checked his watch.

She diverted her gaze toward Lee, who sat across from her.

He seemed closer to her age, maybe in his early thirties. His slightly mussed, dark brown hair looked styled. He took dark-framed glasses from the pocket of his peach, short-sleeved dress shirt and put them on.

Kathy came into the room followed by the two young men Hayley remembered meeting at the interview. While they took seats at the far end of the table, the sensor at the front door toned.

Looking to her right, Hayley watched a man wearing a stern expression hurry in. He appeared to be in his early fifties, slender, with a few gray hairs in his mustache and a receding hairline. Dressed in jeans and a blue T-shirt, he walked with purpose toward the head of the table.

"Those boys are as annoyin' as a splinter in my beehind," the man said, gesturing toward the parking lot.

Remaining in his seat, Roger nodded. "I'm sure Frank's kids are wondering about our new employee." He glanced around the table. "I don't want anything about Hayley or her abilities to leave this room. Frank would have her name all over the papers." He turned to his partner. "Hayley, this is Jim. Jim, Hayley."

Jim reached out and shook her hand. "Good to finally meet ya, darlin'." He cleared his throat. "One thing 'bout this job… we're in the newspaper a hell of a lot."

Hayley nodded, remembering the reports she'd read about Paranormal Search and Analysis. Strange occurrences had begun during Sutterville's downtown renovation a few years back, when

7

mysteries filled the headlines—mysteries she knew she could solve if she could be one of the investigative team—and now here she sat. "I've probably read everything they've written."

"Ever since the ghost-huntin' programs became popular on TV, Frank's been dog-tailin' us—usin' his kids as spies or bookin' the same flight as us when our case is outta town. He's one hell of a pain."

"Frank Thompson owns the *Sutterville Times,*" Lee said. "We've been in business for nine years now, and no one really noticed us until he started writing about our cases three years ago. Frank's relentless. He stops at nothing to get a story. He got past the last psychic we hired."

"Who?" Hayley asked. "I haven't heard of anyone with my abilities anywhere in this state."

"Nate Armstrong from Greensboro. Said he was," Jim said. "Damn jackass pulled a fast one on us. He was 'bout as psychic as the wart on my big toe. Since then, we go by word of mouth. When people find a psychic that's not fakin' it, seems they can't talk enough 'bout 'em. We'd heard 'bout you from the Hastings livin' on the outskirts of town, and the Millers livin' near Redville, then a couple of more people who hired us. Girl, you could make a fortune off your talents."

Hayley shook her head. "It's not like that. I give messages from loved ones. It's necessary sometimes. I've always kept a low profile, kept things confidential, and never charged." Grams always took care of her and had left her an inheritance. Hayley didn't need the money. It had been hard enough approaching a stranger to tell them she'd talked to their deceased son, daughter, or husband. *How on earth could I have asked them for money?*

"No one mentioned your other abilities—seeing the past, present, and the future," Roger said. "When we read your job application, we nearly fell over."

Hayley chose her words carefully, trying not to go into detail. "I've found from past experiences that life's a lot easier by keeping my abilities to myself."

"Rough childhood?" Jim asked.

"You can't even imagine." Nothing was worse than having a vision of someone's death while she stood in front of the class reading a book report or talking to the teacher. From her reactions as she envisioned some pretty gory details, it looked to those who watched her like she'd lost her mind.

"So, what brings you to us?" Roger asked. "Seems you're stepping out of character — taking money for the use of your abilities and possibly exposing yourself to the press."

"I've spent all this time learning to control my abilities. I'm ready now. This seems like the perfect job. Everything I've read about you has been so exciting."

"We're glad ya decided to join us, darlin'," Jim said. "We'll try to keep your abilities a secret as long as we can, but it seems we're pretty popular. Speakin' of our reputation…. Excuse me, darlin'." He turned to Roger. "Have I got news that'll tickle your gizzard!"

"What's up?"

"Just listen while I explain."

Roger stood and knocked his knuckles on the table. "Can Jim have your — ?"

"I'll do that. Just sit." Jim knocked on the table. "Can I have your attention?"

Roger moved out of Jim's way and sat next to Hayley, setting his notepad on the table in front of him.

"I got a call from a friend I know in Florida, Admiral Wayne," Jim said. "The military's come across a puzzlin' situation and needs our help. Seems a Japanese World War II escort vessel's been found on one of those remote tropical islands south of

Guam. The village people say it's haunted."

Hayley felt the excitement rise in the room. While she thought about the situation, a sense of importance nudged at the back of her mind. She assumed the compulsion to listen closely came from her desire to contribute all she could to her first case — the need to be accepted, wanting to be part of the team.

Roger and Lee exchanged glances.

"Where on the island?" Lee asked.

"Grounded upriver."

"Must be a deep river to carry a big vessel," Lee said.

Jim straightened and met Lee's gaze. "Ya want to talk weights and buoyancy? Do I look like Newton? Who knows how deep that damn river was sixty years ago? The ship mighta gone upstream durin' monsoon season when the water was high. Anyway, the admiral told me it's stuck in silt by the river bank."

Roger jotted a note and looked at Jim. "Why wasn't the ship found before now?"

"It's covered with jungle growth...looks like the landscape. A botanist was pokin' 'round and found it. He cut aside some vegetation and climbed aboard. Instead of findin' Japanese remains, he found American."

Hayley looked around the table, getting comfortable with the proceedings, seeing everyone taking notes except Clint and John.

Roger stopped writing. "American? Doesn't make sense."

"Exactly. That's the mystery. The military wants to investigate before lettin' the Japanese know about the vessel. If we take this case, that'll give the military a way in without bein' directly involved. They don't wanna ruffle any Japanese feathers. If everythin' goes as planned, the Japanese won't even know anyone went on board."

"Why should they care who investigates?" Clint raised his hand after speaking. "The war's over."

"I don't think our government would like it if some other country was investigatin' one of our ships," Jim said. "Who knows how the Japanese would react, thinkin' the ship is the restin' place for their heroes? Respect for the dead would probably be high on their list. Might be a sensitive situation." He turned to Roger. "Larry, the admiral, wanted me to run this by ya, to get your reaction. The military's put a priority on this case 'cause it's typhoon season. I need to give him a call to let him know if we're takin' the case."

"Yes," Roger said. "This is great! But we need more details. Call him back. We'll have to contact our other clients. I need to give them an estimated date in order to reschedule their cases."

A flicker of unease ruffled Hayley's senses at the mention of typhoons. "What's the weather look like?"

"You're no doubt pickin' up on the tropical depression that Guam experienced yesterday. That type of weather is common this time of year. Good perception, darlin'."

Hayley warmed at the compliment, but felt driven to be an asset to the team. She closed her eyes and cleared her mind, trying to use her clairvoyance to foresee what they'd be walking into. She perceived nothing but stillness…no visions or sensing of the future. The worry she had about the weather had vanished. *It's probably nothing.*

When she opened her eyes, she was startled to find Lee studying her from across the table. Her composure shattered, her face heated. *Shoot!* How could he, with just one look, fluster her so profoundly?

"Are you all right?" he asked.

She nodded and glanced around. Apparently, everyone sitting at the table, staring at her, wondered the same thing. "I was trying to get a clue about this case."

Clint and John leaned in, elbows on the table. Kathy

stopped taking notes, her attention focused on Hayley and Lee's discussion.

"Get a clue? How?" Lee asked.

"I get visions," she said, trying to explain clearly. "Kind of like a movie playing in front of me. But it's complicated. The future isn't fixed. Since everyone has free will, what I see isn't always what happens. So far, I'm not seeing anything or getting a knowing about the ship."

"Maybe you're just nervous," Lee said, as if he was putting himself in her place. "First-day-on-the-job jitters, so to speak."

"Could be," she said, knowing nerves had never blocked her abilities before, and doubting that was the reason she couldn't perceive anything about the case. *So why didn't I see this?* Surprises were rare, except when pertaining to herself. *Does this mean that because my future's involved with case investigations, I'm barred from knowing their outcome?* She gathered her stirring senses, closed her eyes, and looked for a hint to what had happened to the Japanese crew, trying to glimpse the past instead of the future. Unsuccessful, she opened her eyes again.

Lee spoke up. "When are we going? Will we need shots?"

Jim twitched his mustache. "Shots? Damned if I know. I'll find out. Should be happenin' within days. Some of ya might find it hard to leave on short notice."

Lee stood. "Possibly a ship full of ghosts, halfway around the world…can't get any better than this." He looked at Hayley. "You can go, can't you?"

His anxious expression heated the pit of her stomach and sent her daydreams of him into a spin. *God, help me.* "No problem with me. I'm in."

"Clint, John, and Kathy, any of you have a problem with leaving right away?" Roger asked.

They shook their heads.

"Well, if anything comes up, let me know," Roger told them.

"That's it. You can have the chair back, Roger," Jim said. He raised his chin. "I smell coffee."

"There are muffins over there, Jim," Kathy said, pointing to the alcove.

A broad smile lit Jim's face. He crossed the room and returned to the table with a couple of muffins and a cup of coffee. "I'll go call him back. I know Larry. He'll be as anxious as a one-eyed cat watchin' two rat holes."

After Jim backed out the door, holding his drink and snack, Roger stepped to the head of the table, grinning at Lee. "Can you believe we've snagged a military case?"

Hayley watched Lee's reaction—the line of his chin, his sensuous lips forming a smile. She felt excitement radiate from every cell of his being. "It's almost too cool to be true," he said.

Roger looked down the table at Clint. "You and John go ahead and take your lunch break, and bring Hayley with you. You might take her to Lucy's."

She noticed his devious smile and raised a brow.

"It's a haunted restaurant, built in the early 1900s," Lee told her.

Yes, I know. I've never been there on purpose. This ought to be interesting.

CHAPTER 2

Sitting in the backseat of Clint's car as he drove by Sutterville's Main Street Park, Hayley looked out the window at the clouds rolling in. The breeze from the coming storm rustled the leaves of the maple trees as a bent old man and an elderly woman strolled through the park with their arms interlocked. Pigeons took to the air from the gazebo in the center of the green. *A gloomy summer day for the living.*

Clint drove the twenty-five-mile-an-hour speed limit down Main Street, now and then looking at her through the rearview mirror. She wished he would stop. His glances made her uncomfortable.

"There're a lot of haunted places in town," Clint told her. "Jim and Lee helped renovate some of the old houses around here. People who don't believe in ghosts were surprised after the renovations started. We received plenty of calls from nonbelievers insisting ghosts don't exist, but asking for our help anyway. Mr. Windly at the hardware store told Jim he was hearing footsteps. He thought it was squirrels." Clint chuckled.

"What did Jim tell him?" Hayley asked.

"He said, 'When ya can hear a squirrel's footsteps, it's time to

14

kiss your nuts good-bye,'" Clint said, imitating Jim's voice.

Hayley laughed. Even if she didn't know Jim well, she could picture his response.

"It's really fun when we can turn a skeptic into a believer," John said. "Good thing we have all the tech equipment to provide proof. You know what they say—seeing is believing."

"I know what you mean." She remembered her mother's face when she had told her that Gramps was sitting at the end of the dinner table. Her mom had nearly choked on her food, chastised Hayley for her cruel humor, and broke into tears. *Neither my mom nor my dad believed.* After their deaths, they returned to tell her they loved her and that they were sorry for treating her so badly, calling her crazy, and sending her to a shrink. *Maybe I'd be skeptical, too, if I didn't have my gifts.*

"Lucy's was built in the early nineteen-hundreds," John told her. "Looks pretty much the same as it did back then. The old-time feel of the place and the good food—not to mention the ghost—bring in lots of customers. We're considered regulars there, but over the years, we've never brought in our equipment to document the haunting."

"Why not?" Hayley asked.

"Everyone knows it's haunted. And the owners are happy about it. So we're not really needed."

Clint pointed toward an old two-story brick building. "There it is."

Windows dressed with green shutters stood out against the building's white façade. A horizontal sign reading Lucy's Restaurant hung above the first-floor window.

Hayley sensed the energy inside, the presence, the spirit waiting patiently. *Maybe for us.*

John turned to her. "Back then, they served mostly drinks with food on the side. The original owner, Dora Appleton, ran it with her son and his wife. When Dora died, they say she didn't want to leave. She's been around ever since."

Clint parked the car in the restaurant's small lot. As they entered Lucy's, they looked around for a place to sit. An old-time maplewood bar with a decorative wall mirror ran along the entire right side of the room. Booths with green-checkered cushions lined the left wall, and dining tables with high-back spindle chairs filled the center area. In the back, to the left, stood a stairway with a smooth maple railing, a newel post displaying a pinecone finial at its foot. Along the back wall, a large kitchen hid behind double doors.

"Let's sit in the corner," Clint said. He pointed to a booth on the far side. "We can see the entire room from there. Maybe you'll spot Dora."

Hayley surveyed the room, looking for a lingering spirit, feeling unseen eyes focused on them from upstairs. She turned to see a woman in her fifties with curly, light brown hair and plump pink cheeks hurrying to their table. Her smile deepened her laugh lines and brightened her eyes as she handed them menus. "Hi, guys! See you brought a friend."

"Hayley," Clint said, "this is Lucy. She and her husband, Dale, own this place. This is Hayley, Lucy. She's one of us now. It's her first day."

Lucy wiped her hands on her apron before reaching out to shake Hayley's hand. "Hi. It's nice to meet you. You've got your hands full working with these two." She winked. "You guys must be half loony. You wouldn't find me chasing ghosts. The one we have spooks the daylights out of me. Sure keeps the customers coming in, though. We've had lots of people tell us they've seen her shadow."

"Hayley can see ghosts. We thought she might see Dora," John told her.

Hayley gasped inside. *So much for keeping a low profile.*

Lucy's eyes widened as she took a step back. "Really? Take a look around, honey. I've seen her a couple of times myself… nearly scared me to death." She moved aside and gazed out around the room. "You're lucky you got here before the lunch crowd. There's only a few tables taken, but in about twenty minutes, this place will be full. Do you see her anywhere?"

Looking past the tables and chairs, Hayley slowly scanned the restaurant. "Not yet." Although she sensed a presence near the kitchen.

"Let me take your orders so you won't be late getting back."

As soon as Lucy stepped away, Hayley leaned across the table and asked in a lower voice, "How could you just blurt that out? Weren't we told to keep my abilities quiet?"

"There's nothing to worry about," Clint said. "Lucy and Dale are good people. They won't talk behind your back."

"I hope you're right," she said. She searched the room again for the lingerings.

The dining room seemed hushed. A couple at a table whispered to each other, glancing their way. The laughs at the bar were low and muffled. A man with a scruffy beard peered over his shoulder at them. A shiver went up her spine. *They can't be looking at me. Am I just being paranoid?*

"People act like this all the time," John said. "We're celebrities."

He seemed to be reading her thoughts. "Do you hate it?"

"No. It goes with the job," Clint said.

Up until she died, her grandmother had cooked the meals, and Hayley had preferred it that way, so she didn't have to eat in restaurants. *I appeared mental trying to look normal in public while avoiding annoying spirits. Going to school was bad enough.* She hadn't wanted the rest of the town pointing at her.

17

She watched Lucy disappear through the kitchen's swinging double doors. Seconds later, they swung open again, and the plump woman hurried off toward the bar. Walking around the counter, she nudged a man washing glasses. While wiping his hands on a bar towel, he nodded.

"That's Dale. They're talking about us," John said.

Clint looked toward the bar. "Might be." He turned to Hayley. "So, besides seeing the dead, you can see the future, too?"

She nodded, wondering where this was leading.

"If you can see the future, can't you play the stock market?" Clint asked. "Why do you need to work? You should be rich."

"It doesn't work like that. There's a devine code that doesn't let me see my own future or profit from playing the stock market. I have to go through the good and the bad in life just like you."

"That doesn't seem fair," John said.

"No one like me knows the big picture," she said. "Psychics have to work for their money giving readings, writing books, holding seminars, or doing reality shows. If they want to find out about their own future, they have to go to another psychic."

"If it's not for yourself, can you see anything in the future?" John whispered to her.

"Depends," she answered, suspicious.

"Could you tell me who's going to win the game tonight so I can win our bet? It wouldn't be for yourself, so you wouldn't be breaking the rules," John said.

"That would be cheating, John," she told him.

"So?"

He seems to be intuitive, so why's he worried about winning? In her mind's eye, she glimpsed their past bets and sensed a profound importance attached to them. Their gambling was definitely a life-link...a chain of events leading to a major occurrence. For some reason she couldn't see the outcome, but sensed that whatever was going to happen would be critical.

"Things happen for a reason." Her guide Elaina's words were drilled into her. "Just know that everything has purpose," she'd told Hayley many times, "and purpose is not yours to know." She was always there with wisdoms and to protect her from danger.

John waited for her answer.

"So, I don't help people cheat," she said, not wanting to explain life-links. The fewer people who knew about links meant the fewer who would try to manipulate events. She knew things had to happen naturally, or a person's purpose could be jeopardized. Hayley glanced at the bar. "And I don't usually tell people about my abilities."

"Why not?" Clint asked.

"I don't like being judged."

"Who cares what other people think?" Clint said. "Sometimes you have to be brave to be yourself."

She raised a brow. He was right. She'd heard Grams telling her the same thing over and over. "You know, you're pretty smart for someone so young."

His mouth flew open. "Young!"

John snickered. "Guess she told you."

She felt her face flush. "I didn't mean it as an insult. I just meant you're smart."

"Oh, don't worry about it. He's used to getting picked on," John said. "His dad always kids him because he's the only one in his family with red hair and freckles."

Clint glowered. "Thanks a lot, jerk!"

Hayley studied Clint, then closed her eyes to glimpse the past. "Your grandmother on your father's side, Isabelle," she said.

"What?" Clint asked.

"Your dad's mom passed the gene to you."

"But he had brown hair," he told her.

"Brown hair with red highlights. If you trace his side of the family back a few generations, you'll find redheads."

"Wow! You are freaky," Clint said.

She grinned. "Told you."

Clint raised his chin. "Well, anyhow, Roger, Lee, and Jim wouldn't have hired you if they thought you were a nut case. Didn't you see Roger's face at the meeting? He's excited you've joined our team."

"I haven't seen him this way since we built his computer system and taught him how to use all the tech equipment," John said.

That struck her wrong. "So he thinks I'm his new gadget?"

Clint's expression turned serious. "Get real! Roger is the most sincere guy you'll ever meet. And not one of us on this team thinks you're weird."

"Except us," John said, flashing a grin.

She sensed their sincerity. She realized if she judged Roger without knowing him, she'd be judging him the same way she thought others judged her, like the church ladies who gathered for prayer meetings next door to Grams. *Once they heard I had visions, they called me a sinner.*

Glancing toward the bar, she saw Lucy hurrying back to their booth with two framed pictures, her eyes flashing with excitement. When she reached their table, Lucy's voice had risen a couple of octaves. "Dale said Dora's been around. She scared off a customer about forty minutes ago." She handed Clint the pictures. "I took these down from the wall near the bar. They're photos of Dora and her family."

Hayley saw a young woman by the kitchen where she'd sensed a presence earlier. Clearly it wasn't Dora, a much older woman. She nodded. "Yes, I see her. She's by the bar. Do you know you have two lingering spirits?"

Lucy paled and glanced around the room. "No. Are you kidding?"

"There's also a younger woman back by the kitchen. Same period clothing—a floor-length skirt, long-sleeved blouse buttoned at the neck, and her hair is pinned up in curls."

Clint handed the picture to Hayley.

"This is the other spirit," she said, pointing to the photo.

"That's Rose, Dora's daughter-in-law," Lucy said. "She was about twenty-five when she died. Story is—"

Hayley raised her hand. "Wait. Let me see if I can get an impression of what happened to her. If I'm right, let me know." Closing her eyes, she prayed for protection and mentally surrounded herself with white light to shield herself from imposing emotions. She cleared her mind, allowing her acute perception to sense the past energy in the atmosphere around her. She viewed the past as if watching a movie in her mind. A young pretty lady walked along the balcony overlooking the main floor of the restaurant.

"I see Rose walking toward the stairs. A man, who looks a few years older than she, is storming out of the door behind her. He's got a beard, a mustache, and disheveled long sandy-colored hair. It's her husband. He's reaching out, grabbing her shoulder, stopping her on the top landing. They're arguing because she's pregnant. She's crying. He's grabbing her by the hair." Hayley gasped. "He pushes her down the stairs. Rose is lying on the floor, dead." When the vision ended, Hayley took a deep breath, shaking off the negativity she felt from the husband and the disgust she had for him. Then she opened her eyes and looked up at Lucy.

"You can see all that?" Clint said. "Cool."

"You're as right as rain, dear. They say Dora's son reported he had found her that horrible morning at the foot of the stairs and called for help, but it was too late. She was already dead." Lucy waved, calling her husband to join them, and lowered her voice to a whisper. "They called it an accident until they found out she was expecting a baby. Then it looked more like foul play. Everyone knew Thomas Appleton hated kids." Lucy shook her head and shrugged. "But they didn't have proof."

Hayley shivered, hoping he wasn't a lingering spirit. *He can't be here. Lucy and Dale would definitely know if he were.*

Dale finished waiting on an old man sitting near the door and rushed over.

"Did she see her?" he asked.

"We have two. Dora and Rose," Lucy told him. "And she had a vision, Dale—a vision of how Rose was killed."

"Well, I'll be."

"How exciting," Lucy said. She searched the room.

"Where are they?" Dale asked. "Can you point to them? Maybe if I know where they are, I can see them."

"Dora's over there by the bar," Hayley said, pointing. "And Rose is standing near the kitchen by that table at the end."

Clint and John rose from their seats to look over the back of the booth. Dale and Lucy squinted, staring out into the dimly lit room.

"Can't see them," Dale said.

The others concurred.

"I'll go get your orders," Lucy told them. "I know you have to get back."

Dale looked over his shoulder at the front door when a few customers walked in. Three of the people sitting at the bar turned to locate him. "Oh, shoot! Better get back to the bar. Enjoy your meal."

Hayley nodded. "Nice meeting you."

Watching Lucy move past the tables close to the kitchen, Hayley saw her stop before reaching the double doors, Rose standing next to her.

"Rose, are you there?" Lucy asked. She shook her head and hurried through the kitchen doors.

While John surveyed the room, hunting for signs of the ghosts, he asked Hayley, "Why can you see them sometimes and not others?"

She thought for a moment, finding a way to explain. "It has to do with a dimensional veil. It's like there's a separation between them and us. Picture it as a divider with several layers. It takes energy for them to move forward through a layer, so they have to pull energy from wherever they can. That's why it gets cold around them. They're pulling the energy from the air. The more layers they step through, the easier it is for me to see them. You can see them, too. They just have to step through more layers."

Hayley jumped when Lucy set their three orders of hamburgers and fries on the table. Coming toward them from the bar, Dale carried three glasses of cola. He set them on their table, then rushed away when another customer entered.

Lucy stood by Clint, gazing at the far end of the bar. "Do they look like their pictures? Are they transparent? What are they doing?"

Hayley took a drink to wash down her food. It surprised her how comfortable she felt, maybe for the first time in her life, telling the team and someone other than Grams what her gifts allowed her to see. She smiled at Lucy. "They appear exactly like their pictures, only slightly transparent." She spotted them across the room. "Rose is looking at Dora, who's staring at us."

Lucy strained to see.

Noticing Rose's unsettled face, Hayley sensed trouble. "I think it upset Rose when you said her name on your way to the kitchen. She doesn't seem too pleased about it."

"Why would that bother her?" Clint mumbled with his mouth full.

Hayley picked up a fry and dipped it into the ketchup on her plate. "I don't know."

"Well, back to work," Lucy said after another group of customers arrived. She left their bill on the table. "Give me a wave, you guys, if you need anything."

Seeing that John and Clint had eaten their meals, Hayley hurried to finish.

"This would be a great place to give you hands-on training," Clint said. "Maybe we can talk Roger into it. It would be your last chance before we go on that military case."

Unable to speak with a mouthful of fries, Hayley nodded.

Reaching across the table, John picked up the check. "My turn to buy." He pulled out his wallet.

"How much do I owe?" Hayley asked.

"Nothing. I've got it." He laid cash on the table.

"Thanks," she said, and looked at Clint. "Training? In what way?"

"Since no one but you can see and hear ghosts," Clint said, "you'll need further evidence to support your encounters—something visual or audio to show the military. So we'll be teaching you how to use our equipment. They're easy to use. But if you need help, we always work in pairs while investigating, so someone will always be close by."

Hayley moved her empty plate away. "I hope he goes for it. It sounds fun."

Clint looked at his watch. "I guess we better get back." He wiped his mouth with a napkin and slid out of the booth.

Stepping aside, John allowed Hayley to follow Clint.

Halfway to the door, she saw Dora appear at the end of

the aisle, giving Clint an intense glare. Hayley grabbed Clint's shoulder, pulling him back. "Stop! Wait."

"What?" He froze, reached out in front of him, and yanked his hand back. "It's cold. Is it Dora?"

"Yes." Hayley stepped in front of him. She felt the air around her get colder and sensed an attack. "Dora, stop!"

Dora flinched, her eyes widened, and her open mouth closed. With pursed lips, she glared at Hayley. She turned, took a step, and disappeared. One by one, pictures on the wall crashed to the floor. The lights in the restaurant flashed on and off.

"Way to go, Hayley," Clint said gruffly. "You made her mad."

"She was going to attack you."

"Attack? Wow."

"I surprised her. She didn't realize I could see her." Hayley led the way toward the exit, not waiting for anything more to happen.

Lucy and Dale stood at the end of the bar talking to a wide-eyed customer. The lights continued to flicker.

Embarrassment and regret flooded Hayley, feeling she'd caused all the damage. She hesitated before leaving. "It's my fault. I'm sorry," she told them.

Lucy gave her a reassuring smile. "It's all right, honey. This kind of thing happens now and then. There's not much we haven't seen."

Glasses behind the bar hit the floor and shattered. Customers sprang from their seats, spreading out into the center of the room among the tables and chairs. Hayley flinched at the sound of breaking glass. Dale and Lucy ran back to their customers and tried to encourage them to stay.

They'll probably ban me from the restaurant.

"Come on, let's get out of here," John said, standing aside to let Hayley go first.

Once she stepped out the door, she heard Clint gasp and scream behind her. She moved aside just as he flew out the door, sailing into John. Both tumbled to the ground.

Hayley stared, mouth open, after the door slammed, rattling the glass in the front window. Her body shook as adrenaline rushed through her. The lingering spirits were exhilarating, unlike the mild-mannered spirits she normally encountered, who only wanted her help to give messages to their families.

"Are you guys all right?" she asked.

John got up, rubbing his elbow.

Hayley offered Clint her hand. "Wow, she's angry."

Clint, with her assistance, stood and brushed himself off. "Yeah! Damn, that was wicked cool! She sure would make a good bouncer." He looked over at the car. "Let's go! I can't wait to tell Roger about this."

In minutes, they were in the car and halfway to the office.

Hayley sat in the back. She brushed her hair behind her ear and caught Clint's glance in the rearview mirror. "I hope he doesn't get too upset about what just happened," she said.

"Don't worry about Roger," Clint said. "I'll tell him you saved my life."

He slowed down as he turned into the parking lot, then parked. They climbed out of the car quickly, hurrying to report their encounter.

* * *

Roger called a meeting after lunch. He stood at the head of the table and cleared his throat. "Tonight we'll be taking a little trip over to Lucy's restaurant. She said they'll be closing early, but even so we're looking at a long day." He scanned the team. "If I let you go home now, can everyone be here around eight o'clock?" There were no objections. "Okay, but be back on time so we can train Hayley."

Lee leaned toward her. "You've sure had a thrilling day so far. I hope we have as much excitement tonight."

Her heart pounded. *Is it because he's so close or because I'm going back to Lucy's?* "I hope so, too! I guess we'll see."

CHAPTER 3

Hayley opened the front gate to her home, gazing lovingly at the old Victorian with its pale green siding, cream and eggplant trim, and gingerbread details. The turret, capped with a coned roof, had four bow windows looking out over her rose garden. She took a deep breath, smelling a floral scent sweeping over her yard.

Small, lacy sweet Williams covered the ground around the foot of the old apple tree. Along the picket fence on both sides of the yard were hollyhocks, white daisies, Virginia bluebells, foxglove, and other flowers whose names she didn't know.

She walked toward the front door and stepped up to the wraparound porch, where a planter of pink geraniums hung on the railing. From her purse she removed her house key and let herself in. To her, it felt like a hug to come home.

After climbing the staircase, she headed to her bedroom to change clothes. When she reached the door she turned on the bedroom light. An old water oak grew outside her window, blocking the light entering through the sash window.

A breeze rustled the lace curtains. She slipped off her Mary Janes, walked across the cool hardwood floor, and stood at the open window looking out at the backyard. She pictured herself on a tire swing hanging from the sturdy oak, and playing horseshoes in the sandy trench across the grass near the birch trees. It had been like this since she was little, seeing herself growing up here, even though she never did. She and her parents had lived down the street. When her grandmother died, Hayley took her inheritance and bought this house, finally making it her own and filling it with Grams's furniture.

Grams…the only person in the world I can tell my secrets to. And the only one who really knows me.

A familiar squeak came from the rocking chair behind her. Smiling, she turned, noticing her clothes she'd draped across the chair were now folded neatly on the end of her bed.

Her grandmother, eighty-two when she passed on, had materialized and sat in the rocker next to the fireplace. In spirit form, Grams appeared no older than thirty—a phenomenon Hayley always had to adjust to. Today she wore a short-sleeved dress with a daisy print, and her curled blonde hair fell softly on her shoulders. "You're back early," Grams said.

"Yes, but I have to return later for some on-the-job training."

"Oh, sounds fun."

Hayley sat on her bed, thinking. *I wasn't as nervous this time. But this thing with Lee…I felt like I was in high school.* She glanced at Grams. "Have any wisdoms you'd like to share with me?"

"For instance?"

"Like how to block these inappropriate feelings I'm having for one of my bosses."

"Sorry. You know the rules, dear. I can't divulge your future. You have to go through the same romantic trials and tribulations every other woman experiences."

Hayley looked down, kneading her hands in her lap. "Shoot, I knew it. Trials and tribulations. I'm going to cross the line and get fired, aren't I?"

"It was only a figure of speech, dear. Not a clue," Grams told her. "You won't be getting anything out of me, so don't even try."

"But—"

Grams held up her index finger. "Just do what you've always done and follow your intuition. If things work out the way you want, that's good. And if they don't, that's good too, because whatever is supposed to happen will." Grams stood. "I have to go now, so have fun tonight." She walked toward the door, her image fading with each step until she disappeared.

"But, Grams, what about the case?" Hayley asked. "Why can't I foresee what we'll be walking into? Was I right about the weather, or was that uneasiness a warning?"

No reply.

She shook her head. "I'm talking to myself."

The room was silent, except for the rustling of curtains. She walked to the window and closed it, mumbling, "It's always the same advice. 'Things happen for a reason' and 'Follow your intuition.'" She strolled to the end of the bed and started to unbutton her blouse. "I'm not following my intuition. I'm following my hormones."

She took off her blouse and tossed it on the rocker, then unzipped her pants. "A thousand things could go wrong. I don't know anything about romance. I've never dated or kissed a man." She took her pants off and tossed them onto the chair as well. "I'll just block all thoughts of him. I've blocked a lot worse...death, pain, and sadness. How hard can this be?"

Hayley grabbed her blue jeans and yellow T-shirt from the pile of folded clothing on the bed, pulled them on, and took her sneakers out of the closet. While she sat on her bed putting on her shoes, she checked her watch. She had hours before she needed to go back to the office.

The excitement of returning to Lucy's and showing the others her talents churned through Hayley's stomach. One moment she felt like giggling, and the next like throwing up. She stood in front of the mirror to remove her silver hoop earrings and her watch. No jewelry, she remembered, laying them on the dresser.

Glancing up, she stared at her reflection. A week ago she'd trimmed her light brown hair and cut her bangs to just above her brows, keeping them out of her face. She realized that wearing her hair long had become a habit she'd had since her high school years. Back then, she'd gone to extremes hiding behind long hair with bangs that swooped in front of her eyes, helping her to shun eye contact. Afraid of leading an admirer on, she'd felt guilty returning a smile. It would give an admirer the wrong idea, just as her outward appearance gave him the impression she was normal. As much as she wanted a boyfriend, she believed it was better just to walk away before she scared him off.

But Lee was unlike anyone she'd met before. He knocked her resolve right off its foundation. It was unsettling. She glared at her refection. *Stop it! Stop thinking about him!* Clenching her fist, determined to block every thought of Lee, she turned and left the room.

The old wood floor groaned as she headed for the staircase. Her hand slid along its smooth maple railing when she remembered too late to avoid the fifth step. The step's tread bowed from the weight of her slender body. Its loud creaking made her cringe. *I have to get that fixed.*

The late afternoon fled during housework and a couple of loads of laundry. By the time she looked at the clock again, the sun had begun to set.

Hayley grabbed her purse and headed out the door.

While she drove through town, she saw some of the shops on Main Street had closed for the evening. The old lampposts shone dimly in the last rays of daylight. Soon the streets would be empty and Sutterville would look like a ghost town, which, Hayley knew, it basically was. It brought back memories.

She couldn't count how many times she'd been downtown while growing up, but there wasn't once that she hadn't seen a lingering spirit. Some had been solid and harder to distinguish from the living, while others varied in translucency. The lingerers who knew they were dead were the worst to encounter. When she'd enter a store, they would approach her and blind her with visions of their deaths. Twice she was nearly possessed. Thank God, Elaina had stepped in to protect her. That's when she realized she could trust her.

All of her childhood she'd seen Elaina standing nearby—in the park, on the street, in her bedroom. But the dead scared her as a child, although Elaina never approached. *She waited until I wasn't afraid of her any longer.* "I know you're still watching over me. I sense your presence, even though I can't see you. You're not fooling me. I know you're just standing back and letting Grams think she took over for you."

Hayley turned the corner and pulled into the office lot. *It's funny. It's not the dead I'm worried about anymore; it's the living.* She parked and climbed out of her car.

CHAPTER 4

Hayley found the team ready to go. She rode to Lucy's in one company van with Roger, Lee, and Jim. Kathy, Clint, and John went in the second van.

At the restaurant, while the other paranormal investigators waited in their vehicle, Hayley got out of the van with Roger, Lee, and Jim.

Jim hesitated. "Go ahead and go inside. I'll catch up with ya shortly."

She followed Roger and Lee to the entrance. While she looked through the diner's window, green curtains drawn to the side, she thought about Dora's madness and the frenzy of bar glasses shattering just hours ago. She tried to sense the spirit's presence. Things seemed calm, with no signs of paranormal activity.

Dale unlocked the door to let them in.

Lucy took off her apron and hurried over. "Come in, come in," she said. "We were just talking about you."

"Have a seat at the bar," Dale offered.

"Has there been any more trouble since lunch?" Roger asked, taking Dale's suggestion.

Hayley sat next to him, while Lee took the seat beside her.

Dale followed Lucy behind the bar. He walked to the far end, brought back a stool, and set it by her, but she seemed too excited to sit.

"After the door slammed on their way out, the place went quiet," Lucy said. "Not a peep." She looked at Hayley. "It must be exciting to be able to see ghosts."

"How come you can see Dora and Rose and we can't?" Dale asked.

Hayley took a deep breath, knowing she had to get over this fear of telling others about her abilities. But she'd built a wall around herself for too many years, and faked being normal. Grams was right. She needed to stop worrying about what people thought of her. If she wanted to keep this job, she had to be honest and tell them everything.

"As far as I know, everyone has a spirit guide. That's a spirit whose job is to watch over each of us and help us through our lives. I've been told by my guide Elaina that my mind is the same as anyone's, but, like a radio, I'm tuned to a vibrating frequency. Most people call it intuition."

"Intuition? So, everyone can tap into that frequency?" Dale asked.

"Yes. It's like singing…everyone can do it, but some are more talented than others, and some don't try."

"Can you see your spirit guide? Is she here now?" Lucy asked.

"I used to see her, but since my grandmother died, Elaina stands back and lets Grams help me. I guess Grams is in training." Hayley smiled. "And I only see her when I need help."

"Kind of unsettling to know someone's always watching you," Dale said. He glanced around. "See Dora and Rose anywhere?"

Hayley scanned the room. "Not yet."

"From what Hayley's told us," Roger said, "you're experiencing an intelligent haunting."

"There's more than one kind?" Dale asked.

"There are four," Lee said. "Intelligent is when the ghosts respond to your actions or questions. Residual is when the haunting is leftover energy, a memory so to speak, that plays over and over. In that case, there'll be no communication between us and the ghosts. But we can capture their conversation on our voice recorders. Then there's poltergeist. It's an intelligent haunting where the ghost interacts with objects, moving them, opening cabinets, moving furniture, being a nuisance basically. And the fourth is demonic, and we all know what that is."

"So, do you see this stuff happening around you all the time?" Dale asked Hayley. "It would totally freak me out."

"It did scare me as a child because I didn't have any control. You'd be surprised how many spirits are around us all the time. Since they knew I was able to see them, I was bombarded with visitations, not to mention the constant visions I'd have of their deaths. It's taken me years to learn how to control all of it." As a little girl, she'd huddled in the corner of her bedroom at night when spirits came to her. To hide from them, she threw pillows and bedcovers over her head and covered her ears with her hands to shut out their voices. "Now I'm able to turn my gifts on and off when I feel like it."

Wide-eyed, Lucy raised her hand to her cheek. "Visitations? Sounds scary. I'd be a nut case."

"They were mainly from spirits returning to see their families and needing my help. Not the scary stuff you see in movies." She looked at Roger. "I guess you guys work more with the lingering spirits, or ghosts as you prefer to call them. That's a little different from what I've been used to."

"What's the difference?" he asked.

"When people cross over, they retain their personalities, but their burdens and negativity are left behind. They're able to tap into a universal knowledge. But since the lingerings only know what they've learned in their previous life, they're unenlightened and left with their good and bad traits. For instance, a lingering man who used to beat his wife would still be a violent person."

"Do you think that's what we'll find here?" Lee asked. "Is Rose's husband haunting this place, too?"

"Not that I know of, although I haven't been anywhere but in this room."

Roger turned and surveyed the room. "Do you see Dora or Rose yet?"

Hayley looked toward the back of the restaurant. "I think I see something moving by the kitchen," she said in a low voice. The sound of the front door opening startled her. She turned to see Jim walking their way.

"Jim, tell the others to bring in the equipment," Roger whispered.

Jim leaned in. "Why's everyone whisperin'? Tryin' not to spook the spooks?"

Roger chuckled. "Seems like a good idea. Nothing's worse than an angry apparition."

Jim studied Hayley. "Whatcha plannin' to do to piss 'em off?"

"I'm planning to ask Dora why she's so mad."

"Well, hell, that oughta do it. The last time I asked a woman why she was so mad, I had to duck. She missed me with a meat cleaver by an inch," Jim said.

"Sure you don't want to stay?" Roger asked, sarcasm in his voice.

"No. That monitor in the van will give me a front-row seat. I'll be able to see things as they're happenin'. Anyway, I don't want to be 'round when things start flyin'. Better you than me."

* * *

While the others set up the equipment in the restaurant, Hayley stood outside by the front window. She gazed at the full moon as it peeked in and out from behind the billowing clouds. As a warm breeze lifted the edges of her hair, the same uneasiness about the weather she'd sensed at the meeting nudged her consciousness. *Am I sensing something or not? Why can't I be sure?*

"Think we'll get rain?" Lee asked, walking up behind her.

She kept her focus on the sky, trying to keep her mind on the threat of a storm and off Lee's handsome face, biceps, and his…. "I wish it would rain; it's been too long."

"Actually, it's nights like this when the air is electrically charged that there's a lot of paranormal activity. They're able to draw as much energy as they need to materialize. Look who I'm telling. You probably know all that." Lee looked at the sky. "But you're right…we sure could use some rain."

He leaned on the porch railing, inches from her. The heat rose in her cheeks, and she felt self-conscious.

"You said you weren't seeing or getting a knowing about the ship at the meeting this morning," Lee said. "What's a 'knowing'? Where does that come from?"

She lowered her head, realizing most people found intangible concepts hard to believe and hoping he wasn't one of them. "When I was young and things were scary and confusing, my guide wanted to help, but I tried to ignore everything, including her. I just wanted to be like everyone else." She lifted her chin. Her reminiscing gaze met Lee's warm eyes. Hayley took a deep breath and went on. "Finally, I decided I had to start asking questions. So Elaina helped me figure things out. From what she told me, there's a phenomenon called Akashic. It's a divine universal library. It's not written knowledge, but more of a knowing. Somehow, I'm able to tap into it."

"How knowing?" Lee asked.

"It's all knowing. There are no limits. It encompasses time, space, and spirit. Everything."

She expected the usual comments — You're crazy. That's hard to believe. You're as weird as they come — but he said nothing.

"Is it hard for you to tell the living from the dead?" he asked. "Do you see them that clearly?"

"I guess if they're far away I might be fooled. But usually it's pretty easy to tell the difference. The deads' spirits vibrate on a different frequency. I'm sensitive to their vibration. Plus, they suck the energy out of the air in order to materialize, so it's always cold."

Jim wandered around the corner from the parking lot. He stood beside them, glancing up at the passing clouds. "It's been so dry, the trees are bribin' the dogs," he said. "Well, we're all wired up. There're IR cameras everywhere, even in the kitchen." He turned to Hayley. "Ya know what an IR camera is, don't ya, darlin'? It's one of those cameras that sees in the dark. We're 'bout ready to turn the lights out."

"Why do we work in the dark?" Hayley asked.

"Our EMF detectors and our other devices can't detect the difference between an energy form and electronic equipment," Lee explained. "In order to pinpoint the ghost, we have to shut down the power coming from other sources."

Lee reached around her with a guiding gesture, his hand brushing the small of her back, making her pulse quicken. She held her chin up and looked straight ahead, hoping he wouldn't notice his effect on her.

"Let's go in and see what Roger has planned," he suggested.

Jim stepped across the electrical wires trailing over the threshold and running to the van. Reaching over, he held the restaurant's door open to let them go in. "Watch your step. I'm goin' out to the van. I'll see ya guys later."

When Hayley followed Lee inside, she looked around for the resident lingering spirits Dora and Rose, but found no sign of either.

In the corner booth by the front window, Dale and Lucy sat facing the center of the room, watching the team set up. A large coffee pot rested on their table, as if they expected a long evening.

By the doorway in front of Hayley and Lee, Roger leaned over a table covered with equipment. He glanced up at them.

"We're ready to turn the lights out." He gathered the team. "Okay, Clint and John, I want you guys over by the bar — take a digital camera and an EMF detector." Roger held the meter out to Hayley. "EMF means electromagnetic field. You'll learn about that later. Lee, take Hayley to the kitchen. Give her a voice recorder. After she's comfortable with that, show her how to use something else."

Lee picked up the EVP recorder and passed it to Hayley. "You just have to push this button down and keep the recorder running until the investigation is over. It's a simple voice recorder, but it'll pick up spirit voices and noises we don't hear with the normal ear." When he straightened, a blush touched his cheeks. He hurried to add, "You're extra-normal and don't need the recorder at all."

He's about to find out how extra-normal I am.

Roger cleared his throat. "Investigate everything to make sure there's not an explanation for a cold spot or anything else that seems out of the ordinary," he told Hayley. "Your number one lesson is, 'Don't jump to conclusions.' We want to know for sure that it's not an anomaly." He pointed out the infrared cameras taped above the front door. "Each section of the restaurant has an IR camera, and Jim's out in the van watching on the monitor. We investigate in pairs, so one person can take pictures while the other takes a reading. Try to get Dora and Rose to talk to you. Ask questions and wait for an answer."

Hayley nodded.

Roger turned toward Kathy. "We'll take the front. Okay, guys, turn out the lights."

Lee lit the way with his flashlight, leading Hayley past the bar and along the back wall to the kitchen's double doors. "Do you see anything?" he asked, searching the darkness with his flashlight.

"Not yet. Wait! Did you see that?" She pointed to the swinging doors.

He followed her gesture. "No. What?"

"That door opened a couple of inches, then closed."

Lee cracked the door. Frosty air washed across their faces. He hesitated, peeking inside, and whispered, "I wonder if Dora's in there waiting for us." He shined the light into what little he could see of the kitchen. "Why do you think she's so angry at you?" He moved so she could see inside.

"I thought about that. It must be because I can see her," she whispered.

"I wonder why that would upset her?"

"Guess we're about to find out." Hayley scooted out of his way and let Lee go in first. Shivering from the cold, she snuck into the kitchen behind him.

Lee shone the light into every alcove. "Can you see anyone? Are they both here?"

"Maybe it would be a good idea to describe what we see so we can compare the differences." She held the EVP out to catch his description.

"Okay," Lee said, looking across the kitchen. "I see a misty vapor in the corner. What do you think it is?"

"It's Dora. I see her as a full-bodied apparition. She has her hand on her hip, and she's glaring at us."

"Try talking to her."

Hayley held the voice recorder out in front of her, and Lee flashed the light in the spirit's direction. She kept her voice pleasant, trying not to sound threatening. "Dora, why are you mad?"

Above the counter a hanging pot rack swayed, causing the pots and pans to bang together…ready, Hayley feared, to fly off their hooks.

She and Lee backed away, moving to the far end of the kitchen, and stood behind the stainless steel island. From a small window overlooking the alley, a faint light from the moon, peeking through the clouds, penetrated the darkness.

"Duck!" he shouted.

Something flew toward her, and she threw up her arms to protect her face. Lee's hands clenched her waist, pulling her down. She cringed as a large pot flew past. It crashed against the wall, missing the infrared camera taped to the top shelf by inches. Her heart pounded. Clamping her eyes shut, she nuzzled her head against Lee.

Determined to catch the voice of the irate spirit, she rose slightly and held the recorder above the countertop.

"Get out!" Dora screamed.

Hayley darted back down, her body shaking. *This is so cool.* "Did you hear her?" she whispered.

"No," he answered in a low voice. "You're doing good, Hayley. Maybe we'll be able to hear her later when we play back the EVP."

Slowly, they rose to peek. Lee shone the light into the corner about fifteen feet from them.

"I don't see her anymore," Hayley said. "All I see is a mist where she stood."

41

"I see it, too."

Hayley glanced up at the window. The clouds drifted away from the moon, and its light streamed into the kitchen.

On the far end of the island, the vapor drifted toward a long butcher's block counter to the left of the sink. From the cabinet below, Hayley heard drawers fly open, the clattering sound of silverware, and kitchen utensils hitting the floor.

Lee flashed his light toward the noise. He grabbed Hayley again. "Get down!"

They ducked just in time. A wooden rolling pin hit the stainless steel sink behind them.

Trying to find a comfortable crouching position, Hayley lost her balance. Lee's arms went around her, stopping her fall. She looked down at his protective grip, wishing he wouldn't release her, fearing this would be the only way she would ever have his arms around her.

He didn't let go. His strong arms held her tight. At the sound of metal hitting the cabinet behind them, she leaned into him again.

The moment Lee began to speak, an object bounced off the wall, landing next to him. He pointed the flashlight at his foot. "Damn! Look at the size of that knife!"

The hair on her arms stood on end. *This is more than I expected.*

The room grew silent.

"Is it over?" Hayley asked, not wanting to leave Lee's side. In the moonlight, his expression looked warm, caring, and concerned. It melted her heart.

Lee stood, flashing the light into the corner and nearly fell backward, dodging a pan coming toward his head. Once he dove back down, his arm went around Hayley's waist. Her arm wrapped around his back.

"Guess not. Thank God for the moonlight," he said, concern

in his voice. "Looks like she's trying to kill us."

"I think she's just about depleted her energy," Hayley said. "She can't keep this up for long."

Quiet filled the chilly room. They huddled, waiting for Dora's next move. Hayley's heart pounded in her ears, her cheek just inches from Lee's. With his arms around her, she was sure he could feel the adrenaline rushing through her veins.

She turned toward him, her breath in his ear. "Do you hear that?"

"What?"

"I think it's my heart."

He cleared his throat. "Are you sure? I thought it was mine."

The double doors swung open, and they watched the mist rush out. The room warmed. The metal pot rack creaked as it slowed its sway. Only two pans remained hanging.

They stood.

He flashed the light around the room. "Come on." Grabbing her hand, he led her through the darkness to the door where Dora had exited to the dining room.

CHAPTER 5

Lee cracked open the swinging doors and peeked into the main room. Hayley waited behind him in the dark. With her hand still in his, he led her out of the kitchen into the dining room. Outside the double doors, they stood with their backs against the wall and stared into the unlit room.

"My eyes have adjusted," she told him.

"Mine have, too." Lee let go of her hand but stayed close, looking ready to defend.

Through the dimness, she scanned the area for signs of anything unusual. "I see Clint and John by the bar, and Kathy and Roger by the front window, but I don't see Dora anywhere," she said softly. "I think she's gone."

"Now's a good time to get out of here. I'll tell Roger to call off the investigation before someone gets hurt."

"Please don't. We'll be leaving for our military case within days. This is my last chance to learn how to use the tech equipment. I can't be part of the team if I use only my abilities. What I see or feel is just personal experience."

The same protective look he'd worn in the kitchen crossed his face. "But it's too dangerous."

44

"I can't feel her presence, Lee. Dora threw her little tantrum, and now she's gone. The military wants hard evidence, so I need this training."

He looked around the room, then whispered, "Okay, she's gone. I'll take your word for it. You hold on to the EVP, and I'll go up front to get a camera. I'm taking the flashlight. Will you be all right in the dark?"

"Go ahead. I'll be fine."

"I'll be right back."

While she rubbed her cold arms, Hayley kept close to the wall, watching his flashlight beam lead his way between the tables and chairs. She heard voices in the front of the room.

In the stillness, Hayley could see Lee standing by the front table unzipping a bag.

Her breath fogged.

He shone his light into the bag and pulled out the camera while he talked to Roger. They stepped outside, maybe to discuss the attack in the kitchen. She shivered and noticed the growing cold around her.

A choking gasp filled Hayley's lungs as she slammed against the wall and shot upward, her feet dangling above the floor; above her head, her arms were pinned to the wall. She swallowed hard, squeezing her eyes shut, waiting for the pain. It didn't come. Her pulse raced. Hayley dared to open her eyes and gagged a scream. She searched the darkness looking for help, wondering what Dora would do if she yelled out.

About eight feet away, she spotted Rose standing near the dining tables. Hayley's voice shook. "Rose, stop her!"

Unexpectedly, Dora released her, letting her drop.

"Oh," Hayley cried out when she fell to the floor. "She'll kill me, Rose! What did I do to her?" she asked, pain shooting through her outstretched legs.

45

Rose's brows furrowed, and her sweet smile turned to a snarl. "You're trying to make us leave," she hissed.

Hayley cringed and stared into the eyes of Dora's accomplice. "No, Rose! No! You're wrong."

Rose came at her. The apparition's twisted face sent shivers up Hayley's spine. She held her arms up, shielding herself. "Wait, Rose! I can't make you go away!" Hayley's body trembled. "Let me explain, Rose, please."

The apparition stopped in midair. Her transparent image hovered inches above the floor. She wore a long-sleeved blouse with a high collar buttoned at the neck. With her hair pulled up, a few small curls dangled down the forehead of her angry young face. Her full-length skirt shimmered into vapor. Her feet became unrecognizable in the mist.

Hayley brought her knees to her chest and straightened her back, trying to still her shaking body. She searched her mind for some kind of logic…something that would make sense to a one-hundred-year-old spirit.

She looked up at Rose. "I'm pretty sure you know you're a spirit and, except for me, people can't see or hear you. With our equipment" — Hayley held up the EVP to show Rose, then pointed toward the bar where John aimed his camera her way, filming the disturbance — "we can take your picture and put it on TV so people can see and hear you. We won't hurt Dora or you."

The sound of breaking glass made Hayley flinch. *Dora.* She glanced toward the bar, then back at her attacker. "It's like advertising, Rose. We're just trying to get more customers to come in. Dora should like that. How about a truce?"

She noticed a glint of sweetness soften the sharp edges of Rose's face before her image shimmered into mist and trailed off into the gray shadows.

Hayley could see Lee's flashlight heading toward her. She

raised her hand to block the blinding light.

"Hayley!" Lee lifted her from the floor, supporting her, guiding her to a chair at a nearby table.

She couldn't stop shaking.

"What happened? Are you okay?" He pulled out a chair and sat next to her.

"Dora pushed me against the wall, shoved me up it, and held me there." Hayley saw his stunned face in the dim light. "I'm okay. I'm not hurt, just a little shaken."

Lee turned his light to the front door. "I'm taking you out of here."

"No, Lee, wait." She put her hand on his arm. "We can't leave. Dora's out of control, and I'm worried about Lucy and Dale."

The voices across the room grew louder. She looked up to see Roger heading their way. He squatted next to Lee's chair, his flashlight illuminating the table. "What happened?"

Lee stiffened in his seat. "Dora attacked her. She hauled her up the wall and pinned her there."

Roger studied her face. "Damn! Are you all right?"

Hayley nodded.

"Lee told me about the attack in the kitchen." Roger looked at the double doors. "I guess that room is soundproofed so whatever noise they make in there doesn't bother customers. We didn't hear a thing." He stood. "I asked Lucy and Dale to wait outside until we're through in here. These attacks are too aggressive. I suggest we get the lights on and start packing things up."

"No, no! I'm not hurt, Roger. She just scared the hell out of me." She laced her fingers together to hide their telltale shaking.

Lee looked at Roger and shrugged.

"I'm worried about Lucy and Dale. I explained things to Rose and asked her for a truce. I want to make sure it's safe before we go."

"Did Rose tell you why Dora's acting like this?" Roger asked.

"They thought we were trying to make them leave."

Roger raised a brow, scanned the room, then sighed. "Okay, we'll wait a few minutes." He directed his flashlight beam at the bar. "I'll find out from Clint and John if there's been any sign of them. And I'll get everyone else out of here."

Hayley watched him walk away. His image faded to gray in the darkness.

Lee sat back in his chair, his hand nudging the flashlight, spinning it around, highlighting his face.

Hayley stared into his brown eyes. Her pulse quickened. After everything they'd gone through tonight, she was surprised to feel her cheeks flush. *Damn! How do I get over this?*

She looked toward the entrance where the equipment lay on the table. "If everything seems to be okay, do you think you can finish my training?"

Lee looked at the floor and chuckled. He smiled as he studied her. "You're a stubborn woman."

"I'm fine now."

He threw his hands up in resignation. "Okay. I give up. Let's take a walk by the bar. I'll show you how the thermal imaging camera works."

When they reached the front of the room, things were still.

"Everyone's outside," Lee said. He picked up a large camera with a wide-view screen and showed her the camera's sensitivity by aiming it at electrical objects. On the camera's view screen, the energy's varied temperatures showed up as an array of colors.

"Since ghosts are energy beings, this will capture their image," he said.

As he explained the meaning of the spectrum of colors they walked, rounding the corner toward the staircase. A chill stopped them.

Lee grabbed Hayley's hand. "They're here!" He looked at his camera. "They drained the batteries. They're getting ready for another attack. Let's go."

She pulled away. "Wait, Lee. I think they're going to materialize."

"Good time to get out of here."

"Maybe there's a reason."

"Yeah, I bet I know what it is. They can hurt you worse if they're solid." Reaching for her hand again, he took it and turned, heading to the door, his hand tightening around hers. "Let's go." He began to lead her away.

Hayley jerked Lee to a halt. Her hand slipped from his. "Maybe the truce worked."

"There's a fifty-fifty chance of that happening, and I don't like the odds." He motioned her to follow. "Come on, Hayley."

She glanced back at the staircase. The cold air turned to a mist. "Look, Lee." He stared, then moved to Hayley's side, placing his hand on her shoulder. While standing her ground, she gave him a hard look. "I'm not leaving."

The front door opened.

"Come here, Roger!" Lee called out.

Roger rushed over, stopping when he came to the wall of cold air. He looked up at the infrared camera hanging above the curtains behind the booth where Lucy and Dale had been sitting earlier. "I hope we're getting this."

The space in front of them grew frigid as the ghosts gathered energy from the air. Two clouds oscillated into misty forms and then grew in width and height, wavering until their transparent features became solid and detailed, allowing everyone to see them.

Dora's image formed next to Rose's at the bottom of the staircase. The short, stocky woman wore a flowered blouse buttoned at the neck, a long skirt, and had her hair pulled neatly into a bun. Her face was peaceful, but stern. Rose stood beside her, smiling. Turning, together they floated up the stairs, gradually disappearing as they reached the landing.

"It worked," Hayley said softly.

Lee stared at the staircase. "I guess it did."

Roger rubbed his arms. "The hairs on my entire body are standing on end. I can't believe we got that on camera." He flashed his light on Hayley. "Are you okay?"

"I can't quit shaking," Hayley said. "This is one of the most exciting nights I've ever had."

"It's the adrenaline," Roger said. "It hits you like the thrill of a roller coaster. It's addicting."

Lucy and her husband peered inside. "Can we come back in now?" Dale called out.

"Guess so. Show's over," Roger shouted.

The couple walked across the dining room, stood by Lee, and looked up at the staircase. "We saw Dora and Rose on the monitor in the van," Dale said. "That was damn cool catching those two materializing. Can't wait to show the footage to the customers."

A grin spread across Roger's face. "What a night, huh? I'm sure it'll be quieter around here now. Hayley explained why we were here. They thought we were trying to make them leave."

"Wouldn't want that. We lose them, we lose business," Lucy said.

"As I mentioned," Roger said, "we'll be out of town for a couple of weeks, but when we get back, we'll bring you a copy of everything we gathered tonight."

"Bring it by when you're ready," Lucy said. "But don't take too long. I don't think I can stand the wait. I'm excited to see and hear everything again."

"With or without your evidence, she'll be talking about

tonight for years," Dale said, giving her a wink and chuckling.

Lucy put her hands on her hips. "And you won't be?"

"Thanks for letting us come in." Roger shook their hands. "We'll take care of everything once we're back."

"We appreciate that. Thank you," Lucy said.

Roger turned to Lee and Hayley. "I'll get the guys to pack up."

Clint and John took the IR cameras down and rolled up the extension cords. With the end of the investigation, they returned the equipment to the van and everyone headed for the office.

* * *

Once Hayley pulled out of PSA's parking lot, heading for home, she began to relax.

Totally amazing! I'm addicted! What a rush! And Lee…I'm sure there are statistics stating it's not a good idea to tell one of your bosses that you want him and want him now *on the very first day of your job.* She yawned. *Okay, hitting on Lee is off limits, but I can still dream about him.*

CHAPTER 6

The next morning, after parking her car, Hayley walked to the office. *Great day.* When she approached the glass front door, she stopped and thought maybe she'd spoken too soon. Inside, she saw Kathy darting out from behind the reception desk, putting her fingers to her lips. Cautiously, Hayley opened the door and entered.

Kathy blocked Hayley's path. Her dilated pupils betrayed her anxiety. "I disconnected the door chime so you could come in without them hearing you."

The look on her face made Hayley's heart skip. "Why? Where is everyone?" She looked around for any telltale signs of trouble. "What's wrong?"

"They're waiting for you in the back room." She leaned toward Hayley and kept her voice soft. "Remember yesterday when I told you about Jim's sense of humor? I just want to give you a warning before you go back there that he and the guys get a real kick out of embarrassing each other. Now you're part of the team, that includes you, too." Kathy looked down, then gazed at her with pleading eyes. "Whatever happens, don't quit."

52

Hayley thought back to the night before. *I can't remember doing anything to get embarrassed about.* Still, the way Kathy was acting made her stomach flip. *She has to be blowing this out of proportion.*

Confident she'd done nothing wrong, Hayley walked toward the sound of conversation, while Kathy, wearing a mobile earphone and carrying a notepad, followed her.

In the back room Jim sat at the computer, Roger next to him. Lee stood behind them talking casually. Off to the side, Clint and John discussed a baseball game that would be on that night. As soon as her two young co-workers noticed her, their conversation stopped and they avoided eye contact with her. Clint put his headset on over his curly red hair, then quickly rolled his chair to his computer. John also turned to his work. Their suspicious behavior sent shivers up her spine.

Lee, Roger, and Jim looked up as she came in. Scanning the room with her senses, Hayley didn't detect any threats. Still, she kept her guard up as she approached.

"Good to see ya, darlin'," Jim said. "We've been waitin' for ya." He swung his chair around to face the computer. "We'll be goin' over the results of last night." He winked at Roger.

Kathy whispered in Hayley's ear, "I've seen that look before."

"I think we'll begin in the kitchen." Jim started the footage. The infrared cameras on a shelf in the far end of Lucy's kitchen captured Lee and Hayley crouched behind the island, avoiding Dora's attack.

Roger moved his chair closer to Jim and looked over his shoulder at Hayley. "This is really exciting stuff. So, you could see Dora? Your perception is better than the camera's. It isn't picking her up. We can see only a wave of mist just before she threw that pan at you."

"She appeared solid to me." Hayley, not seeing what Kathy was so flustered about, gave the blonde a questioning glance.

Biting her lip, Kathy nodded, then shifted her weight from one foot to the other.

"I'm glad we had a camera in there," Lee said. "I didn't see her myself—just the things flying at us."

Jim grimaced. "One thing 'bout that. If ya know the ghost is mad, don't stand in front of the damn camera." He forwarded the footage. "That flyin' pan came inches away from crashin' into an expensive piece of equipment." He looked up at Lee. "I'm surprised ya don't know that by now. Ya must be a slow learner."

Lee straightened slightly and shot a glare at Jim. "Must be."

"Now, let's go in for a closer look," Jim said. With no menace in his face, he said to Hayley, "Ya might wanna come a little closer, darlin'."

Kathy put her notepad to her mouth and cleared her throat.

Hayley stared at her, then at Jim, wondering what he was about to do.

Baffled by mixed messages, Hayley moved closer, nearly rubbing elbows with Lee. She studied the monitor while Jim zoomed in on the footage of her and Lee at the beginning of Dora's rampage. Hayley and Lee stood in the darkness behind the island in the kitchen. A large pan flew straight at them, and Lee pulled her out of harm's way.

"Notice the handwork Lee is displayin'. Faster than fiddlin' fingers, he grabbed Hayley 'round the waist," Jim said.

Instant embarrassment flooded though Hayley. *Oh no! He's turning an innocent act into something intimate. Did they figure out how much I wanted it to be true?* Red-faced, she wished she could run and hide. Then she noticed that Lee stood with his arms crossed, glaring at his partner.

Jim scratched his chin. "I can understand ya tellin' her to duck, but don't ya think she can manage that on her own?" He replayed the scene in slow motion.

"You had to be there," Lee said, his brow furrowed. He rubbed the back of his neck and studied the floor.

"Okay...so, now ya got her to duck. Watch your smooth moves." He played the footage of Lee putting his arm around Hayley during another round of assaults. "That was slicker than frog's hair. I didn't think ya had it in ya, Lee. What exactly's goin' through your mind?"

Hayley cringed. She had thought about Lee's touch all night, over and over replaying his arms around her. The only place Lee's behavior was intimate was in her dreams. *If they knew how much I enjoyed those touches he's being chastised for, they'd fire me.*

When Jim stared up at him, Lee's face flushed tomato red. The lines on his forehead deepened, and his jaw hardened. He opened his mouth to speak.

Jim turned away, then nudged Roger. "He looks like the cheese fell off his cracker."

"I was just being protective," Lee said firmly.

Jim gave him a lopsided grin, looking as if he was enjoying Lee's defensive attitude. He played the video forward. "Ya sure are bein' protective. You're protectin' that girl all over the place."

Hayley felt helpless. She wanted to say something to defend Lee, but kept silent. Kathy had said they liked to joke around and embarrass each other. *If this is a joke, I don't get it.* She watched a mix of expressions cross Lee's face.

He put his hands on his hips. "Is this really necessary?" Pinching the bridge of his nose, he stared at the floor, then gave Hayley a sidelong look. Another blush crossed his face and reddened his ears. He grinned sheepishly at her. His expression made her giggle.

"I wouldn't laugh if I were you, girl," Jim said. "This is the part where the knife flies at ya." He hesitated, gazing up, as if in thought. "I wonder if Dora has any livin' relatives?" Clearing his throat, he focused on the video. "Where was I? My train fell off its track. Oh, yeah. Watch Hayley's hand as she flinches away from the knife. Notice the smooth movement of her fingers slidin' down the small of Lee's back and fittin' snug as a bug into the back of his pants."

No! Holy – Hayley stood stone still with eyes wide. Her open hand went to her chest as her jaw dropped. She felt the blood running from her feet to the top of her head. The video showed, close-up in HD, her fingers slipping down into the gap under Lee's belt.

Her hands covered her mouth, then moved to her eyes. "I had no idea—"

Jim interrupted her. "You two give a new meanin' to the term 'hands-on trainin'.'"

Hayley stood, stunned.

Jim swung his chair around, laughed, and his mood turned mildly serious. "I just wanna point out how everyone reacts differently when they're scared. Kathy, bless her heart…." He looked at her with puppy eyes and a small smile. "She's been in just 'bout everyone's arms—even mine."

Kathy rolled her eyes, slapped the note pad against her leg, and huffed.

"It goes with the territory," he said. "It has nothin' to do with that there 'sexual harassment.' Sometimes when we're scared, we all do or say things we wouldn't normally do." He looked toward Clint and John, who quickly turned away in unison, back to their work. Jim laughed. "Look at 'em. They're afraid I'm gonna go down the list of their embarrassin' moments."

With a nod of agreement, Roger said, "We've all had our moments—even me. The point we're trying to make is don't worry about your reactions. If you end up in someone's arms, we don't take it personally."

Although noticing Lee's posture loosen, Hayley was still reluctant to relax.

Kathy moved closer. "Take a deep breath. I know how you feel. It helps if you think that they came from a different planet."

Roger turned back to the computer. "Now we're done with our training evaluation, I want to tell you guys this is one hell of a video."

"It sure beats anythin' I've ever seen," Jim said. "Hell, I nearly needed diapers when that big knife came flyin' at the screen. I jumped so high, I fell backwards in my chair. I was lucky I didn't break my beehind. Never knew I could move so fast, gettin' back up to see if ya guys were still livin'."

They watched the beginning of the video—the attack in the kitchen. Then they viewed the footage of the dining room—Hayley, thrown against the wall. Going over the details, she told them exactly what she saw while they compared it to what the camera had captured.

"That woman was as mad as a bobcat bein' poked with a stick. I've never seen such a thing...I mean from a ghost," Jim said. "Ya know what impresses me, though, is how Hayley kept hold of that recorder the whole time." He glanced up at her. "Good girl, darlin'."

Kathy touched her earphone, listened closely, then left the room. She hurried back. "Jim, the admiral's on the phone."

He moved his seat back and stepped past Lee. "Thanks, sweetie. I'll take it up front."

"While we're waiting for Jim," Roger said, "let's get ready for our morning meeting."

* * *

Hayley took her seat at the conference table. Lee sat across from her. He turned as Kathy walked up beside him and began asking him questions.

With Lee's shoulder turned towards her, his sinewy biceps peeking out from under his short sleeves, Hayley's imagination chose to undress him. Clamping her eyes closed, she prayed. *Oh, God, please help me. I'm turning into a pervert.* When she opened her eyes, she peered around trying to find something to focus on besides Lee.

The enticing smell of coffee drifted through the office and, except for Lee's conversation, the room was quiet. Lee smiled at her and turned back to his discussion with Kathy. Hayley sat silently, her eyes diverted downward, focused on his notepad.

She fidgeted, lacing and unlacing her fingers on her lap, then suddenly realized what she was seeing. With its cover folded over, Lee's notepad revealed on an open page, written in script, her name scrolled out in beautiful handwriting, followed by a short sentence. Like a schoolgirl wishing the football jock would miraculously fall head over heels for her, Hayley stared at the graceful lines of her name on the page and hoped for a miracle.

Is he thinking about me, too? Her heart pounded as common sense fought with her wishful thinking. Squinting, she tried to read the words. Impossible. The writing was upside down. She struggled against the urge to reach over and turn the pad toward her.

While he sat sideways in his seat, the sudden movement of placing his arm on the table made Hayley's heart skip. Her eyes darted away from the pad. When his arm relaxed and his hand fell across his notes, execrations filled her mind.

What the hell am I doing?

She gazed over her shoulder at Roger, who stared out the window, his back to her, a loud noise from the parking lot keeping his attention. Relieved he was distracted, she swallowed hard and continued to snoop.

While watching Lee out of the corner of her eye, she waited.

One of his fingers flexed, then another. His hand lifted slightly while he spoke. She nonchalantly leaned closer to his writing. Her eyes strained to read the words, then followed the muscular curve of his arm to the soft skin of his neck.

Why am I torturing myself? How can someone like him be thinking about me?

Hayley forced her attention back to his notepad, and he turned. Her heart jumped into her throat, and she looked up. Holding her breath, she watched him straighten himself in his chair. She reminded herself to breathe as her eyes were drawn to his writing.

Lee caught her gaze and flipped the notebook closed.

Her heart nearly stopped.

When her eyes met his, the thing she least wanted to happen, happened—blood rushed to her cheeks. *Damn!* Hayley felt the heat as her face flushed…she was sure it was as bright as a red neon sign, proclaiming, "Look what you do to me." She tucked her hair behind her ear as she tried to calm her vital signs.

She diverted her eyes, then looked at him, finding his attention still on her. She felt guilty, embarrassed, nervous, and irritated with herself for being so irrational. *He's one of my bosses. He's supposed to make notes. He probably wrote, Hayley sees dead people.*

Lee cleared his throat, picked up his pencil, and toyed with it. "I didn't mean to be rude, turning away from you. I had to answer Kathy's question."

Hayley nodded.

He stared at his notepad as if in thought, then gazed at her. "So, besides seeing ghosts, do you have any other talents, like clairvoyance or telepathy?"

"I'm a bit clairvoyant, not telepathic. How about you?"

Lee mumbled under his breath.

She feverishly prayed his answer would be no. *Please, God, don't let him be telepathic. I'd die from embarrassment!* She hesitated. *Damn, if he is, he can hear me now.*

He tossed the pencil down and leaned back in his seat, shaking his head. When he raised his head, a smile pulled up one corner of his mouth, a smile that dissolved any intentions she had of thinking rationally. "No. I don't have any of those talents. It would be great to see ghosts, though. I write scary stories for a magazine once a month. A talent like that could be useful."

Not wanting her voice to sound shaky, she cleared her throat. "Oh, that's interesting." *How can I work with him if I can't control my emotions? This is going to be a real problem.* She saw Jim was once again standing at the head of the table.

He looked at the team. "Okay, our secret mission is underway in the mornin'. We've been instructed to get our equipment ready. When we reach the ship, there won't be any electricity, so we'll take everythin' but the infrared cameras."

Kathy raised her hand. "How long is this job going to take?"

"It'll be 'bout two weeks."

Clint leaned forward. "What time in the morning?"

"I was gettin' to that. Two vans will be pickin' us up 'bout nine. So don't be later than eight-thirty. They'll take us to Greensboro Airport, where we'll board a private jet. From there, we'll fly to Florida and pick up the admiral."

"Will Admiral Wayne be heading our investigation?" Lee asked.

"No. Brass gave him permission to be our host and to hook us up with his nephew, Paul. He's the botanist who found the ship and is gonna be our guide. Thankfully no one but us will have a say in our investigation."

"That's good! We don't want any military interference," Roger said.

Jim nodded. "Larry, the admiral, said we'll be on our own when the helicopter drops us off on the island."

"Perfect," Roger said.

"So, where was I?" Jim scratched his chin and looked at his notations. "Oh yeah. After pickin' up the admiral, we'll be headin' for our first layover in Coronado. It's a little city near San Diego. Next will be Hawaii, then Guam."

"Cool," Clint shouted. He turned to John. "Know how to surf?"

John shook his head. "No. But maybe we can—"

Jim cleared his throat loudly. "Quiet down, guys. I'm not finished. From there, Paul will take us to the Japanese ship. Once we get on board, we gotta do as much as we can, as fast as we can, then hightail it out of there."

He hesitated and read his notes. "You'll need to bring light clothes for our stay in Coronado, Hawaii, and Guam. But once we get to the remote island, you'll need to wear long-sleeved shirts and long pants for protection from bugs, 'cause we'll be hikin' through a jungle. Make sure you wear sturdy shoes and your clothes are cotton. Larry said the jungle's hellish hot."

Roger stood. "Remember, this is a secret mission. No one is supposed to know what we're doing or where we're going. Have any of you told anyone about this?" He looked around as each person answered with a shake of the head.

"I need to keep in touch with my parents or they'll worry," Kathy said.

"We can keep in touch with folks," Jim answered, "but if they ask, just tell 'em we're on a case. That's all they need to know."

"Jim, Lee, and I will stay and pack up the equipment," Roger said. "Everyone else can go home and make necessary arrangements. And remember to be here no later than eight-thirty in the morning. Be on time!"

CHAPTER 7

Not long after Hayley's head hit the pillow, a collage of images streamed through her mind. When she slipped into a deeper sleep, a vivid dream played like a video, pulling her in, making her the lead character, a man who was an officer in the navy.

Hayley, entangled in Lieutenant Sanders's being, followed the shoreline with two seamen. Hearing his thoughts as if they were her own, she knew they searched for a miracle. He thought about the captain giving him an objective — to find a way off the island and bring help. It wasn't just an order; it was a mission of the heart, a cry to God. The crew *must* be saved. They were dying one right after the other.

Glancing over his shoulder, the lieutenant noticed one of his seamen faltering. The eighteen-year-old, sweating and shivering, trudged through the sand, not able to keep up. Finally, he staggered and collapsed on the shore.

Lieutenant Sanders went to him and knelt, visions of his crew's agonizing deaths filling his mind. "Hang in there, Palmer. You're going to be okay. Just get some rest."

Seaman Morris, standing beside them, swiped at his runny

nose with his palm and brushed away his tears.

Fever burned Palmer's body while he rested on the sand, straining to speak. "I'm sorry, sir. I'm sorry, sir."

Hayley felt the lieutenant's throat tighten, the choking back of his tears, the stinging in his eyes as he tried to keep his composure while he gave comfort. "It's okay, Palmer. The sun's setting. It's time for us to stop and get some rest. We'll camp here for the night." He stood and walked down to the surf.

Hayley felt the wind flutter against his white T-shirt when he removed his khaki shirt. When he dipped the cloth into the brine, she felt the coolness of the water. After wringing out his shirt, he returned to the seaman's side. The moonlight glistened off Palmer's sweaty face as the lieutenant placed the cool cloth across his hot forehead.

He pulled Morris aside. "I have to go on. It doesn't look good. If the malaria affects him like it did the others, he'll be gone by morning." He looked into Morris's wet eyes. "I don't want you to take it on yourself to return him to the ship. I know he's your best friend. I'm really sorry, but when he goes, report to the ship and get help to take him back."

While Sanders walked away from his men, Hayley felt the tears streaking down his cheeks. With the back of his hand, he wiped them away. When he closed his eyes, it seemed her eyes shut, too. His chest heaved and he took a deep breath, fighting to regain his strength, as she experienced the same physical and emotional reactions. He was torn, leaving them. How could he walk away when they needed him? How could he not when there was a chance to save the crew's lives? His torment overwhelmed her.

The lieutenant hiked until he could go no farther. His fatigue drained Hayley as it consumed him. Pain shot through her aching bones when he crumbled onto the sand. While he looked to the heavens, the sound of the surf lulled him to sleep. In his dreams, he replayed the recent days.

After their ship had been hit by the Japanese fleet and the crew had made it to this island, the marooned shipmates now were being killed by another enemy. Malaria invaded and had killed one-third of the crew. They needed to find a way off the island. He had to bring help before everyone died.

At sunrise, Lieutenant Sanders vaguely heard the waves in the distance. Hayley shivered along with him and felt the sweat drenching his face, the pain arching his back and darting through his stiffened legs. He knew the symptoms.

Thoughts of his men ripped through his mind. "Please, God, don't let this happen. I have to bring help. Please, God." Over and over he attempted to get up, but his body wouldn't respond. He drifted in and out of consciousness.

"Please, God, please, God," he moaned.

* * *

Hayley struggled to break free of the nightmare—one of the common unpleasantries she suffered from being gifted. But this time there seemed to be a confusing difference. She didn't merely witness a death. This time, she was sucked into the lieutenant's existence and forced to experience his agony.

While she relived his last hours of life, she suffered with him while inhaling the sea breeze and hearing the crashing waves. The moment he took his final breath she awoke, gasping for air. Tears streamed down her cheeks. She opened her eyes to see a breeze ruffling her bedroom curtains.

She checked the clock. "Seven-thirty. What happened to the alarm?"

Straining to sit up, she grimaced. Her body ached. Sharp pains darted through her legs and up her spine. Hayley groaned. "Ow…damn!" She scooted to the edge of her bed, reached for the lamp on the nightstand, and turned it on. In the light, she examined her arms and legs—no bruises, thank goodness. She pulled her pillow to her chest and hugged it until the pain subsided.

What happened? I spent years learning to be a bystander and to separate myself from trauma. Why did I become the lieutenant? Why couldn't I block his pain? Elaina taught me how to shield myself. I mastered it! I know I mastered it!

She placed the pillow at the head of the bed and wished for more sleep. With a tired moan Hayley stood, walked across the cool wood floor, and grabbed her robe from the back of the rocking chair. Yawning, she draped her robe over her tired body, stuck her feet into fuzzy yellow slippers, and headed for the stairway.

Coffee. I need coffee. She reached the fifth step and eased herself over it, not wanting to be reminded by its creak that it needed fixing.

Across from the foot of the staircase, she caught her reflection in the mirror. Her tangled light brown hair stuck out in all directions. "I look like a deranged cockatoo." Too tired to care, she halfheartedly patted down the spikes, hurried to the kitchen, put the coffee on, and trotted upstairs to take a shower.

By the time she'd finished dressing and drank a cup of coffee, she had twenty minutes to get to the office. After placing her makeup and toothbrush into the suitcase she'd packed the night before and taking it downstairs, she took a run around the house to make sure things were locked and appliances turned off. Satisfied she'd taken care of everything, she grabbed her purse, the suitcase, and dashed out the door.

CHAPTER 8

When pulling into the parking lot, Hayley noticed duffel bags and luggage piled near the office entrance. She glanced at the clock on the dash—eight-thirty. Perfect timing.

Hayley quickly parked and got out of her car, sensing critical eyes bearing down on her. Gazing to the right, she scanned the wooded grove and to the left, Henry's Hardware—no one. Living or dead? Since her abilities didn't come with instructions, her deceased grandmother and Elaina had helped her write a user's manual. In the simplest terms, not expecting Hayley to learn scientific principles, Grams told her that everything in the universe is made up of energy, constantly moving and vibrating, each at its own rate.

"Everyone is an individual, but most humans have similar vibration frequencies. Yours, dear, is far different, and because of that, your aura is seen as a beacon by the departed."

"I glow?"

"Yes, dear."

"If I recall, vibrating frequencies can be altered."

"You're catching on, dear."

It was a eureka moment when Hayley realized frequencies

could be manipulated, if only for a short time. It allowed her to eliminate her glow in order to finally have control over unwanted visitations. The prying eyes she sensed couldn't be a spirit's because she'd turned off her beacon and was closed for business.

Looking over her shoulder, she witnessed three gangling boys gawking at her from across the street…the same kids who were skateboarding the day before yesterday.

Through the office window, she noticed Kathy sitting behind her desk, waving a donut in one hand, holding a cup of coffee in the other. At the conference table, Roger appeared engrossed in packing equipment. He pointed to a few bags at his side when Lee came from the back room.

Lee grabbed a suitcase and a duffle bag and headed toward the front door. With one bag under his arm and another in his hand, he reached the office door and held it open for Hayley.

Catching herself staring at him, Hayley waited for the annoying blush she always experienced when he was near. It didn't happen. Instead, she fought the urge to kiss him good morning. She bit her lip. *So much for wishful thinking.*

Lee smiled. "Good morning."

"Good morning, Lee." She glanced over her shoulder. "I noticed we're being watched."

"Yes. Frank and his kids are a real nuisance," Lee said. "Most of our customers want to keep their personal lives out of the papers. Now this. Our case is supposed to be a military secret. It's going to be tricky getting out of here without being followed." He stepped out of her way, allowing her to enter.

While Lee carried the bags outside, she studied his tight behind and sighed. *He looks as good from the back as he does from the front. Mmm.*

When she turned away, Hayley saw the expression on Roger's face that told her he knew what she was thinking. He cleared his throat and looked down, grinning.

Her face heated.

Roger laughed lightly as he zipped up a laptop case. "Good morning, Hayley."

She smiled nervously, wondering how guilty she looked. "Good morning."

He turned toward Jim, coming from the back room. "Jim, would you show Hayley where to park her car, please?"

"Sure. Little lady, just drive your car through those big double gates, and I'll meet ya in the back."

On her way out of the office, she tried to avoid Lee. Sensing Roger's gaze, she stared at the ground, chastising herself on the way to her car. *How stupid am I? I hope Roger doesn't say anything to Lee. What am I thinking—the boss's partner? Could he fire me for inappropriate thoughts? Damn, how embarrassing. What in the hell am I doing?* She opened the car door and slid inside. *I wish I could see my own future. Is it asking too much to have both the perfect job and the perfect man?*

Making sure not to run over any luggage, she maneuvered her car around to the side gate. The gates rolled back, and she drove forward. Two garages remaining from a prior car dealership flanked the paved backyard. She remembered being there as a child with her grandparents when they had brought their car in for repairs. Seeing the garages now, she felt as though she had been transported back in time. Everything looked the same, except cars weren't being repaired. The three company vans and Kathy's red Toyota GT were parked in the stalls.

Jim pointed to an empty space. "Just pull in there, darlin'."

She swung her car inside.

After she turned off the engine, Jim approached her car. "This is a fine security system we've got here. You won't have to worry 'bout nothin'."

Hayley popped the trunk, got out of the car, and went around to get her baggage.

"We're still waitin' for Clint and John. After they get here, I'll lock up." He reached into the trunk and lifted out her bags.

They were walking toward the office when Jim stopped, setting her things down. "We'll just wait out here a bit and see if they'll pull in."

Good. I'd rather not go inside and face Roger right now. "How long have Clint and John been working here?"

"About four years, I'd say. Since they were in high school. They're Roger's nephews and both computer geniuses, who're goin' to Duke University now. They're just workin' here durin' school breaks." He glanced at the gate. "We would've been lost without those two. They chose the equipment we needed and set everythin' up for us."

"Is Kathy a relative, too?"

"No, but we've adopted her. Lee's an only child, but he thinks of Kathy as a sister. To me and Roger, she's like a daughter. And, I guess, John and Clint fight with her like siblings. Hell, we're just one big happy family."

They faced the gate as the nephews drove in. Because their windows were rolled down, Hayley heard the boys arguing. Clint pulled his car into the garage, climbed out, opened the back door, and pulled out their luggage. After John slammed the car door shut, he went around and yanked his bag out of Clint's hand, his voice echoing in the courtyard. "Just wait until I win," John shouted. "Next time you're going to be sorry." John's eyebrows were missing and his dark locks gone; his head was bald and pink.

"A bet is a bet, and shaved means shaved," Clint said smugly.

Jim's jaw dropped while he gawked at John. "What in hell did ya do?"

"He lost a bet on the ballgame last night," Clint said simply.

Staring at John, Jim shook his head. "Boy, I thought ya couldn't get any uglier, but I was wrong. What possessed ya to do a thing like that? Your uncle isn't gonna like this one bit. Clint, grab Hayley's other bag."

Jim reached into his pocket, pulled out a remote, and closed both garage doors. Turning, he opened the office back door, allowing Hayley to go in first.

She kept quiet and held back a smile while she walked down the hallway.

"It's not my fault he lost," Clint said flatly.

"I can't believe the two of ya are related to Roger. Your genes must of come from the shallow end of the pool," Jim said to John, "Boy, you're lizard-butt ugly—walk backwards."

Clint laughed.

"I wouldn't laugh if I were you, boy," Jim said. "You've got to be dumber than dirt to do this just before we leave. Ya know how your uncle likes to make a good first impression."

When she entered the main room, Hayley went to stand by Kathy and Lee at the reception desk. Sneaking a peek at Lee's face, she looked for signs of Roger's tattling that she'd checked out his tight rear end. Lee's reaction to her was the same as always, nothing out of the ordinary. She breathed a relieved sigh. *Thank God, Roger didn't tell him.*

Not seeming to notice their entrance, Roger zipped up a black duffel bag, grabbed its handle, and lifted it from the conference table. He turned, lowered the bag to his side, glanced at John, and froze, eyes widened. The bag slipped from his grip, dropping onto the burgundy carpet. "What in hell did you do?"

Jim stepped between John and his uncle. He held out his hand, as if trying to stop Roger's words. "I said that already. These two boneheads were bettin' on the baseball game last night, and John

70

lost."

With luggage in their hands and under each arm, his nephews hurried to the front door, putting their bags down with the others. They turned to face their uncle.

"We've worked hard to create a professional image. That's why we got this case. You know as well as I do how people look at us as if we're crazy. Now look at you." Roger took a deep breath. "Damn it, Clint and John, couldn't you have waited until we got back?"

Hayley felt tempted to tell him about the life-links that spurred the cousins to bet. But things could change if she spoke. The cousins' actions had to play out. For now, she had to keep her secret.

"Well, let's try to look on the bright side, Roger," Jim said, calmly.

"What bright side? There isn't any bright side."

"If you're worried 'bout the admiral seein' his bald head, ya don't have to. He's seen more shaved heads in the military than a pediatrician's seen baby butts. As for John's eyebrows, maybe he won't notice. So, let's just calm down now."

With frustration written on his face, Roger said to his nephew, "How could anyone not notice his shaved brows? He looks damn ridiculous." With a surrendering groan, Roger ran a hand through his hair, then shrugged. "All right…the admiral's your friend. But don't expect me to be happy about this." He pointed to the equipment bags. "Take everything outside, you two."

John pushed past Clint when he went out the door. "Cheater," John said.

"Loser," Clint retorted.

Roger swiped his hand across his face, and Jim caught the gesture. "Don't worry, Roger. I'll take care of 'em." He grabbed the bag at Roger's feet, then met Clint at the door. "Ya two are annoyin' every hair on my backside. I don't wanna hear another word comin' out of your ugly faces, or you're gonna come up missin'." He pointed outside. "Get movin', bonehead."

After Clint went out the door, Jim turned to Roger and winked.

A wink? Hayley studied Lee. He stood with his arms crossed and a straight face.

Roger grabbed the remote, closed the curtains, then bent with laughter. Next to her, Lee began laughing, too. How could she have read them so wrong? Weren't they upset? She looked at Kathy.

"I gave up trying to figure out men a few years ago," Kathy said.

After catching his breath, Roger straightened. "I almost lost it a couple of times. That had to be one of the funniest things I've ever seen. But I was serious about their timing."

Almost lost it a couple of times? I didn't even see that. Am I blind?

"Do you think they're as bad as we were when we were young?" Lee asked, wiping his eyes.

"Hell, no," Roger said. "Not even close."

Kathy shook her head.

"You guys better wait outside. I have to lock up," Roger said.

Outside, when Lee walked away, leaving her standing with Kathy, Hayley thought about yesterday, the video, and Lee's embarrassment. Had she read Lee correctly then? A lump of sadness formed in her throat. Insecurity spurred her imagination. Closing her eyes, she remembered a trick Grams had taught her to remove negative energy. She cleared her mind, then mentally envisioned white light surrounding her. When she opened her eyes, Kathy was studying her.

"Just trying to center myself," Hayley told her.

"Do that often?" Kathy asked.

"I guess I do. Especially when there's so much going on." Without thinking, she glanced at Lee.

Kathy nodded. "You can talk to me about anything, you know. I'm not judgmental."

"I'd like that," Hayley said. *Lee, the cousins' betting. Secrets, always secrets. I can't tell her anything.*

After Roger stepped out of the office to lock the door, Jim called to him, "They're here."

Two black vans pulled up. The drivers got out, clean-cut men in civilian clothes.

"I thought we were being picked up by the military, Jim," Roger said.

"We are. Ya know…incognito, secret mission. Remember?" Jim motioned at the kids across the street. "Wonder if they'll try followin' us."

* * *

Fifteen minutes into their drive to the airport, Hayley received a knowing and didn't question it. Her knowings were always pure truth. "Roger, Frank Thompson is following us."

Roger pulled out his cell phone. "Jim, Hayley said Frank's following us." He looked into the van's side mirror, trying to see beyond the second van, listening to Jim's reply. "He is? Damn pest. Thanks." Roger told the driver, "Someone's following us."

"Know who it is, sir?"

"Frank Thompson, owner of the *Sutterville Times,* the local newspaper. Been trailing us to all our cases."

"A reporter. He can follow us to the airport, but he can't trace the jet," the driver said. "Don't worry, sir. We'll take care of him."

Roger put his phone away.

Hayley sensed his concern. So far, he and the team had kept her name and abilities out of the newspapers. Eventually Frank Thompson would find out, as persistent as he was. But this case was top secret. She feared Frank could blow everything.

She closed her eyes again, trying to envision any difficulties. Beside her, she heard whispers.

"No, Lee, she's not sleeping. She's meditating."

Hayley opened one eye and peeked at Kathy, gave her a smile, then closed her eyes, cleared her mind, and tried again.

CHAPTER 9

At the airport's guarded gate leading onto the tarmac, the driver flashed his security clearance to pass through.

"We only have two vehicles. The car behind us is a news reporter. Think you can stall him?" the driver asked.

The guard leaned down to the open car window. "No problem," he said in a low voice. He waved both vans through.

Before turning a corner onto the field, the driver slowed, allowing Hayley and the others to watch Frank Thompson's dilemma. Roger looked back at Lee. "Looks like it's working. The guard's not letting him through."

"Can't we get him arrested for stalking?"

"No," Roger said. "Frank's only dangerous and threatening to himself. Anyway, I think reporters have immunity to stalking laws. If they didn't, every paparazzi in the country would be behind bars." He turned to the driver. "Any chance he can follow us from here?"

"None, sir. We've got your back."

"Frank's going to be livid," Lee said.

Hayley looked out the van's windshield when the driver circled in front of a hangar. A two-engine private jet stood silently on the tarmac. Steps connected to an open door. When the vans halted, two men exited the plane.

After the investigators climbed out of the vehicles, the drivers started to unload their luggage.

Hayley stayed at Roger's side. He walked forward, shaking the hands of the pilot, David Gates, and co-pilot, Steve Duff.

"It's a Challenger 605. Flies at Mach .82 with a four thousand nautical-mile range," Steve said. "I'll give you a tour while Captain Gates talks to the tower." He stepped aside, allowing them to board.

Hayley waited to walk with Lee.

Steve followed them in and stood by the galley at the front of the cabin. "We'll be flying to Florida on the first leg of your flight. When we stop to pick up Admiral Wayne, the galley and bar will be fully stocked with meals and a variety of drinks. Until then, there are a few drinks and snacks for you once we're in the air."

While the co-pilot explained, Lee reached around Hayley, claiming his seat by setting his laptop onto a hinged leaf table with two seats on each side.

Jim, standing behind Roger, leaned forward. "This jet is sweet."

"Yeah," Roger said. "Wouldn't mind getting one of these for Christmas."

"I'll keep that in mind."

Steve led them down the center aisle. "All of your seats swivel," Steve said, "allowing each passenger to participate in group meetings. There are web hookups throughout, and TVs are stationed at several locations. The TV in the rear is equipped with a variety of games."

"Guess John and I'll sit in the back," Clint said.

"There are two restrooms." Steve took them to the rear of the plane. "One is located just outside the cockpit, and the other is here. The door next to it leads to storage." He faced them. "Any questions?"

"Is this a military jet?" Roger asked.

"No, sir. It's privately owned. We're aware you're being followed."

"You know about that all ready? That was fast."

"If being followed is what you're worried about, there's no need. Your mission has been financed by an untraceable source. Anything else?"

"What happened to our friend?"

"He didn't have the necessary clearance and was turned away at the gate."

"Bet Frank loved that," Lee said.

"Feel free to ask if you have any more questions. We'll be taking off shortly, so please be seated and buckle up." Steve turned and headed toward the cockpit.

While she sat by Kathy on a light brown couch near the back, Hayley rubbed her hand across the seat's soft leather. She admired the richness of the wood side tables, and the feel of sitting in someone's living room. While mentally counting the seating capacity, she glanced around, looking for Lee. He sat alone in the seat he'd claimed across from the galley.

With their arms full of luggage and equipment, the van drivers entered the cabin, taking the team's items to the storage area. After a few trips, they wished everyone well and left the plane, closing the hatch behind them.

The engines began to whine. Hayley fastened her seatbelt and laced her fingers together, trying not to be nervous. *This is really happening. I'm flying halfway around the world. If I had foreseen this, I never would've believed it.*

The pilot announced over a speaker, "We're ready for takeoff. Make sure your seatbelts are fastened. Once we're in the air, you'll be free to walk around."

* * *

"Anyone want a drink? Hayley, Kathy, Jim?" Roger asked.

"Yes, please. I'll have a Coke," Hayley said.

He headed toward the galley and stopped to talk to Lee.

"There's an Internet hookup beside me. This is perfect," Lee said, unzipping his laptop case. "I can do research for my magazine story." He glanced over his shoulder. "You guys comfortable back there?"

"Yeah. When you're finished with your work, you should join us," Roger said. "Want anything to drink while I'm up?"

"Not right now, thanks."

Jim swiveled his seat. "What 'bout me? Am I invisible?"

"I just asked you, remember? Or is old age getting to you? What do you want?"

Jim whispered to Hayley, "Can you use your gift and see if there's any beer?"

She nodded. "There's a couple behind the sodas."

"Beer," Jim told Roger.

"Are you deaf, too? The co-pilot said the bar will be stocked when we get to Florida."

"There's a couple behind the sodas," Jim said.

Roger reached into the refrigerator, moved things aside, and pulled out a Budweiser. "How in the hell did you know that?" He glanced at Hayley, then at Jim. "Cheater."

Jim's eyes widened with surprise. "Ya sure have a way with twistin' the facts." He touched a finger to his head. "Ya underestimate me. I've got more brains than a camel's got spit. Want me to tell ya the future?"

"No. Want to see if you can fly?" With a can of beer in one hand and two sodas in the other, Roger walked back to his seat. He handed Hayley her drink, set his and Jim's cans on the side

78

table between them, and sat.

Jim closed his eyes without asking for Hayley's insight. "I see a woman prettier than an angel. She's tellin' me that you're gonna spill that soda down the front of your shirt." He opened his eyes and grinned.

Roger popped the lid of his soda. When he took a sip, the plane hit turbulence. His drink ran down his shirt.

Jim's mouth gaped. "Well, I'll be dipped in donkey dung. I knew I had some gypsy blood in me."

Hayley burst out laughing.

Roger sprang from his seat, hurried up the galley, then came back wiping his shirt with a napkin. "I don't know about gypsy blood, but I do know you're mental."

Jim popped the tab and took a sip of his beer. "Ah, good stuff. Thanks, Roger."

"Don't mention it."

Kathy touched Hayley's arm. "Welcome to the nuthouse."

While trying to keep her eyes off Jim's dumbfounded expression so she wouldn't start laughing again, Hayley changed the subject. "What got you interested in hunting ghosts, Roger?"

He checked out the seat. Not finding anything spilled, he sat. "While I was at Duke, I was drawn to Rhine's off-campus research. They were doing clinical testing with mediums and learning about ghosts and the afterlife. I couldn't get enough." He looked over at Jim. "I've known Jim since I was twenty-one. He came over to help my parents with some renovation problems. After he found out how interested I was in ghosts, he took me to a few haunted houses around town."

Jim smirked. "Couldn't get rid of him. He was pesterin' me all the time. So I took him to every scary house I'd been to. With his sweet disposition, he finagled the owners into lettin' him use his camera. Worked pretty good. Got some decent shots of ectoplasm. Back then we didn't know 'bout infrared." Jim looked at Roger and Lee. "We were havin' one hell of a good time."

"My parents were best friends with Lee's," Roger said. "We've always been like brothers, even though I'm ten years older than he is. When I started hanging out with Jim, Lee came with us."

"It was so fun scarin' Lee. You could hear his knees knockin' clean in the other room. I can't tell ya how many times he peed his pants."

Lee looked up from his laptop. "Ah—let's not go there."

While Hayley laughed, she saw Steve step out of the cockpit and approach Roger. "We'll be landing at Jacksonville Naval Air Station in twenty minutes, sir," he told him.

"Where will we be heading next?" Roger asked.

"Coronado, across the harbor from San Diego, sir."

"How long's the flight?"

"Four-and-a-half hours, sir."

"Thank you."

Steve went back to join the pilot.

With a grin under his graying mustache, Jim leaned toward Roger. "Looks like we're gonna be part of the jet set."

Kathy set a book down on the seat, stood, walked up front, and talked to Lee. "Can I use your computer a minute?"

"Sure, go ahead." He saved his work and slid out of his seat to let her sit.

Hayley's pulse beat wildly when Lee sat on the couch next to her. *Okay, I can't sit next to him and I can't look at him without having palpitations. I'm pathetic.* While she tried to control her vital signs, she rose and took her empty soda can to the galley.

When she found the trash container, Hayley tossed the can, then pulled another soda from the fridge. She said a prayer while she returned to her seat. *Please, God, just shoot me. Or, maybe you can just shock me every time I think of him, like those devices that stop dogs from barking. Spiked hair's in now. No one would think it's unusual. All I'd have to worry about would be the sudden yelps I'd be making every couple of seconds and the smoke coming out of my ears.*

She sat again, sipped her drink, and gave her attention to Roger and Jim's discussion about the navy. "Were you ever stationed in San Diego?" she asked Jim.

"Yeah. I went through boot camp there."

Kathy swiveled her seat toward them. "Then you'll know that the Hotel del Coronado nearby is famous for its ghosts. It's haunted by a woman who took her life while staying at the hotel in the late eighteen hundreds. And in San Diego, across the bay in Old Town, the Whaley House was built on top of the gallows."

"I don't think they're gonna let us get sidetracked," Jim told her.

"How long have you known the admiral?" Roger asked Jim.

"Since he was knee high to a gnat. We were best friends. After high school, we joined the navy. He went to Annapolis, and I went to boot camp. San Diego's changed a bit since then."

"What year was that?" Roger asked.

"In nineteen-seventy-three. After San Diego, I was stationed in South Carolina. That's when Larry and I met up again. We ended up servin' in Nam together. I was enlisted for only eight years, but he made it a career. He always liked the navy better than I did."

Roger folded his arms across his chest. "How'd he know about us? Have you been making up stories? Maybe exaggerating things a little?"

"Hell, no. Would I do that? I've been tellin' him 'bout our ghost huntin' for years. Ain't nothin' new."

"Must have made a good impression on him," Roger said.

Jim scratched his cheek. "Well, I did talk to him the day we did a background check on Hayley. Next thing ya know, he called me 'bout this Japanese warship."

Roger gave him an appraising look. "How much did you fabricate about Hayley's gifts?"

"Not a bit. No need to. She's amazin' just the way she is."

"I know what kind of storyteller you are. I can imagine how you might have turned Hayley into some kind of superhero. I'm telling you right now not to put this case on Hayley's shoulders."

"I'm innocent. Just ask Larry."

At the mention of the admiral, Hayley's stomached fluttered. A vision skirted across her mind in undecipherable pictures. It seemed her abilities were being blocked somehow. But why? Five days ago, before she started this job, she had no problem seeing the past, present, and the future. Now, nothing was coming to her. She couldn't read Lee's or any of the team members' lives.

That isn't exactly true, she corrected herself. She could see Clint's and John's life-links. But only up to a point. Her attempts to see their futures were being blocked, too. Now she was barred from knowing anything about the admiral. *What's going on? Am I losing my abilities? Please, God, don't let that happen! Not now.*

The pilot announced to prepare for landing and buckle up.

CHAPTER 10

After touching down at Jacksonville Naval Air Station, Hayley knelt on the couch and looked out the window. A black car with flags attached over each headlight waited on the tarmac. The driver opened the passenger's door and a man wearing blue jeans, a Hawaiian shirt, sunglasses, and a nautical hat climbed out.

That has to be the admiral. Hmm. There's something about him. A muddled whisper out of a foggy memory swept across Hayley's thoughts. Shivers went up her spine. Something about the admiral triggered a memory that floated on the edge of her mind, just out of reach. She tried to touch the thought and experienced a flicker of déjà vu. When she pushed her hair behind her ear, the feeling faded and the elusive memory disappeared.

Lee slid in on her left to share her window.

She felt the heat from his cheek as he leaned to look out at the tarmac. The heat of a flush crossed her face. The warmth from their bodies fogged the window.

Lee wiped away the haze with his hand. "Guess we're a little hot-blooded."

You have no idea. "Guess so." She reminded herself to breathe.

"What's wrong?" he asked in a low voice.

"What makes you think something's wrong?" she asked, staring at the admiral, trying to understand the elusive smudges of memory he provoked.

"You looked troubled when you saw the admiral. Do you know him?"

"No." Hayley watched the admiral speak to his driver. "Have you ever had déjà vu?"

"All the time," Lee whispered.

"Are you feeling anything now?" she asked.

"Nothing I can put my finger on. I think it might be just the intrigue of this whole thing—the mystery of the ship and its crew."

"Maybe that's what I'm feeling—kind of a sense of secrecy."

"Yeah, could be," Lee said.

They pulled away from the window. She sat on the couch while Lee and Roger joined Jim at the front of the cabin to greet their host.

The tall, middle-aged man ducked through the door. He pulled off his glasses and placed them in his shirt pocket. A warm smile crossed his face when he removed his hat and swept his fingers through his thinning brown hair. Then he threw his arm around Jim's shoulders.

Jim examined his friend's face. "Ya haven't changed a bit. Your ugly face can still scare the warts off a toad." He turned to Lee and Roger. "This is Admiral Lawrence H. Wayne, US Navy. Larry, these are my partners, Roger Hudson and Lee Franklin."

The admiral shook their hands. "Nice to meet you guys. I've heard a lot about you and your team."

"Hope it was accurate," Roger said, raising a brow at Jim. "Let me introduce you to everyone." He ushered Admiral Wayne to his nephews. "This is Clint Waverly and John Brighton. They're

84

our electronics geniuses."

The admiral shook Clint's hand, but hesitated when he came to John. He rubbed his chin and smiled at the bald young man. "Lose a bet, son?"

John stood with his shoulders back and a stoic expression on his face. "Yes, sir."

"It happens to the best of us. I hope you win next time."

"Thank you, sir." He relaxed his stance and glanced at Clint.

Jim nudged Roger. "See, I told ya their shenanigans wouldn't bother him. I'm psychic."

"The word's psycho." Roger turned toward the couch.

Hayley and Kathy stood.

"This is Kathy Lane, our historian," Roger said. "I think you two have spoken."

"Yes," Admiral Wayne said, taking Kathy's hand. "Good to meet you."

"And this is Hayley Johnson. She's our newest addition. Her specialty is communicating with and seeing ghosts."

The admiral raised his eyebrows, then shook her hand. "Jim told me all about you. You may not know this, but you're the reason the military agreed to hire the team."

Her eyes widened as she felt a blanket of burden wrap around her shoulders. She looked at Jim and furrowed her brows. "I had no idea, Admiral, sir."

Jim looked at her innocently and shrugged.

"You can call me Admiral or Larry. It doesn't matter to me." He patted Jim's shoulder. "Sit next to me. It's really good to see your miserable face instead of talking to you on the phone."

Everyone found seats.

Admiral Wayne faced his long-time friend. "You look excited."

"If I had a tail, I'd be waggin' it." Jim picked up the empty beer can on the table beside him and shook it. "Happen to bring any more beer with ya?"

"I've got a couple of men stocking the galley. There'll be plenty to drink and eat once they're finished. You may have seen the catering truck."

When the young sailors boarded, Hayley inhaled the aroma of food.

"That smells great, doesn't it?" Admiral Wayne asked. "We have ham, roast beef, and chicken—vegetables and potatoes with gravy, or rice if you prefer. Help yourselves."

"Thank you. Maybe later," Roger said. "Right now I'd like to ask a few questions about our case. How many days do you think it will take to get to the ship?"

"Four, maybe five, counting today," Admiral Wayne said.

Jim rubbed his chin and nodded thoughtfully. "That's not too bad. How close is the Japanese ship to Guam?"

"About six hundred nautical miles. Hundreds of remote islands are around there. It's no wonder it took this long for the island to be officially recorded."

"How many bodies were found on board?" Roger asked.

"Six. Americans. Found in berthing." A sober expression crossed the admiral's face. "Officers and crew, each taking a bunk in the enlisted quarters—that's never seen. Another mystery."

"No sign of Japanese?" Jim asked.

"None. With your help, I hope we'll find out what happened to them."

"Where were the bodies taken?" Roger asked.

"JPAC, Joint POW/MIA Accounting Command, took the remains to CILHI, the Central Identification Laboratory in Hawaii," Admiral Wayne said. "After the bodies are examined for cause of death and officially identified, they'll be returned to their families for burial."

"Hopefully we'll be able to provide some answers," Roger said.

The copilot approached Admiral Wayne. "We're ready to take off, sir."

"Thank you. I guess we'd better buckle up."

"How big of a ship are we talking about?" Roger asked, securing his seatbelt.

"It's a Japanese escort, which isn't a large vessel. Approximately two hundred fifty feet aft to bow with a thirty-foot beam. Maybe you can visualize it better if I said it's about three-fourths of a football field in length. The botanist who found it is my nephew, Paul Perkins."

Roger nodded. "We're all eager to get in there to investigate. Will you be going with us to the ship?"

"No," Admiral Wayne said. "I'll be handing you over to Paul once we reach Guam." He turned to Hayley. "Tell me, how long have you been seeing ghosts?"

"All my life."

Jim's eyes twinkled. "Let me tell ya 'bout this little lady."

Hayley sat back in her seat and sighed, hoping he wouldn't go into the embarrassing details about her hands-on training.

"Ya wouldn't believe how she managed to wrap two mean ghosts 'round her finger," Jim started.

She listened as he elaborated on every detail. It seemed like a different story to her since she didn't have a chance to think about things at the time, her mind preoccupied with thinking of ways to avoid being killed.

"Ya should've seen how high I jumped when that pan flew at the camera. And never in all my years have I seen a ghost throw a knife at anyone."

Hayley could see how Jim convinced Admiral Wayne that she could solve their mystery. He told a good tale. By the time he finished the story, she was a heroine.

Jim looked over at Hayley. "Guess our girl's got a way with ghosts."

"So, where will we be staying tonight?" Roger asked.

"Hotel del Coronado, just outside San Diego." He smiled. "And it's haunted."

"Kathy mentioned that place. Looks like we might be in for an interesting evening."

CHAPTER 11

After washing her lunch dishes, Hayley wiped her hands on a towel and stepped away from the galley sink. She noticed Lee sitting alone, working at his computer.

I'll take a chance. Maybe if I flirt just a little, something not too noticeable, I won't make too big a fool of myself.

She watched Lee's face as he typed. He pushed up his dark-framed glasses while he read his work. His brows lifted, and the creases in his forehead deepened. Then his expression changed to a frown. Hayley sank into the leather seat across from him. His eyes widened momentarily, then he refocused his attention on the computer monitor.

"Hi. Just one second." He forged ahead with his work. Between his struggle to compose his story and the deletion of unwanted sentences, he looked over his glasses and smiled at her, then went back to his editing.

In a moment, he turned away from his work. "Sorry, I didn't mean to be rude, but I had to finish a thought."

She looked at his computer to avoid making eye contact,

trying to keep the telling blush away from her cheeks. "What are you working on?"

"A short story for a magazine. The last few days have been so crazy that I haven't put much time into it. My deadline's tomorrow." He shook his head. "I write one every month, but I'm having a hard time with this one."

"What kind of story are you writing?"

"A ghost story. I've blended my two passions together — ghost investigation and writing."

"How much have you written?"

He shrugged his shoulders and shook his head. "Not much. I can't seem to get a grip on a storyline."

"What you need is a ghost writer. I have lots of true stories I can tell you. If you like one, you can use it. But you might have to change things a little to protect the identity of my friends."

"Really? You wouldn't mind?"

"No. It could be fun."

His smile widened. "Great! Why don't you sit next to me, and we can play with some ideas?"

Hayley slid into the seat beside him. She started with the story about the Hastings and how their deceased relative helped them find their property deed hidden in the false bottom of a drawer. Next she told him about the spirit of a little girl she had met at the cemetery, and how she'd helped her find her way into the light, allowing the girl to cross over and be with her mother. Halfway through she hesitated, giving him a puzzled look.

He peered over his glasses. "What?"

She studied his face while she tapped her finger on her chin. "Are those reading glasses?"

"Yes." His brows narrowed.

Hayley saw a confused look spread across his face. "You have that Clark Kent thing going on," she said in a matter-of-fact tone.

He looked over the top of the dark rims. "'Clark Kent thing'?"

She focused on his work to avoid eye contact, trying to cover any traces of flirting. "Yeah. You know, a mild-mannered ghostwriter who takes off his glasses and becomes a handsome Superman," Hayley said nonchalantly.

"A handsome Superman, huh? And could you be Lois Lane?"

She held back her instincts to shout, "Yes, yes, yes," and smiled. "I was just stating a fact."

When Hayley looked down at the monitor, out of the corner of her she caught his amused smile. She went on with her stories until he decided to go with the first one.

He typed a few sentences, changing her story a bit. "Why don't I make the ghost the family's great-aunt, Hildy? She can show them where the deed is to save the farm."

"That's good. It can be hidden in a closet behind a wall panel."

They played with the storyline, letting their imaginations fly. They laughed and came up with one crazy idea after another until tears rolled down Hayley's cheeks.

Hayley got up from her seat, grabbed napkins from the galley, then threw all but one on the table and dabbed the wet streaks on her face. Finally getting serious, they came up with a finished tale.

An hour after Hayley had joined him Lee reread the draft. "Fantastic! All I need to do is copy-read, then send it off. Thanks for your help. I really appreciate it."

"My pleasure."

He set his glasses on the table, then swiveled his chair toward her. "So, does your clairvoyance tell you if you'll like working for us?"

"I don't have to see the future. I already know I like it. The only thing that would change my mind is being told to do something I'm not comfortable with."

"Like what?"

"Like staging."

"Staging?" Lee said.

"Using fishing line, for example, to make a door look like it's opening or closing by itself. Or faking a recording to make someone think it's a lingering spirit."

"I wouldn't be comfortable with that either. We take our investigations seriously. The infrared cameras and going over the evidence would tell us if someone was faking results. We'd catch it, I'm sure."

Hayley nodded, studying his handsome face. She felt comfortable sitting next to him, although her heart still raced when their eyes met.

He toyed with his glasses. "We expect everyone to be professional and to concentrate on their job. That's one reason I don't want employees dating each other," he explained hesitantly. "I want them to keep their minds on their work. Not to mention how uncomfortable things would be if it didn't work out. A situation like that could cause someone to quit."

He glanced at her.

Hayley couldn't believe what he had just said. She turned away, shaking her head.

"You're shaking your head. I guess you don't agree with me."

She faced him, looking into his questioning eyes. "Have you ever heard of life-links?"

"No. What's that?"

"Okay, let me give you a hypothetical example." She thought a minute. "Let's say you asked me out on a date, and we decided to meet at a very nice restaurant."

He raised a finger, tapping his head. "A very nice restaurant…

got it."

"In this story, your passion is architecture. You wait at the restaurant, but I never show up. Sad, huh?"

He nodded.

"Okay, but as you sit alone, waiting, you scribble on a napkin the plans of a house you've been envisioning for days. After realizing you've been stood up, you go ahead and order your meal. Now, as you wait for your food, you have time to detail your drawing. When your dinner is being served, your napkin falls to the floor. An architect having dinner with a client just across from you picks up the napkin. What seemed to be a bad situation leads to the job of your dreams."

"One thing leads to another."

"Exactly. Situations link together. If you didn't ask me out, you wouldn't have gone to that restaurant. And if I didn't stand you up, you wouldn't have sketched the house. It's a natural chain of events." She stared into his eyes. "Life-links only happen when things are allowed to occur spontaneously and someone's allowed to follow an instinct. Even if it's something as simple as a date. Your 'no dating' rule, although made with good intentions, would block the natural chain."

"Life-links. Wow! That's interesting. Okay, I'll reconsider my views on dating." He sat back in his chair. "So tell me — what was the reason you stood me up?"

She looked at him and teasingly smiled. "Hypothetically? I must've been hit by a truck."

With a small smile, he met her gaze. She saw a slight blush on his cheeks.

"If I ask you to go out on a date with me tonight, would you?" he asked.

His words melted her.

Lee cleared his throat. "Just a glass of wine on the beach

while we watch the sunset."

Her heart raced. "I'd like that very much."

"It's a date then." The plane banked to the right, catching his attention. He glanced out the window. "Wow! Take a look at that."

She moved back to the window seat across from him and looked out. Seals surfaced in the ocean off Coronado, while some made their way to the jutting rocks along the beach.

When their plane flew over the peninsula, Hayley saw the size and grandeur of Hotel del Coronado. The plane circled and landed at adjacent North Island Naval Air Station, then taxied to a hangar. With their bags in a van and their equipment left securely on the plane, they were chauffeured to the hotel.

The Victorian overlooked the ocean. The closer they approached, the more impressive the hotel became.

CHAPTER 12

As their military chauffeur drove the van up the hotel's curved driveway, Hayley looked out the window at Hotel del Coronado, better known as the Del to locals, she'd read. The white Victorian's fanciful balconies and spindle railings contrasted with the red roof. Architectural angles of the rooftops and the array of small dormers gave the appearance of several hotels combined. She could imagine the enormous red-roofed turret on the hotel's beach side being seen for miles from ships at sea. *Beautiful.*

While she gazed at hibiscus, banana trees, and tall palms, fond memories of residing there flooded Hayley's mind. Her thoughts confused her. This was her first visit to the hotel.

"I'm getting a weird feeling about this place, Lee," she said, not taking her eyes off the building.

He leaned closer, peering out at the Del. "What kind of weird feeling?"

"I'm getting memories of living here, but I've never been here before."

"You must be picking up the energy from the resident ghost. You should write this down. Keep a journal of anything unusual."

The driver parked under the porte-cochere. As Hayley

stepped out of the van and followed the others to the lobby, her paramnesia grew stronger. She regretted not having the ability to block unwanted thoughts. All she could do was take note of the impressions and try to concentrate on other things.

Studying the richness of the lobby's oak and mahogany woodwork lining walls and ceiling, her eyes slowly adjusted to the dimness. She wandered the lobby with Lee, hoping to spot the Del's lingering spirits.

The red floral carpeting led to a grand staircase connecting to the rooms upstairs. Left of the staircase stood an Otis hand-operated cage elevator. An attendant dressed in Victorian clothing and wearing a pillbox hat held the sliding cage door aside.

"Hayley, do you see him?"

"He's real, Lee."

"Darn!" He looked around at the decor. "So much dark wood. It feels like we're in a cave."

Kathy walked up and dangled a room pass in front of Hayley. "I get one, and you get one. We're roommates. Our bags have been sent to our rooms. And Roger's taken care of the tip."

Hayley held out her hand, and Kathy dropped the magnetized keycard into her palm. "Thanks."

Kathy stepped into the elevator with Hayley and Lee. "I need a new bathing suit, so I asked the woman behind the desk where I could find one. She said they have shops downstairs, but if I can't find what I want, there's a store down the street."

"Sounds like fun. I might join you," Hayley said.

When they reached the third floor, the elevator operator slid open the brass door and they stepped out. The three of them strolled to the end of the hall and turned the corner.

"So, what room are you in?" Lee asked Hayley.

"Three-oh-one," she told him. *Why in the world did I say that?*

"No, that's not right," Kathy said. "Look at your key. We're in 3361. How about you, Lee?"

He looked. "I'm two doors down from you."

"Do you know what time we'll be going to dinner?" Kathy asked him.

"Roger wants us to meet in his room at four." He looked at Hayley. "I guess I'll see you later."

"Yeah, see you." Hayley put the keycard into the lock and opened the door. The bellman had brought up their bags and placed them near the chair in the corner.

Kathy followed her inside. "Are you going to buy a bathing suit, too?"

"Yeah, I think I'll need one for tonight." Hayley crossed the room and opened the louvered doors leading to the balcony. "I'd like this one," she said, pointing to the bed closest to her.

"Okay." Kathy picked up her luggage and set it on the bed nearest the bathroom. "So, don't tell me...Lee asked you out."

Hayley turned in surprise. "How did you know?"

"I heard Roger and Lee talking in the office while you drove your car around back this morning." Kathy unzipped her suitcase.

"Damn! He must've told him."

"Who told who what?"

Hayley shrugged. "Oh—Roger caught me admiring Lee's tush." She grabbed her suitcase and placed it on a luggage rack next to the TV console, opened the case halfway, reached in, and removed her sneakers. She went to the edge of her bed, sat, and changed her shoes.

"That's not the first time," Kathy said.

Hayley paused, tied her shoelace, and looked up at Kathy. "What do you mean?"

"Well...."

Patiently, Hayley watched while Kathy pulled out a pink scarf and tied it around her blonde hair. Finally, Kathy continued,

"The argument wasn't exactly about that."

"What argument?" Hayley asked.

Holding up the mirror, Kathy applied pink lipstick, pulled a tissue from a small package, and carefully wiped the corner of her mouth.

"Come on. You have to tell me."

Kathy laughed, dropped the tube back into the small bag, and tossed the bag into her suitcase. Before speaking, she crawled to the middle of her bed and wrapped her arms around her knees. "It was almost an argument. Roger told Lee that he was tired of the way he was acting."

"Roger was mad at Lee?"

"No, not mad…irritated. Lee couldn't keep his eyes off you when you walked out of the office to park your car. Roger called his name three times before he snapped out of it."

"Lee was watching me?"

"What was driving Roger nuts was Lee's crazy idea that if he asked you out and things didn't work out, you'd quit. So Lee came up with a 'no dating' rule."

Hayley nodded. "Lee told me about that rule."

"I guess he figured if he couldn't ask you out, he would convince himself to keep his thoughts on business. Only it didn't work. He couldn't keep his mind off you."

Surprised, Hayley studied Kathy's face, noticing a glint of humor in her eyes and the edges of her mouth turning up. "You're not serious."

"Roger told Lee he's been looking at you as much as you've been watching him, and if he didn't ask you out, then Lee could just stay home," Kathy said.

"I'm sure he was just joking."

"He wants Lee to be happy. He told him not to worry and just go for it."

"Hmmm." Hayley felt confused. "So, Roger had to force Lee to ask me out?"

"Lee lost his entire family in one year. It was traumatic. It's been fourteen years since then, but he still has a problem with getting close. He's had his share of dates, but he's never had a girlfriend longer than a month. Roger was ecstatic when you took this job. He's like a big brother to Lee. Therefore, if it came down to his own happiness or hurting Roger if you left, Lee would make the sacrifice. So Roger gave him a shove."

Kathy climbed off the bed and giggled as she grabbed her makeup bag, comb, and brush. "Lee looks like a lost puppy when you're not around," she said, walking into the bathroom and leaving the door open.

A smile crossed Hayley's face. "So, he watches me?"

Kathy peeked out from the bathroom. "It's totally obvious, Hayley. Get a grip. You can't keep your eyes off each other. Everyone knows that except you two."

Hayley sat on the edge of her bed, the last few days going through her head, her brows narrowing as she remembered every detail. *This can't be.* She stood, then sat again. "On a scale from one to ten, how embarrassed should I be?"

"Don't do that to yourself, Hayley. Everyone loves Lee. It's been a long time since he's gone out with anyone. He's been immersing himself in those magazine stories and making excuses that he's just not interested in dating." Kathy came out of the bathroom and walked over to her. "You can't believe how happy everyone is that he's going crazy over you."

Hayley couldn't repeat the word fast enough. "'Crazy'? You'd really say 'crazy'?" *That's impossible.*

"Crazy, nuts." Kathy patted her on the leg. "Let's go shopping."

"I can't believe it!" Hayley said. She stood, grabbed her purse, and followed Kathy to the elevator. While they rode down to the hotel's shops, she couldn't stop thinking about Lee. Still in a daze of disbelief, she didn't realize the elevator door had opened.

Abruptly, Kathy took Hayley's hand and pulled her along. "Come on. We're going to find you a bathing suit that'll make Lee drool."

CHAPTER 13

After shopping, Hayley and Kathy joined the rest of the paranormal investigators and Admiral Wayne in Roger's room at four o'clock. Looking at the hotel's directory, they decided to have dinner at the Sheerwater Restaurant facing the beach.

The team split up, some taking the stairs, others the cage elevator, everyone instructed to meet on the first floor in front of the restaurant.

Through the brightly lit hallway, Hayley and Lee followed the row of shops to the right. After making their way around hotel guests, they came to a spacious lounge. The hardwood floors flared out into a sunny room. Columns, spaced throughout, reached up to a white-beamed ceiling. Light streamed through the wall of windows facing the beach. Small mahogany tables with rounded-back chairs rested on Persian rugs among indoor palms.

Hayley hesitated when she entered the room, Lee at her side. "I'm picking up memories," she said.

He glanced around. "From this room?"

She looked toward the Victorian, hand-carved mahogany bar. The enormous piece of furniture took up a fourth of the room. The back bar's spindles and mirrors lined the wall.

A wave of familiarity washed over her. "I think it's the bar." She turned to Lee, who was studying their surroundings. "Having someone else's memories in my head is really annoying. I wish I knew whose thoughts I'm getting."

"Maybe they're residual. Just the strong energy of memories left in the walls of this old place."

Hayley pushed the paramnesia to the back of her mind. "I don't want to deal with this now. Let's follow the others."

Across from the bar stood the entrance to the Sheerwater, where the group waited to be seated. They followed the hostess through the main dining room to the lanai. A table for eight allowed the team to sit together.

The hostess gave them menus. A waiter filled their water glasses.

Hayley gazed past the large canvas umbrellas on the lanai and beyond the lawns bordered with low hedges to peek at the ocean. She relaxed, smelling the salty air and listening to the rhythm of the waves. While the others considered their orders, she scanned her menu. "I recommend the roast lamb."

Without looking up, she could feel the others staring at her.

"Hayley's been recalling memories of her previous stay here," Lee explained. "Only she's never been here before."

"Must be really strong if she's recommending the hotel's food. Can you describe how you're feeling, Hayley?"

She laid her menu on the table and took a deep breath. "It's a knowing. I can see the meal and remember the taste. It's a memory from someone else's past."

"Do you think you're picking up the thoughts from a resident ghost?" Roger asked.

She nodded. "Could be. Maybe it's a favorite dish."

Roger looked across the table. "Kathy, what information did

you find about ghost sightings?"

Kathy reached for a spiral notebook by her purse. She flipped through, coming to a stop at a page marked by a folded corner. "There seem to be six ghosts seen throughout the Del. A little boy and girl run up and down the halls. An old caretaker walks through the dining room. A Victorian lady moves across the dance floor in the ballroom. But the ghosts seen most are a maid and Kate Morgan."

"That's quite a few," Roger said. "Tell us about Kate."

"I read that in 1892, around Thanksgiving, a twenty-four-year-old woman by the name of Lottie Anderson Bernard, later found to be Kate Morgan, checked in. She told the desk clerk that her brother would be joining her shortly. After five days, her brother never showed up, and her body was found outside on the stairs leading to the beach with a gun laying beside her. It appeared she had shot herself."

"What kind of activity has there been?" Roger asked.

"Everything from flickering lights and mysterious sounds to disappearing bedcovers and flying objects."

He turned to Hayley. "Can you pinpoint the time period of the memories?"

"No. I have no idea. But it doesn't feel recent."

"How old is the hotel, Kathy?" Roger asked.

She flipped a page of her notebook. "A couple of retired gentlemen from the Midwest came here in the late eighteen-eighties. There were two landmasses back then, Coronado and North Island. They bought both, then built the hotel. The military purchased the north island in 1917. After World War I, the owners of the hotel had financial difficulties and the property was sold to John D. Spreckels."

The waiter approached and asked if they were ready to order.

"Not yet. Give us another few minutes." Roger opened his

menu. "We'd better focus on ordering or we'll be here all day."

Kathy set her notes down.

The table fell quiet while they went over their menus.

After the waiter returned and took their order, Roger looked across the table. "When did they connect the island with the peninsula, Admiral?"

"It was during the nineteen-thirties. They dredged the harbor to allow bigger warships to enter, then used the dirt to fill the gap between the two landmasses."

"Are any of these facts stirring up memories, Hayley?" Roger asked.

"No. Not yet."

"After Pearl Harbor was bombed, the only residents at the hotel were military," the admiral said. "No one wanted to vacation here because they thought San Diego would be bombed next. The number of military men and women staying here, awaiting orders, saved the hotel from closing. The hotel might have served roast lamb from the time they opened and all through World War II."

Roger nodded. "They could've had a ranch close by where they got their meat. Any other memories besides the food, Hayley?"

"I had a familiar feeling as I walked past the bar."

"That won't help pinpoint the time either," Kathy told them. "The bar was brought from Pennsylvania by ship around Cape Horn in 1888, the year the hotel opened. If it had been installed much later, we could've narrowed the timeline."

Jim rubbed his chin. "Ya know, that bar's 'bout as old as Larry, but in better shape."

"Don't start with me, Jim. I have friends in high places that can make the date on your birth certificate read 'older than dirt.'"

"Why, Larry, that would be dishonest."

"I still owe you for some of those hellish jokes you sprang on me when we were young."

Hayley noticed Clint and John sitting forward in their seats, listening closely, and she laughed to herself.

"Them days are gone," Jim said.

"True, but some things are hard to forget. For example—"

Jim held up his palm. "Hold it, Larry. Don't be lettin' the cat outta the bag. We've got a couple of lightweight jokesters here," he said, pointing at Clint and John. "And I'd rather not give 'em any good ideas."

"No one could be as ornery as you," Admiral Wayne said.

"Not anymore. I'm sweeter than whiskey in punch nowadays. I've mellowed with age. Just ask Roger."

"Don't bring me into this." He glanced over his shoulder at the waiter with his arms full of plates. "Just in time."

Hayley and Lee had ordered the recommended roast lamb.

Finally making his way around the table, the waiter placed the last order of a hamburger and soda in front of Clint.

"Clint, is that all you're gonna eat?" Jim asked. "Have ya looked at yourself lately? If ya stand sideways and stick out your tongue, ya look like a zipper. I've seen more meat on a hockey stick."

"I'm just not hungry."

"Think you're getting sick?" John asked, with mock concern.

Maybe he is. Hayley studied Clint's posture, wondering if his health was the major event of his life-link. This could be serious. *I'll try to foresee his future later when I'm alone.*

"Maybe you should rest," John added.

Clint glared at his cousin. "You'd like that, wouldn't you? You think you'll be able to meet girls without me? I'm the chick magnet. Not you."

"In your dreams."

"You don't sound sick," Roger said. "Have a stomachache or anything?"

"No. I'm just not hungry. What's the big deal?" Clint said.

Roger shrugged. "We're a long way from home. Just wanted to make sure."

As Jim picked up his fork and knife, ready to cut another slice of meat, he turned to Lee. "This steak is so good my taste buds are applaudin'. How's the lamb?"

After taking a bite, Lee nodded. "Good choice!"

Hayley raised her fork to have a taste. The slice of lamb fell off the tines and slid down the front of her blouse. "Oh, no!" She lifted the meat from her blouse, then tried to wipe off the gravy. "I think I might've ruined this blouse."

Quickly Lee dipped his white cloth napkin into his water glass and leaned toward her. With a reddened face, he hesitated an inch away from Hayley's breast. "Ah…I think you should do this." He handed her the damp cloth.

While she dabbed, the spot spread.

Kathy took the hotel's brochure from her purse. "The hotel can clean that for you."

"I think I'll let them. After I eat, I guess I'll go upstairs and change." She returned the napkin to Lee.

"I'll go with you if you want," he said. "I'm expecting an email and left my cell phone in my room."

"Thanks, Lee. I feel really weird about this place."

* * *

Hayley laid her knife and fork across her empty plate, then dabbed the corners of her mouth with her napkin. Sitting back in her chair while the others finished their meals, she thought about the strange feelings she'd experienced earlier, planning to write about them in her journal.

When she looked at Roger, something unexpected happened.

She saw a vision of him kissing a woman with long dark hair. It was as if she'd stepped into a romantic movie. The movie ended abruptly, her reality returned, and no one at the dinner table had noticed her momentary trance state.

Great. I'm getting visions of Roger's future when I haven't been able to read him since we've met. Why now? Did the hotel's weird energy trigger it? What's going on? I need to talk to Grams.

CHAPTER 14

After dinner, Hayley and Lee walked along the hallways beneath the Del's lobby. They stopped to read a brief history displayed under glass, telling of the hotel, Coronado, and North Island, and then continued on.

Off the hall, they came to the elevator next to a wide, dimly lit staircase. From somewhere above a cool breeze drifted down, catching Hayley's attention. Gazing up the stairs, she saw the bustle of a long black lace dress disappear within the elevator shaft. She left Lee's side and wandered to the bottom of the stairs. With her foot on the last step and her hand on the railing, she sensed a presence and decided to follow.

Lee released the elevator button and waited for its arrival.

The elevator door slid open and a short man in a vintage uniform slid the brass cage door aside. "Are you going up, sir?"

Hayley began inching her way up the stairs.

Lee hesitated. "I guess not. Thank you."

The operator closed the cage.

Following Hayley's lead, Lee turned away. "Do you see something?"

She put her finger to her lips, and whispered, "Do you have

your digital camera with you?"

Reaching into his pocket, he pulled out a small camera. "Yes. How did you know?" He mumbled, "Stupid question."

Hayley peeked behind the elevator shaft at the deserted staircase. "I thought I saw the bustle of a woman's black lace dress." She turned and shrugged. "Gone."

Lee took pictures from all angles while he climbed the stairs, trying to capture any signs of paranormal activity.

Lifting her chin, Hayley noticed a sweet fragrance. "Do you smell perfume?"

He moved to her side and sniffed. "Yes. Strange. It's only in this small area." He snapped a shot of the area above her. "Do you see mist or anything like that?"

"No," she said. "Not a thing."

They continued toward the lobby. A young lady sitting behind a small desk at the landing asked if she could help them.

"Did you see a woman in a bustled black lace dress come by here?" Hayley asked.

"No. Sorry." The woman laughed lightly. "Bet you saw Kate Morgan, our resident ghost. She wanders the entire hotel, and has no problem letting people know she's around."

Hayley peered up at the balcony encircling the lobby. "Come on, Lee. Let's go up to the next floor and take some photos."

They rushed around to the right side of the elevator and climbed the stairs to the next landing.

From above, Hayley gazed out over the railing. The enormous chandelier, hanging from the mahogany-beamed ceiling of the second floor, seemed to float over the center of the busy room below.

Lee adjusted his camera lens. "Let's get some shots of the lobby and take a few on our way to our rooms," he said. "When I get to my room, I'll download these pictures into my computer and see if we caught anything interesting."

Hayley scanned the crowd of people below…some checking in, while others roamed the lobby. She squinted into the shadows. "I don't see her. Let's head up to our rooms."

Aiming his camera toward the ceiling and the dark paneled walls, Lee took a few more shots. "I think I've got enough. I'm right behind you."

They climbed one more flight of stairs.

Wide-striped gold-and-cream wallpaper brightened the narrow hall. They followed the hallway to the right, which led to the rooms on the street-side of the hotel. Along the way, Lee angled his camera, snapping photos of the empty corridor.

They came to an out-of-the-way staircase connecting to the courtyard below.

When they came to the first door on the left, Hayley turned away from Lee and tried to enter the room. She rattled the doorknob and scowled, then searched her pockets. "How do I get in?"

He hurried to her. "What are you looking for and whose room is this?"

"It's mine. I can't find my key." She took a deep, frustrated breath, jiggled the handle again, and put her hands on her hips.

Lee looked at the floor and picked up her keycard lying next to her feet. He held it up to her, but she didn't respond. "Ah… what kind of key are you looking for?"

"You know what a key looks like. A shiny piece of metal with teeth." She looked at the doorknob. "Where's the keyhole? Who changed the lock on my door?"

Lee took her picture, then snapped shots of the area around her. "What name did you write on the register when you checked in?"

Hayley thought for a second, and looked at the number on

the oval plaque on the wall next to the doorframe. The room's number read 3326. Confused, not knowing what had just happened, she stepped back and shook her head. "This isn't my room. What was I doing?"

"Looked like you were trying to get into someone else's room. You do know hotels don't use metal keys any longer? Are you aware we're not even close to your room?"

She realized where she was and watched Lee's face. *If he didn't think I'm strange before, he will now.*

"I think you were possessed, and it might have something to do with Kate Morgan. How do you feel?"

Knowing she'd lost complete control to something or someone shook her. And looking like a fool in front of Lee made matters worse. "I can't believe I spontaneously reacted to someone else's memories." She looked at his concerned face. "It's one thing to remember their favorite dish on the menu, but to physically react like this is really scary."

Lee put his arm around her shoulder. "Come with me. I'll make sure you get home safely." He guided her to the end of the hall and around the corner. Every few steps, he asked if she was all right.

"I'm fine. Really. But whoever is messing with my mind is more than annoying."

"I can understand that," he said, lowering his arm as they reached her door. While she unlocked her door, he looked over her shoulder. The door clicked open.

Hayley spun around and faced Lee, feeling self-conscious and a bit of a freak. *How long will it be before he runs the other way?* "Thanks for walking me home."

"I can't imagine what would've happened if I hadn't been with you." He studied her face. "I'm going back to my room. Will you be all right?"

"Yes. Seriously, I'm fine."

"I'll bring my computer back, and we can go over the pictures with Roger. It won't be long. I'll knock on your door when I'm ready."

"Okay, I'll see you in a few minutes."

She watched Lee walk away, then went inside and closed the door. "Perfect. I'm alone. Grams, I need you."

While standing in the center of the room, Hayley turned in a circle, wondering if her grandmother had heard her call. She glanced over her shoulder.

Grams sat in a chair near the balcony, wearing a blue summer dress. A white headband pulled her blonde hair back away from her bangs. "Yes, dear?"

"Did you see what happened to me in the hallway?"

"Of course."

"Who was controlling me? Who's getting inside my head?"

"Sorry. You know I'm not allowed to interfere in your life."

Hayley's mouth gaped. She couldn't believe what she'd heard. "'Interfere'? You're joking, right?" She walked over to Grams and stood in front of her, totally confused. "I just want to know how to stop this from happening." Her grandmother's stoic expression made her realize Grams was serious. Hayley threw up her arms. "I don't get it. You've always helped me. What's different now?"

"You can't have all the answers, Hayley. You have to live your life the same way everyone else does."

Hayley stepped backwards until she found the edge of the bed and gingerly sat. *Can't have all the answers? What's that supposed to mean?* "But I'm not like anyone else. Besides not being able to block unwanted energy, I'm having trouble reading the people around me. Am I losing my abilities? Am I becoming normal?" She stood and paced the room, torn between wishful thinking and the feeling of dread. "I've wanted to be normal all my life, but not this way." She faced Grams. "It's life threatening. How am I going to deal with this? I need to shield myself."

"You'll get through this, dear. All I can tell you is that you will find the answer. I can't say anymore. Love you."

"Wait. Is this going to mess up our military investigation?"

"You don't need me, dear. You'll be just fine. Love you." With that, she disappeared.

"I love you, too, Grams." Hayley crossed her arms. "Well, I guess I have to figure this out on my own."

CHAPTER 15

While standing at the entrance to the lounge, Hayley spotted Jim and the admiral drinking beer at the bar. Jim waved.

Hayley waved back and nudged Lee. "There's Jim and Admiral Wayne." She looked around for the others. "I don't see Roger."

"Let's check outside." Lee waved toward the bar, then, taking her hand, led her out the glass double doors to the patio, where he looked for the others.

She glanced down at his hand in hers, and her gaze traveled up his arm to the soft skin of his neck, then lingered at his handsome face as he looked over his shoulder. *After what happened earlier, now his hand's in mine, he put his arm around me while he walked me to my room, and I have a date with him later. Grams, wherever you are, pinch me.*

The ocean's salty breeze brushed against Hayley's face and whipped her light brown hair, bringing her thoughts back to the moment. She looked up at the cloudless sky. The afternoon sun had dipped into evening.

It can't be later than five-thirty. It's June. The sun should set around eight.

She smiled, thinking about tonight and Lee. While gazing toward the west, she spotted Clint, John, and Kathy coming from the beach by the hotel. "Well, there are the guys and Kathy," she said, "but where's Roger?"

"Let's try over by those tables," he suggested.

Lee walked hand-in-hand with her to the shaded tables, only steps from the Sheerwater. They found Roger sitting under an umbrella out of the sun, sipping a drink.

Lee set his computer on the patio table, pulled out a chair for Hayley, and moved his chair closer to hers. After they sat, he took her hand again, giving it a gentle squeeze, and asked in a low voice, "Can I get you anything?"

She shook her head.

Roger set his drink on the table, leaned back in his chair, and folded his arms, scrutinizing them. "What's going on, you two? You look like you've seen a ghost."

"You're not far off. We had a very interesting walk to our rooms," Lee said. He opened his laptop and booted it up. "I'm going to go over the pictures we took on our way upstairs."

Hayley's attention was drawn to the Sheerwater's lanai, where earlier she'd experienced someone else's memories of the restaurant's roast lamb. Nervously she looked for any of the hotel's deceased residents, knowing she couldn't block their attacks on her. *I feel like their puppet.*

"Are you going to fill me in on what happened? Hayley looks a little shaken."

Lee focused on the computer screen, his fingers darting across the keyboard. "Once I pull up these pictures, I'll start from the beginning."

When a hand appeared on the back of her chair, Hayley jumped and peered up at Jim.

"Sorry, didn't mean to scare ya." Jim glanced at Lee. "I saw ya draggin' her by the hand with that protective look on your face. What happened?" He and Admiral Wayne set their beer glasses on the table, then pulled up chairs.

Not wishing to lead the conversation, Hayley sat quietly, wanting Lee to speak. *I can't tell them. I didn't feel any different or sense anything unusual. Was I possessed? I can't explain it.*

Lee looked up from the computer. "I'll start with what happened in the hallway. This first shot was taken down that hall." Lee pointed inside. "On the staircase leading to the lobby, Hayley thought she saw Kate."

"Well, knock me down and steal my teeth. Did ya get her picture?" Jim asked.

"We can only speculate," Lee said. "Unfortunately, Kate stepped behind the elevator shaft, and Hayley only glimpsed her bustle."

Jim turned to the admiral. "I heard gettin' a picture of Kate is like tryin' to shoot a gnat off the head of a hummingbird. Damn spook disappears before you can get a shot."

Lee enlarged the photo and then swiveled the laptop toward Roger. "This picture shows a vaporous cloud hovering above Hayley on the staircase."

Roger studied the photo. "This is wicked cool. I can't believe you captured this." He pushed the laptop toward Jim.

Jim moved the computer closer to the admiral, reached into his pocket, and pulled out a pen. With the tip, he pointed to the faint shape in the photo. "This is an energy vapor. Ghosts don't always appear as people. Sometimes they travel as vapor. Mostly they choose to be orbs, 'cause it takes less energy to take that shape. But whatever shape they decide on, we don't usually see 'em with the naked eye. They show up after we develop the pictures." He gave the laptop back to Lee.

"Interesting," the admiral said.

Lee pulled up the next photo, then turned the screen so Roger could see. "This was taken on the second floor, overlooking the lobby."

Roger nodded. "Great shot, Lee." He got up and took the computer to the admiral, setting it in front of him. "This is what Jim was talking about. See these orbs? They look like bubbles, but they're not. Each one is believed to be an entity. When Lee was taking this picture, he couldn't see them."

"Very impressive," Admiral Wayne said. "I've never seen anything like it."

"We know of six spirits from our research, and it looks like they're all in the lobby at the same time," Roger said.

"Gettin' all these ghosts together is like herdin' cats," Jim said. He turned to Hayley and Lee. "Good job, guys."

After his laptop was returned to him, Lee brought up the pictures from the third-floor hallway. "We left the balcony and headed to our rooms. Just as we turned the corner and came to room 3326, next to the first stairway, Hayley was possessed."

Everyone gasped.

"What?" Roger asked, taking his seat. "You're not serious."

"Hayley insisted it was her room and searched her pockets for a key. I mean a real key, not the keycard they gave us. She kept pushing and pulling on the doorknob."

Jim stared at her in amazement. "How long was she possessed, Lee?"

"Two or three minutes."

With a glint of sympathy in his eye, Jim smiled and said, "Don't worry, darlin'. I know how you're feelin'. I was possessed once myself."

Roger glared at him. "No, you weren't! You were just trying to cover up the reason why you drove the company van over a ditch and into the lake."

"I was possessed, Roger. I swear."

A gust played with Hayley's hair until the wayward strands fell across her lips. Irritated at her vulnerability, she brushed her hair behind her ear and inhaled deeply to calm herself. "I felt absolutely sure it was my room, but the lock was different." She shook her head. "It's scarier than hell having no control over what's happening to you." She brushed her hand down her arm. "I'm getting goosebumps."

"What else did you notice?" Roger asked.

"Now that I think about it, I'm pretty sure the colors of the hallway and carpet were different."

"Sounds like you were reliving the past," Roger said. "I don't think you necessarily had to be possessed, though. Maybe you were wrapped up in a memory left in the walls of this place."

Hayley looked around when Kathy, Clint, and John joined them. The boys turned, watching a couple of well-endowed, bikini-clad blondes stroll toward the beach.

Jim cleared his throat. "Stop gawkin' and close your mouths. Ya look like a couple of carps."

John looked away, took his baseball cap off, folded it, and stuck it under his belt. Swiping his hand across his bald head, he glanced at his cousin.

Clint smiled, ran his fingers through his red hair, looked up, and whistled.

A sneer crossed John's face.

Roger glared at them. "Don't start, guys."

While looking over Roger's shoulder, Kathy examined the photo and pushed her sunglasses onto her forehead. Her platinum blonde hair was neatly pulled into a braid. "What room did you say it was?" she asked Lee.

"3326."

"Kate's room is 3327," Kathy said.

"Maybe it was." Lee checked the photo again. "No, I was right."

Roger rubbed his chin. "What are your plans for tonight, Lee?"

"I'm taking Hayley on a date. We're going to have some wine and watch the sunset on the beach." Lee looked up from his laptop and a boyish smile crossed his face.

Hayley looked at Lee's dark wavy hair, then into his brown eyes, and followed the curve of his strong jaw down to his muscular arms. Her annoyance from the episode in the hotel began to melt away.

"You'll probably be going up to your rooms before then, so why don't we go with you?" Roger said. "That'll give us a chance to see if she'll be possessed again. We'll let Hayley lead."

While Lee studied Hayley's face, he laid his hand on hers. "Are you okay with that? Do you think you'll be all right?"

The expression on his face reminded her of his concern for her at Lucy's. *Am I a burden?* "Sure, Lee, but I don't see why it should happen again. Especially now that I know what to expect."

"Well, why don't we go up and see?" Roger suggested.

The seven investigators and the admiral left the table and headed toward the elevator. When they reached the third floor, they let Hayley lead.

"Just relax," Lee said. "Try to clear your mind and follow your instincts."

Hayley nodded. This time she would protect herself. She closed her eyes and mentally surrounded herself with white light before walking along the narrow hallway. The others kept their distance while she approached the room next to the staircase.

As she had before, she stopped and reached for the doorknob, finding the door locked. She jiggled the handle and started to reach in her pocket for a key. The phenomenon diminished, letting her regain control. When she realized this wasn't her room, she took a step back. "Damn! I can't protect myself."

Lee rushed over, took her hand, and led her away from the room. The others gathered around.

"It didn't look like you were possessed," Roger said. "I think you started to react about five feet from the door." He walked back down the hall. "Come here and see if you feel a pull or a sense of a memory as you move toward the door."

Hayley went to the spot where Roger stood, then tried stepping farther away and walking toward the room again. "I'm not getting anything. There's not a memory or a pull of any kind."

"Hmm," Roger said, examining the area around them.

"Kate's room is across from this one," Kathy said. "I don't think it was her."

"You're probably right. Kate making Hayley go into the room across from hers doesn't make sense," Roger said.

Vexed that her abilities weren't providing insight into who was controlling her, Hayley stood with her hands on her hips. "Then who? This is a lot different from me picking up images and seeing the past. I didn't have any control over what I was doing. It's unnerving."

"I wouldn't count Kate out," Lee said. "This is too close to be just a coincidence." He thought for a moment. "How about her maid?"

"That's a definite possibility," Roger said.

Jim put his finger to his chin and stared Lee in the eye. "Ya need to take Hayley on that date and get her mind off things."

A blush touched Lee's cheeks. He glanced at her and gave her a sheepish grin. "I think I can manage that. I'm bringing wine."

Jim gave him a wink. "Good plan."

CHAPTER 16

Now that the manipulation by ghosts had subsided, Hayley stood in her room, inhaled the salty air drifting in through the open balcony doors, and giggled. This was the first time since they'd been at the Del that she felt relaxed enough to enjoy the moment.

I can't believe I'm here. How cool is this? From the Atlantic to the Pacific. The first leg of our journey. And tomorrow, Hawaii. Wow! She gazed at her reflection in the mirror and giggled again. *Who knew?*

A breeze stirred the curtains. She noticed her journal lying on the bedside table. The entries she'd made of her stay at the Del so far were bothersome. Their layover in Coronado had been arranged by Admiral Wayne.

I hope he doesn't book us into anymore haunted hotels.

She thought back to when she'd originally seen him through the plane's window. *That's strange. I had the same familiar feeling when I first saw Admiral Wayne as I'm getting from this hotel. Well, isn't that just great. I'll have to add that little mystery to my "What in the hell's going on?" list.*

Hayley flipped the page and read the entry about Lee. From

the first time her eyes met his, she couldn't stop thinking about him. If Kathy hadn't told her that Lee was just as crazy for her, she wouldn't have guessed, though. He never let on. *How could I have been so naïve?* She placed her journal back on the nightstand, then turned to get ready for their date.

She rummaged through her shopping bag and selected a teal bikini and an outfit to throw on over it. After changing into her bathing suit, she tied the strings at the back of her neck and stepped in front of the mirror. The bikini brought out more than the blue of her eyes.

If he had trouble keeping his mind off me before, I'm afraid he's in for some sleepless nights now.

She reached for the light blue halter-top and white shorts, tossing them on over her swim suit, and headed to the bathroom to apply finishing touches. While combing her hair, Hayley heard a knock. She slid the comb into the back pocket of her shorts and went to the door.

Lee stood holding a pile of towels and a brown picnic basket. His gaze went from her bare legs to her blouse's plunging neckline, where it lingered. He cleared his throat. "You look nice."

When he moved aside, allowing her to step out into the hallway, the tower of towels leaned and the crowning towel tumbled to the floor.

They bent at the same time.

Her knees turned to jelly as their eyes met. His lips were inches away from hers. She stood. With a deep breath, she steadied herself, then reached out. "Let me help you."

He gave her the fallen towel.

Hayley folded it, then held out her arms while he stacked a few more on top. "Thanks. I've got everything else," he said.

"How did you get all this?"

"I gave the concierge a little something." With his hands full,

122

he managed to point a finger at the pile she carried. "We've got blanket beach towels." He tucked the few towels he still carried under his arm and lifted the basket lid. "For our sunset snack — wine, cheeses, salmon, and crackers."

"Sounds good." She almost choked on the word "good." How many times had she dreamed about a date on the beach? The word was "romantic."

He escorted her to a staircase connecting to the beach.

While they strolled toward the tall palm trees along the manicured lawns beside the seashore, Hayley noticed that the crowds of visitors who had relaxed and enjoyed the hotel's laid-back atmosphere had thinned. Only a few people had stayed to catch the sunset.

The blue of the sky faded to a lighter hue. She knew it wouldn't be long before the wisps of clouds above the horizon would become aflame with color.

She walked with Lee across the smooth sands of the beach to find a place to unfurl their blanket. They chose a comfortable spot a few feet from where the sands were moistened by the ocean's waves.

She slipped out of her blouse and shorts and folded them, laying them next to the towels. When she turned she found Lee pulling his white T-shirt over his head. His arms, not overly sculpted, were well shaped — arms she would love to fall into.

He flung his shirt onto the blanket and glanced at her. "Nice swimsuit."

Noticing his lingering gaze, Hayley blushed. "Thanks." Starting to feel self-conscious, she smiled, tucked her hair behind her ear, and looked out toward the ocean, then back at his broad smile.

He reached out his hand. "Let's walk."

A scene from a romance novel, a page from a fairytale, a date with Adonis—wishes from her most-desired daydreams were being checked off her list when he took her hand. They made their way to the wet, compressed sand right at the water's edge, where they could walk easily.

Piles of boulders, blocking the beach to the east, jutted into the ocean. Hayley looked up at the sound of a seal's bark. Two harbor seals pulled themselves up onto the rocks, squinting into the sun while they rested on the huge stones. She and Lee turned to stroll in the opposite direction. When they stopped to watch the gulls gliding over the ocean, the froth from the remnants of a wave skimmed across their feet.

Lee wiggled his toes. "That feels good, doesn't it? Had you ever seen the Pacific Ocean?"

"No. How about you?"

"A few times, but it's never as fun when you're by yourself." He looked toward the horizon. "Like a lot of things."

"I know what you mean." Hayley followed his gaze. "I've thought about visiting England, but the thought of going alone killed it for me. Have you ever been there?"

He nodded. "Several times."

"So, if we stand here," she said, "where do you think Hawaii is?"

After getting his bearings, he pointed, moving his finger to the left of the Point Loma peninsula. "I'm not really sure, but I think Hawaii would be about there."

"This feels more like a vacation than a job," she admitted. "I can't believe I'm here. A week of traveling to a remote island off Guam...what could be better?"

He took her hand again and they strolled along the wet sands. "Are you having any kind of feelings about our trip to the Japanese ship?"

"I'm still worried about the weather."

"That's an easy fix. I can search the web for weather tracking on my laptop once I get to my room. So, you're not sensing anything about the next few days?"

"Feelings? Like what?"

"I don't know. I guess clairvoyant. Some sort of hint of what we can expect."

"No. Nothing." She peered down at the tide licking her feet.

"Is that normal for you?"

She knew she had to tell him soon that her abilities were faltering. "I never get impressions of my own future. But that doesn't mean I won't be able to see or feel something about our case. I just haven't yet." Guilt and frustration washed over her. *How am I going to tell him? That's why they hired me. I'll be letting him and the team down.*

He stopped walking, dropped her hand, bent down, and picked up a piece of shell. "How about the rest of us? Can you see our futures?" he asked, tossing the shard into the water.

"I'm getting some. Remember what I told you about life-links?" she asked.

"Yes," he replied, giving her his full attention.

"If you tell someone what I saw, it could block the link and it might not happen at all."

His brows narrowed. "Will it change things if you tell me?"

They began to stroll again, moving away from the incoming tide.

"Not if you keep it to yourself."

"Okay. I can do that. So what have you seen?"

"I saw Roger kissing a woman who has long black hair, but I don't know when it will happen."

He stopped. His wide eyes lit up. "Wow! Really? I mean, seriously?"

"Remember, you can't tell him."

"What? Don't you think you can trust me?" He picked her up, cradling her in his arms, and headed out into the water.

She gasped, surprise overwhelmed her, and her heart raced. Giggling, she wrapped her arms around his neck.

Waves hit his thighs.

Hayley held on tightly. "Wait, Lee! No! No!"

Reaching up, he pried her grip from around his neck and tossed her into the shallow water.

Hayley tried to glare at him when a small wave hit her from behind. She wiped her drenched face. "You should come with a label, Lee — warning: known to throw defenseless women into the ocean."

While the cold water splashed over her, she remembered the self-defense classes she had taken in her high school gym class. *Okay, you want to play rough….* She brushed back her hair, then reached up. "Give me a hand, Mister Bully."

He pulled her up. Her wet bikini clung to her. She shivered from the cold.

"Have I told you how much I like your swimsuit?" he asked, his smile almost a smirk.

Hayley folded her arms across her chest. "I'm cold, Lee."

With payback on her mind, she nestled against him as she contemplated her next move. She felt his body mold against hers as he held her. *Now.* Catching him off guard, she stepped to the side, wrapped her leg behind his, and pulled his right leg out from under him.

He fell back into a breaking wave.

"Ha!" She laughed.

Lee leapt out of the water.

Surprised at his quick recovery, Hayley ran onto the dry sand, which hindered her movement. Trying to get back to the wet sand, she turned, but Lee stood behind her. She went to her right and he blocked her. Then she tried to go left, and he blocked her again. Laughing, she spun around to escape.

He grabbed her before she knew it, flipping her back into his arms. "Defenseless, hah!" He turned back toward the water.

"You're not?"

"No, I'm not. I'm just going to help you wash the sand off."

When he reached the water, he set her down. A wave washed over her feet. She leaned over his shoulder when he bent to wipe the sand from her legs.

Gently, he lifted her across his shoulder, carried her back to the blanket, then set her down. Grinning, he shook the water out of his hair.

She flinched, the cold water splattering over her. "Tha-tha-thanks, Lee." Her teeth chattered, and she hugged herself.

Lee grabbed a beach blanket and sat, moving his legs wide apart. "Sit in front of me, and I'll throw this around us." Scooting back, he made room for her. She sat, and he wrapped the beach blanket around them. "Here, you hold the towel," he said, giving her the ends.

She clenched them in front of her and drew in a breath when she felt his warm arms wrap around her bare waist.

"Is that better?" he asked.

"Perfect." *Heaven.*

The waves rushed to the shore and the breeze carried the salty scent. Hayley took a deep relaxing breath and watched the seagulls soar, searching for their evening meal. In the distance, the sun lingered low on the horizon. She leaned into Lee, her hands pulling the beach towel snugly in front of her. She looked up. *Thank you, God.*

After what seemed to be a moment of awkward silence, Lee's lips brushed against her ear. "Would you like some wine?"

She wondered if he could feel her heart race as his breath

sent tingles though every nerve in her body. "I do, but I don't. I don't want to move."

"Are you still cold?"

Hayley cuddled closer. "Not at all." She felt him smile against her cheek.

"I'm sure we can figure this out. Don't move," he said. "I think we need to ditch the towel."

Reluctantly, she let go of the terrycloth edges.

Lee took his arm from around Hayley's waist and tossed the towel behind him. Leaning back, he reached for the basket.

Hayley scooted around to sit opposite him. "Why don't I make some snacks while you pour the wine?"

"Sounds good." He opened the lid, pulled out a bottle of Merlot, and passed her the basket.

She removed the cheese, crackers, smoked salmon, and set them aside. After taking out a plate to use as a cutting board, she sliced the fish into small pieces and glanced at him. "I talked to Grams today," she said, "right after you left me in my room while you answered your email."

Lee held the wine bottle steady on the blanket in front of him. He hesitated before reaching for the corkscrew and looked at her, raising a brow. "Your grandmother? The one that's your guardian angel? She appeared in your room?"

"Yes," Hayley said, continuing to stack the cheese and salmon on the crackers. "She appears whenever I need her."

"So, what did you talk about?"

Hayley set the plate of snacks to the side, then faced Lee. She needed to be honest with him. "Something strange has been going on with my abilities since I took this job. I was able to read Clint's and John's life-link, but I can't foresee where it's leading."

"Clint and John have a life-link? Is it because they're cousins?" Lee asked.

"No," she said. "It has to do with their betting. Each time they bet, it's a link in the chain. But I can't see the event it's leading to. Normally for me, that wouldn't be a problem. I've tried to read you and the others and, besides a tiny peek at Roger's future, I'm not able to see a thing."

"You've been trying to read me?" A grin flickered across his face.

"Don't make me go there, Lee." She blushed. "That's not the point I was making."

His smile disappeared. "Sorry. Go ahead."

"Anyway, I'm afraid I'm losing my abilities. I thought you should know."

"Wow! That sounds serious. Are you worried? You know, being like the rest of us isn't so bad. What did Grams say?"

"She said she couldn't say anything because she'd be interfering in my life. I'm supposed to experience life just like anyone else, without having a clue."

"She wouldn't tell you if you're right about this?"

"She said I'll find out why, but didn't say when. Then I asked about the military case. She said I'll be just fine." *I hope that's what she meant.*

"That's good to know." He pulled two glasses from the basket.

She nodded, meeting his gaze. "This thing that's going on with my abilities has been driving me insane. Normally I would've been able to block the memories I've been experiencing, and I never would've been controlled like I was. It's damn scary."

"Maybe you just need to relax a little and get your mind off everything. Could be stress." He finished removing the cork, poured her a glass of wine, and passed it to her.

Nerves? Maybe. But I doubt it. "You're probably right," she said, reaching for her drink. She took a sip.

Lee patted the blanket in front of him. "Want your seat back?"

She moved back into cuddling position and leaned into him once more, molding herself against his warm body.

He wrapped his arm around her. "Don't worry any more about your abilities, Hayley. Even if the worst happens and you lose all of your gifts, you can't do a thing about it. We've brought all of our equipment. This wouldn't be our first case without using your psychic abilities. And if I'm not worried, you shouldn't be either."

"Thanks, Lee." Hayley sighed, pushed the negativity from her thoughts, and brushed her hand across his. She looked at the horizon, watching the flames of sunset paint the sky. She smiled, absorbing the moment, and sipped her wine.

CHAPTER 17

Sensual thoughts of Lee faded as Hayley drifted on the edge of sleep. Memories from the hotel's haunted past mingled with fragments of elusive dreams. She tossed and turned. Opening one eye, she peeked at the clock—four A.M.

In the early morning darkness, Hayley lay awake. She kept her eyes closed and calmed her breathing. *You are feeling sleepy. With each breath, you are going deeper and deeper and deeper to sleep.* Her sigh turned into a tired groan. She rolled over to take another peek at the clock. *Damn!* In a few hours, she and the rest of the team would be on a plane to Hawaii.

Dreamy thoughts of Lee and their date last night floated across her mind. No, it wasn't a dream. She remembered how he'd held her for the longest time outside her door before saying goodnight. A kiss would've been nice, but even though it didn't happen, the date was better than she could've imagined. As she drifted back to sleep, she envisioned herself and Lee on a remote island, walking along its white sandy beach, while palm trees swaying in the breeze.

Kathy's cell phone rang, pulling Hayley unwillingly away from waterfalls and a rainbow of plumeria. Fighting to stay awake, she heard Kathy's voice.

"Okay. We'll see you soon." Kathy hung up. "Come on; get up. We've leaving this morning, remember?"

Moving in slow motion, but eager to leave, Hayley finished packing while Kathy called the desk.

"They're sending someone up to get our bags," Kathy said. "Roger said not to tip whoever they send. The admiral has taken care of everything. We're supposed to meet everyone in the lobby."

Once someone picked up their luggage, Kathy and Hayley grabbed their purses and left the room. Hayley turned to close the door when Lee walked over to them.

"Good morning." His gaze met Hayley's tired eyes. "You look like you didn't sleep a wink."

"A wink. That's about it."

She, Lee, and Kathy strolled the narrow hallway and took the elevator down. In the lobby, they walked beneath the crystal chandelier toward the foyer, where Roger stood waiting.

"Everyone's outside getting into the van," Roger said. "We should be ready to go as soon as they load the luggage."

Hayley climbed into the second van. She heard Roger, Kathy, and Lee talking to the admiral on the curb outside. Her tired ears couldn't catch the conversation.

Lee slid in beside her. "Well, we're on our way to Hawaii."

* * *

Both vans were waved through the gates at North Island Naval Air Station. Following the narrow roads across the base, they approached the airfield. Hayley glanced out the window and saw the private jet waiting on the tarmac. They circled around and stopped in front of the wing.

The aroma of coffee welcomed her when she boarded. Plopping down into the first seat facing the galley, she yawned.

When Lee sank into the seat next to her, Hayley gave him a tired smile.

He reached over, giving her hand a gentle squeeze. "Sure you don't want anything to eat? They stocked the galley."

"No, thanks. I'll get something after I wake up," she said, fastening her seatbelt.

He leaned across her and closed the window shade.

Not able to keep her eyes open, she crossed her arms and laid her head against the pillowed headrest. Thoughts of their destination drifted in her mind. *Hawaii. I'm going to Hawaii.* She turned her head and smelled the smooth leather, then sighed. *Note to self: When pigs fly and I'm rich, buy a private jet.* She hardly noticed that Lee had left his seat.

He returned with a blanket and pillow. "Here you go. Get some sleep, and I'll wake you before we land." Putting the pillow behind her head, he adjusted it to make her comfortable, then covered her with the blanket.

"Thanks, Lee. How long is the flight?"

"Five-and-a-half hours."

Her hand covered a yawn. "Okay."

She closed her eyes and drifted into a dream that placed her outside the Del. On the walkway, she stood near the Victorian barroom. The crowds of army and navy personnel, who laughed and drank inside, wore World War II uniforms.

She saw the reflection of a naval officer in the mirror behind the old mahogany bar. He walked inside, hearing music and laughter, while feeling the underlying tension in the air from the men awaiting orders.

The sun started to set. She watched the officer approach the bartender. A young man sitting at the bar stood and offered him his seat.

After the officer sat, a beer slid in front of him. He sipped.

Hayley listened to his thoughts of his family. After remembering a promise he had made to them, he left the bar and followed the flickering lights down the hallway to the elevator. The attendant stepped aside, allowing him to enter.

"What floor, sir?"

"Third, thank you."

Through his eyes, she watched him walk the narrow hall until he came to his room. He took his key, opened the door, and went straight to the writing desk, sat down, and pulled out a pen. On hotel stationery, he wrote:

— —

Dear Mom and Dad,

I hope everything is fine at home. I miss you already, even if it's only been a week. I'm staying at the Hotel del Coronado, just a brief ferry ride away from San Diego. I'll be here only a short time. I'm waiting for orders to board ship and go to war. The hotel is full of military personnel waiting for word. I've enclosed a picture of me standing in front of the hotel. Tell Uncle George that the roast lamb is excellent here, and it's my favorite dish. If he ever gets a chance to come to the Del, I highly recommend it. I'll keep in touch as best I can. Give my love to everyone.

Love, Richard

* * *

A tickle on her nose startled Hayley awake. She opened her eyes to find Lee smiling at her. "You'll need to sleep tonight, so you might want to wake up," he told her.

Hayley stretched and hid a yawn with the back of her hand. After taking a moment to awaken, she removed the blanket, folded it, grabbed the pillow behind her head, and passed it all to Lee.

He got up to put them away.

Before he returned, she opened the window shade, sat back, and glanced at him when he took his seat. "I guess I'm still thinking about the Del," she said. "I had a dream of a naval officer named Richard who stayed there during World War II. He wrote a letter to his family telling them about the hotel and the military men awaiting orders."

Lee nodded. "Yes, that sounds right. Do you remember after dinner, the hallway display case we looked at telling us about the hotel's history?"

"Yes. I guess I made a stew from what we'd read and put it all in a dream. I even dreamt the officer's favorite dish was the roast lamb."

"I'm surprised you didn't include Kate Morgan," Lee said. "I hope you're keeping a journal of everything you're experiencing. You should record your dreams, too."

"Yes. I bought a journal in the gift shop at the hotel. I started my entry with a dream I had Tuesday night."

"About what?"

"It was the saddest dream. A lieutenant and two of his men were stranded on an island, trying to find a way off. Everyone in his crew was dying from malaria, and the lieutenant had orders to get help. He died before he could complete his mission. I woke up crying."

"Maybe your dreams were stirred by the news of our case."

"Could be. It was so vivid. My clairvoyant dreams are always of the future, but this dream was of the past, so I don't know if it has validity pertaining to the case." She shook her head. "It's too bad we have dreams we have to figure out."

"I know what you mean. It's like we're given a puzzle or a code we don't know how to break."

They looked up as the admiral approached.

Admiral Wayne, wearing another of his Hawaiian shirts, took the seat across from them. "How are you, Hayley? I heard you didn't sleep well last night."

"Much better now that I've had a nap."

"To my knowledge, the hotel we'll be staying at on Oahu isn't haunted," he told her.

"That's good to hear," Hayley said.

"But the attack on Pearl Harbor took place around that area," the admiral said. "You'll probably be hit pretty hard with strong impressions."

"I understand your concern," Hayley said. "But it won't be a mystery where my thoughts and visions will come from like it was at the Del. I shouldn't have any problems."

"What you see or feel might be intense since there were so many drowning, injuries, and a hell of a lot of other deaths."

"The energy I'll feel should be similar to the energy of the Civil War I've picked up in historic places back home. There shouldn't be anything to be worried about. I'll shield myself if it gets too overwhelming."

"Well, if there's any problem, just let me know, and I'll do whatever I can to help."

"Thank you, Admiral."

"What type of island will we be doing our investigation on… coral or volcanic like Hawaii?" Lee asked.

"Good question. Sounds like you've been doing some research on the composition of the area. The island you're heading to is volcanic—mountainous, rich soil with an abundance of plant life. After Typhoon Sudal hit Yap in 2004, my nephew became involved in a study measuring the forest structure's responses to a severe typhoon—mostly mangroves. That's when he first set foot on the remote island. From what he's told me, the island's beautiful."

The hairs on Hayley's neck stood on end at the mention of typhoons. "Did you check the weather in Guam, Lee?" she asked.

He nodded. "The depression that Jim mentioned yesterday

has been upgraded to a tropical storm, but it's no longer a threat to Guam. The weather should be great by the time we arrive."

"JTWC, the weather central on Guam, updates on a regular basis," Admiral Wayne added. "If there's any threat to our mission, we'd be informed immediately. But since it's a concern of yours, I'll look into it once we're settled in at the hotel."

"I'd appreciate that, Admiral."

"Will we be going to Pearl Harbor?" Lee asked.

"Yes. It'll be our first stop after we register at the hotel. Hopefully, you'll get a little more understanding about what happened, and maybe something you see will help with this investigation."

The admiral rejoined the others.

"Still worried about the weather?" Lee asked.

"Just a feeling," Hayley said. "I'm getting a sense something's developing, but I don't know its intensity."

"In Micronesia, the weather is always a topic, especially now through November," Lee told her. "But like the admiral said, Guam has one of the major tracking centers, and if there's anything we should worry about, we'd have plenty of time to abort our mission."

The uncomfortable feeling she had seemed to vanish while he spoke. She sat back in her seat. "It's only a slight, fragmented impression I'm perceiving. Could be I'm blowing it out of proportion. If we were in danger, I'm sure I'd know."

"Relax. You're trying too hard to foresee our investigation and jumping at shadows."

"It's my first case. I just want to do my best."

"Understandable."

Hearing laughter, Hayley rose and peeked over the back of her seat. Everyone had gathered around and were listening to Jim tell his stories. She settled back down and glanced at Lee.

He took her hand. "And remember, you don't have to do anything that'll make you uncomfortable. If you want to stop or get away from anything that's overwhelming, I'll be right beside you."

He seriously would protect me. I want to kiss him. Just a simple "thank you" kiss. What harm would that do?

She bent and kissed his lips—short and soft, with a subtle linger. She pulled away, hesitating inches away from his lips. "Thank you, Lee," she whispered, then nestled back into her chair.

Before her head could rest against her seat, his face was a breath away from hers. Caught off guard, she blinked, then smiled at him.

He ran his finger across her jaw line to the tip of her chin. "I want to thank you, too." He gave her a tender kiss.

When he was about to sit back, Hayley reached out and touched his arm. "So what are you thanking me for?"

Lee moved closer.

She felt his breath on her face when he whispered, "I'm sure there's something. I'll make a list so I'll have a number of things to thank you for later."

"You don't need a list, Lee. You can…um…thank me anytime you want."

He kissed her once more. "Thank you."

Her heartbeat raced. *Breathe; just breathe.*

He sat back in his seat and laced his fingers between hers.

Warmth spread through her as she looked down at their intertwined hands. She'd dreamt of his kiss more than once. Now the wish had become a promise. She glanced at him out of the corner of her eye.

His brown eyes met her gaze. He squeezed her hand gently.

She nestled back into the seat, closed her eyes, and fought the urge to kiss him again. *I can't wait until "later."*

CHAPTER 18

The plane circled to make its descent to Honolulu International Airport, where it had shared runways with Hickam Air Force Base since the fifties, and landed.

Hayley descended the ramp to the tarmac, walked forward a few feet, and stopped. All around her, she felt the energy of Japan's surprise attack.

Warm and humid air ruffled her hair in a light breeze. Taking a deep breath, she closed her eyes, cleared her mind, and mentally surrounded herself with white light.

Lee moved to her side. "Everything all right?"

She nodded, then opened her eyes and stared straight ahead, the past filling her vision. "Was the base destroyed during the attack, Admiral?"

"Almost. Hickam was Hawaii's principal army air base. When the Japanese Zero fighters and dive-bombers attacked, nearly half of the aircraft on the ground were destroyed or severely damaged. Close to two hundred men were killed and over three hundred wounded. That's not counting the men reported missing."

She stood with a fixed gaze.

"What are you seeing?" the admiral asked.

"I can hear planes and see the attack. It's like watching a movie." She blinked. "It's gone now." She looked across the field to the west. "There's residual haunting. I can see military men running, then disappearing into thin air."

"I wish I could see what you see," Roger said.

Hayley shook her head. "It's probably better you didn't. It's a memory you'd have forever."

"Sounds intense," the admiral said. "After we check into the hotel, we'll be heading to Pearl Harbor. When we get there, you'll probably experience a lot more of the same."

"It's hard to watch, but I'm okay, Admiral. I've shielded myself from the emotional energy." She thanked God her abilities worked this time.

"The drivers are loading our bags into the vans," Lee said. "We'll be on our way shortly."

* * *

Not far from Honolulu International Airport and Hickam Air Force Base, Hayley looked out the van's window and up at the hotel's two high-rise towers. She felt relieved—no familiar memories like those she'd experienced at the Del.

Their two chauffeured vehicles pulled up to the entrance, and the drivers unloaded the luggage. After climbing out of the van, Hayley followed Kathy into the lobby.

"I'll get our keys," Kathy said. She turned and headed over to Roger.

While Hayley waited, Lee walked up. "Our bags have been taken to our rooms. Roger and I will take care of tips."

"Good to know," Hayley said. "Thanks."

"I'll meet you by the elevator. I have to let the others know." He left her and walked to Clint and John.

Kathy hurried back. "We're sharing a room," she said, giving

Hayley a keycard. "It's in the west tower on the tenth floor, and has a balcony with a view of the sea. I'll flip you for the bed next to the bathroom."

"Deal."

They met Lee by the elevator. Hayley flashed her key at him. "I might be directionally challenged, but I think my room's facing west. And it has a balcony."

He held the elevator door. "Dinner, wine, and the sunset?"

"You read my mind," she said as she brushed by him.

* * *

Kathy and Hayley walked into a room with two double beds covered by pale blue bedspreads. Bronze-colored curtains hung across the glass doors leading to the balcony. Their bags sat on the carpet in front of the dresser.

Hayley lifted her suitcase onto one of the beds and searched for something to wear to the memorial. She pulled out a red halter-top.

Kathy raised an eyebrow. "Lee would like that one."

Hayley glanced at the plunging neckline. "Maybe later. It's not appropriate for the memorial."

"I don't know about that. You might attract some sailor ghosts. It could be interesting."

"I prefer a man with meat on his bones."

While looking in the mirror, Kathy ran red lipstick across her lips. "I know what you mean." She puckered, then smacked her lips. "My mom always tells me I should date a man of substance."

"Someone who's not so transparent?" asked Hayley.

"Exactly. Not a Mr. No Body." Kathy laughed.

"I can see that," Hayley said with a giggle. She pulled out a white short-sleeved blouse and tan pants.

They hurried to get ready, left their room, and took the elevator to the lobby.

When the elevator doors opened, Hayley saw their group standing by the entrance. When she and Kathy approached, Lee stopped his conversation with Admiral Wayne, who wore his dress whites.

Lee walked toward them. "Great. You're here. We're ready to go."

* * *

From the hotel, it took only a few minutes to drive to Pearl Harbor.

When she and the team entered the Visitors' Center's Road to War exhibit, Hayley noticed a sailor, his body vaguely transparent, standing with an elderly man and woman looking at an exhibit. She turned to Roger and whispered, "We're not alone here, if you know what I mean."

"Is it haunted?"

"I'm not picking up a haunting. I see the spirit of a sailor wearing a World War II uniform visiting with that gray-haired couple over there." She watched them walk together to the next exhibit.

"Where's he standing?"

"To their left by the exit to the Oahu courtyard. They're going outside. Maybe we can follow. If I guide you to where he's standing and you feel his energy, we can give the admiral a similar experience." She caught the admiral's eye and smiled.

Roger asked Jim to stay with the rest of the team while he, Admiral Wayne, Hayley, and Lee went outside. While twenty or more tourists strolled through the courtyard, the deceased sailor stood by the elderly couple sitting on a bench outside the gallery.

Hayley guided Roger to a spot next to the visiting spirit.

"Four more inches, Roger."

He moved slightly, then looked at the empty space next to him and gave a thumbs-up. After a moment, he walked back to

Hayley and grinned. "That was cool. I felt his presence."

"Okay, Admiral, go and stand exactly where Roger was," Hayley said.

He stood, brushed a leaf from his whites, and took his place next to the couple.

From where she stood, Hayley could tell by the nervous look on his face that he, too, felt the presence. She noticed the red-haired sailor watching Admiral Wayne walk back to her.

The couple stood up and entered the attack exhibit gallery, but the sailor didn't follow.

Hayley's eyes widened. She grinned broadly. "Admiral, he's coming toward us."

While he approached wearing his dress whites, he became solid. He stood at attention in front of the admiral and saluted. "Admiral, sir!"

Admiral Wayne paled as he stared at the young man, a freckle-faced sailor as real as the rest of them. He returned the salute. "It's my honor, son. Thank you!"

The sailor looked at Hayley and gave her a smile and a wink.

"Thank you," she told him, then watched him turn and disappear slowly while walking away.

Shaking, Admiral Wayne sat on a bench. "Can you believe that just happened? I'll never get over this. What a privilege!" He stood with watery eyes and gave Hayley a hug. "Thank you."

"You're welcome. But it wasn't my idea."

"Unbelievable." Roger cleared his voice. He patted the admiral on his back. They started back to the gallery.

Lee ran his finger across Hayley's cheek and brushed a wayward hair out of her eyes. "You have no idea how much you stun me," he whispered.

"Is that good?"

He kissed her softly. "Very." He put his arm around her and

they walked inside to join the others.

CHAPTER 19

With Lee at her side, Hayley moved slowly, studying the exhibits. Photos showed US Navy personnel enjoying big-band concerts and the sailors' everyday lives while they worked and played. A display case held trophies, victory photos, and letters to the folks back home.

She thought of the dream she'd had on the plane during their flight to Oahu, and could see the officer's face in her mind. *It was too vivid to be just a dream.* Hayley had felt the material of his uniform against her skin, the hardness of the bar seat when he sat, and the taste of the beer as he sipped.

I wonder if he died in the war. Maybe he's still alive somewhere.

She glanced at the photos and looked closer at the men's faces. He wouldn't be in these pictures. He had been assigned to a new ship after the attack.

She looked at a photo of a sailor standing alongside his proud mother and father, and thought about the bodies taken off the Japanese ship. "It's irritating." She shook her head. "The deceased they found on board…. I want their families to know what happened to them."

"Your gift to see the past and to block the residual energy

seemed to be working great when we landed here. Maybe earlier you just had a glitch in your psychic abilities for some reason."

"I never have 'glitches.' That's the scary part. But you're right. I was myself again at the air base. Anyway, Grams would've reacted differently if she knew I was losing my gifts, because it would mean I wouldn't be able to see her again. I should relax. Could be I'm the one who's causing my abilities to stop working."

They followed Roger, the admiral, and the rest of the team to the attack gallery next door and began to stroll through the exhibits.

"You know, Lee, history has its own links—history-links," Hayley said, gazing at the photos taken of the raging fires that engulfed Battleship Row on the day they were attacked. "Pearl Harbor was one of them."

He raised a finger. "Don't tell me. Let me try to figure this out. I know at the time Hitler invaded Europe, America wasn't fully committed to the war. Although, we were already helping our allies with supplies."

"Yes, keep going."

They strolled to the next exhibit.

He studied the black-and-white aerial photos. "The attack on Pearl Harbor triggered outrage among Americans and set the stage for our country's involvement in the war. Shortly after the attack, we went after the Japanese in the Pacific and sent troops to Africa."

"Yes, but there's more," Hayley said. "If we'd entered the war without the attack, we would've been using the same ships we used in World War I. When our ships were destroyed and damaged, we were forced to rebuild our fleet. Up until then, the Japanese had the strongest navy and the latest technology."

"I guess Pearl Harbor is the first link in our investigation, too," he said. "Getting any insight on our case yet?"

"No. Nothing."

She glanced to her right and noticed the rest of her group waiting for them, ready to go to the theater to watch a documentary, then to the memorial.

After the video, the team boarded a ferry filled with tourists, which would shuttle them the short distance to the U.S.S. Arizona memorial.

Clouds hung on the horizon to the south, while the skies above them were clear. A breeze blew as they cruised across the channel.

Roger moved to the seat next to Jim. Hayley heard Roger say, "You've been quiet. Anything wrong?"

Jim shook his head. "No. I might look like I'm tougher than a baked owl, but I'm a sponge when it comes to sad stuff—takes the talk right outta me."

"Later on," Roger told him, "the admiral wants us to go with him to visit his sister and her family. Feel like going?"

"You bet." Jim smiled broadly. "I haven't seen her since her weddin'."

"Great. I'll tell the admiral."

The shuttle pulled up to a dock at the memorial. To Hayley, the structure resembled a white bridge floating above the sunken battleship.

In order to protect herself from the emotional energy while she opened her senses to the past, she mentally surrounded herself with white light, then followed the others into the Flag Room.

On one side of the room stood flags of the United States, the state of Hawaii, the Department of the Interior, and the US Army, Navy, Marines, Coast Guard, and Air Force. Across from them flew flags of the battleships anchored on Battleship Row the day of the attack.

In the assembly area, in the middle section of the memorial, where the designer had left the walls open to the elements, Hayley peered into the water and saw a large portion of the U.S.S. Arizona. She looked across the channel and stood with a fixed gaze. "I'm visualizing two attacks. Is that right, Admiral?"

"Yes, they hit us with two waves about an hour apart. Twenty-one ships of the US Pacific Fleet were sunk or damaged. There were a hundred and eighty-eight of our aircraft destroyed, and a hundred and fifty-nine damaged."

"I see the bombing and fires, along with lots and lots of thick smoke. Sailors jumping into the water." She turned toward the other side of the harbor. "There's residual haunting on the shoreline. People are running. Men are being pulled from the water."

Clint looked around the harbor. "Did they destroy everything?"

The admiral shook his head. "No, but the Japanese thought so. They failed to get our aircraft carriers, which were out of port that day." He pointed at the shore. "And neglected to damage the shore-side facilities at the Pearl Harbor Naval Base. We raised and repaired all the ships sunk or damaged except the Arizona, the Oklahoma, and the Utah. While we rebuilt our forces, the Japanese took the American-occupied islands of Wake, Guam, and the Philippines."

Clint asked, "Why did they attack us? Didn't they know we'd go after them?"

"Japan had an insatiable desire to enlarge its empire. They focused all their strength on China. Over the years of conflict, Japan escalated the war from biological warfare and mass murders to their naval plus army and marine land attacks. Lines were finally drawn, creating an alliance among the United States, the Soviet Union, and China to fight Germany's alliance with

Japan.

"The war turned when the US placed an oil embargo on Japan, almost crippling the Japanese invasions. But instead of settling on peace, Japan turned its attention to US and British colonial territories and countries of Asia. In retaliation for the embargo, they attacked Pearl Harbor."

Hayley flashed back to her recent dream of a few nights ago. She turned to the admiral. "Did their biological warfare include malaria?"

"Yes, it did." He looked puzzled. "Why do you ask?"

"I had a dream Tuesday night about American military men dying of malaria on a small island. Maybe it had something to do with our case."

"CIL will examine the bodies found on the ship," Admiral Wayne said. "They should have the cause of death soon."

"What or who is CIL?" she asked.

"Oh, sorry. It stands for Central Identification Laboratory. It's in Hawaii," he explained.

"Would the effects of the malaria show up on skeletal remains?" Hayley asked.

"Don't know. I guess we'll find out."

Hayley turned when Kathy called to Clint and John, pointing at something floating above the sunken hull. "Do you see that?" Kathy asked. She looked over at the admiral. "What's the black stuff bubbling up?"

"Oil continues to leak from the remains of the number three gun turret," Admiral Wayne said. "Some say that when the last survivor of the Arizona dies, the leaking oil will stop." He looked down at the sunken warship. "Eleven hundred and seventy-seven sailors died on this ship, and it's the final resting place for the close to a thousand still buried inside. With the assistance of the United States Navy and the National Park Service, some of the survivors have chosen to join their crewmates after they die. Their ashes are placed by divers inside gun turret number two."

They continued to the Shrine Room where, at the far end, Hayley read the names of the crew inscribed on the marble wall and the names of survivors on the small boxlike structure under the flag. Again she tried to get a psychic connection to PSA's military case. But nothing sparked her clairvoyance.

The shuttle waited to return them to the Visitors' Center. A crewman signaled for them to climb aboard.

* * *

"Where are we going next?" Roger asked the admiral, as the shuttle pulled up to the dock near the museum.

"We'll be traveling the same route we took in pursuit of the Japanese fleet. Tomorrow afternoon, we'll be going to Guam."

From the dock, Hayley gazed across the Pacific. *Guam. I never would've thought I'd be going there.* She looked where she imagined the island and the marooned warship might be. Shivers went up her spine. *What have I gotten myself into?*

CHAPTER 20

Hayley stood by watching the candlelight flicker on a table set for a romantic dinner high above the Pacific on a tenth-floor balcony. White china dishes lay between settings of silver and hemstitched napkins on a burgundy tablecloth. Crystal wine glasses sparkled. To the side, a cart shrouded in white linen stood crowned with silver domes covering plates of mahi-mahi, mandarin-glazed shrimp, rice pilaf, sweet peas with baby carrots, grilled asparagus tips, and fresh bread with coconut butter.

Lee gathered the glasses and set them on the table by one another while he reached into the stainless steel ice bucket and lifted out an open bottle of Beringer fumé blanc.

"So, Kathy's going to watch the game with Clint and John, I understand," Lee said. He filled the glasses, handing one to Hayley. He stood with his back against the balcony railing, studying her face, and tasted his wine, waiting for her reply.

"Yes. She'll be gone a few hours," Hayley said, her gaze traveling down the curve of his neck to his broad shoulders.

She sipped her wine, remembering their last date, and the feel of his skin against hers while he held her close. All day she had thought about tonight. Finally, and only for the second time since they left home, they were alone. She was nervous, anxiously awaiting his promised kiss—a real kiss, steamy, a kiss she'd feel all the way to her toes.

He looked down and smiled.

Can he read my mind? She glanced at her hand holding her glass. The wine was still. *Good. At least I'm keeping my composure.* As she raised the glass to her lips, she jumped, her demeanor shattered by the blare of an air horn from the harbor. Wine trickled down the side of her mouth and off her chin to the plunging neckline of her red halter-top. She held the stemmed glass away from her and watched the golden liquid run down the round of her breast and pool in her cleavage. *Damn it.*

Quickly, Lee handed her a napkin.

Flushed with embarrassment, she noticed where he had focused his gaze. "Seems I should start wearing a bib," she said. "This is the second time you've come to my rescue with a napkin." She wiped away the runaway wine.

"Mind if I help?"

How does he plan to help? She eyed him curiously as she passed him the napkin.

His actions seemed gentle and confident as he took the linen from her, freed the wine glass from her hand, and set them on the table next to his drink. Reaching out, he lifted her chin with his fingertips. Gently he kissed the corner of her mouth. Then his lips followed the liquid path to her chin.

She closed her eyes and held her breath, anticipating his kiss. Instead, his lips feathered kisses across her jaw until his mouth caressed her ear. From her wanton mind to her weakened knees, every nerve in her body ignited in response. She reminded herself to breathe.

"Better?" he whispered in her ear.

Her passion peaked while his heated breath fanned the

flame. Her mind took a moment to process the word. Her mouth couldn't form a sentence. All she could manage in reply was a smile.

Lee held his hand out, and she placed hers on his. He stepped around her and pulled out her chair.

After gathering her composure, she sat quietly and watched while he went to the serving cart and returned with their entrées.

He set her meal in front of her and lifted the silver dome. "Would you like some more wine with your meal?"

"Yes, please."

Lee poured her wine, then adding some to his own glass and took his seat.

"Thank you, Lee." She lifted her glass. Everything was perfect...the warmth of the day, Lee's touch, and his flawless attention to details.

With the sun nearing the horizon, Lee touched his glass to hers. "Here's to sunsets, fine wine, and an evening with you." He reached across the table, took her hand in his, and softly ran his thumb across her fingers. "Remind me to call the TV station and thank them for airing the ballgame."

Hayley whispered in a low voice, "I'll let you in on a little secret. Actually, the game's not on." She took a sip of wine.

He released her hand and sat back. "Okay. Now I'm confused."

"Clint's cheating."

"How?"

"He went to the hotel desk, and they gave him the game they had recorded earlier. Kathy and John don't know it. And of course, John's going to lose the bet again."

"Are you going to tell anyone?"

"No. They're in the middle of a life-link."

"So you don't want to mess up the link?"

She studied Lee's face. Earlier, when she had envisioned Clint's cheating, she was able to foresee bits of his life-link's outcome. She saw him lying on the operating table and his family crying. The trouble she was having with her abilities irritated her. She tried and tried again, but foresaw nothing, sensed nothing. She felt panicked. *Is Clint going to die?* She didn't perceive enough to know for sure.

Hayley looked down at her meal. *I can't be responsible for Clint's death. I can't tell Lee anything. If he says anything to Roger, the link will be severed.* "It's never a good idea to intentionally break a link," she said. "You can never tell if something as insignificant as betting is linked to a major outcome."

"Okay, I'll keep my mouth shut, too."

Remembering another vision, she smiled. "Tonight, Roger's meeting the woman he's going to marry."

Lee covered his mouth with his fist, coughing and gasping as he swallowed his wine. He set his glass next to Hayley's, picked up the bottle, and refilled them. "You foresaw Roger's future?"

She nodded.

"Who is she?" he asked.

Hayley swirled her wine, took a sip, and set the glass on the table. "You'll find out tomorrow. She's going with us to Guam. I do know she's involved in the paranormal, and she's perfect for Roger." Hayley picked up her fork, cut her fish, and took a bite. "This is so delicious."

"How exactly do you perceive the future? Is there a chance you're wrong?"

Hayley set down her fork, glanced up, and took a breath. "Let me see if I can explain. The information I'm getting isn't swirling around in my mind someplace mixed with other thoughts. I just know the information without thinking about it, and see events clearly unfold in a vision. It's always direct, strong, and without doubt. A knowing."

"No doubt?"

"None."

Lee nodded. "So, you don't foresee anything about yourself — even if something bad is going to happen to you?"

"It all depends on what it is. If there's an accident ahead of me on the highway, I'll get the information. But if it's a learning experience or something I'm meant to go through, I have to experience it, just like you do."

"Have you been able to read anyone else in our team besides Roger and his nephews?"

"No, and that's unusual. It must have something to do with that glitch you were talking about."

He smiled.

"What?"

"I'm glad you can't read me. I want things to be spontaneous. What would life be without surprises?"

"You're right. I'm glad, too. It's not often I'm surprised."

They were quiet while they finished their meals. After their last bites, Lee rolled the cart into the hallway, then called the hotel desk. "Another bottle of Beringer fumé blanc, please. Thank you."

Lee moved their seats together.

With his arm around her and a glass of wine in her hand, she and Lee watched the sunset explode in a symphony of colors.

While twilight faded to darkness, they chose a few CDs from the selection he'd borrowed from the hotel and brought to her room. On the balcony, in the flickering candlelight, when she raised her face to his, her hands found the nape of his neck. They swayed to the music.

Before the first song ended, he lowered his lips to hers.

Passion flowed through her veins as she lost herself in the

heat of his kiss, the kiss she had been waiting for. They danced on in a melding embrace, every so often pausing for more lingering kisses.

CHAPTER 21

The morning light streamed in through the restaurant's glass lanai doors as the hostess led Lee and Hayley through the main dining area. Following a path between rattan tables and chairs among potted tropical plants, she guided them toward a conference room overlooking the ocean.

While they trailed, Lee touched Hayley's arm. "Did you see the frond of that palm move all by itself just now? Do you think we have company?"

She counted the days since her first day at work. *How many days has it been? Five.* Roger's words were still fresh in her mind. *You should investigate everything and make sure there's not a logical reason for anything that appears to be out of the ordinary. Your number one lesson is, Don't jump to conclusions. We want to know without a question if it's an anomaly.*

She pointed to another palm tree in the dining room. "That one's moving, too — tell you anything?"

He looked at the hanging fans with wide woven bamboo blades. "The fan. I knew it all along."

Hayley raised a brow and shook her head.

The hostess stopped in front of closed double doors. "Your

friends are inside."

"Thank you," Lee said, then listened. "If you can't hear Jim, this room must be soundproof."

An oval conference table with seating for twelve stood in the center of the room. At the far end, a large picture window looked out over the beach. A photo of a surfer hung on one wall, and a small bronze statue of what might be a Hawaiian king rested on a sideboard.

Roger sat at the head of the table with Admiral Wayne next to him.

The admiral stopped Hayley as she walked by. "I've checked the weather update. The system you seemed to be worried about has formed an eye and is considered a category one typhoon. JTWC is tracking its progress and has told me it's moving to the northwest away from Guam and nowhere near the remote island. It's forecast to miss the Philippines and veer north toward Japan. In a few days, it'll be out of the area completely. Our mission is on schedule."

"Thanks, Admiral. That's good to know," Hayley said, a sense of calm washing over her. *I knew it was nothing.*

She glanced around the table. It appeared the team's gathering seemed unusually spread out, leaving two empty chairs between John and his betting buddy, Clint, and one by the admiral. She and Lee took seats next to Kathy and Jim.

"I guess Roger's future wife isn't joining us," Lee whispered to Hayley.

"Are you doubting me?"

"You're only human," Lee said.

"And if I'm right, what would I be then, an alien?"

"Okay. Let me rephrase…. Everyone makes mistakes."

"Yes, and you know I've been having trouble with my clairvoyance, but not this time. Have patience." She glanced

159

across the table and noticed John sitting with his arms held out as if he were ready to fly away. She nudged Lee.

"Taking up flying, John?" Lee asked.

John sneered.

"I'll tell ya what's wrong with him," Jim said. "Just as I stepped outta the elevator last night, I heard someone screamin' like a banshee. When I got to my hotel room, I was nearly trampled by Clint and Kathy, who were runnin' outta there like their butts were on fire. Inside, I found John doin' the chicken dance and swearin' like a sailor. I never thought he knew so many colorful words. Guess he lost the bet and had to pay up again." Jim shook his head. "This time, Clint waxed John's underarm hairs and ripped 'em all out." He chuckled. "If these guys don't stop bettin', John's not gonna have a strand of hair on his body."

With a reprimanding glare, Roger studied his nephews. "If you two geniuses kill each other, your moms will strangle me for not stopping this foolishness." He sighed. "But it seems nothing I say makes a difference."

Hayley looked down at her laced hands, glad to hear Roger didn't plan on interfering with their betting. She'd try again later to foresee the outcome.

"Looks like we're all here," Roger said. He stood and rapped his knuckles on the table. "We'll start our meeting."

The admiral cleared his throat. "We're not all here yet. I've invited a guest to join us."

Roger raised a brow. "Who?" He took his seat again.

"You'll see soon enough."

The door opened.

Hayley watched Lee's face.

The admiral rose.

His guest, Hayley estimated, stood about five feet, eight inches and appeared to be in her mid-thirties. High cheekbones, long black hair, and the graceful slant of her green eyes revealed her Asian heritage. She wore a forest-green wrap-around dress with a V-neck and short sleeves. A loosely woven tan belt showed off her narrow waist.

Lee winked at Hayley. "I stand corrected. You were right. This ought to be good." He settled back in his chair and quietly observed.

The admiral pulled out his guest's chair. She made herself comfortable next to him.

"Team, this is Dr. Laura Song," Admiral Wayne said. "As you know, Roger, Jim, and I stopped in to visit my sister last night. When I told her about the team's background, she called Dr. Song to join us. I've known Laura all her life." He looked at her, then at Roger. "Not only is she a renowned neurosurgeon, but she's been involved in brain fingerprinting and works closely with our military. She asked to accompany us on our mission and was given full clearance. Just think of her as one of the team." He sat.

Jim gasped, then smiled broadly. "Well, I'll be…."

Surprise crossed Roger's face. "Why didn't you tell us last night when we told you about our case?"

The doctor glanced around the table. Her gaze stopped at Hayley. Laura smiled, then looked at Roger. "Once you left, the thought of an opportunity to learn more about the paranormal gave me so much to think about that I couldn't sleep. I didn't make up my mind until early this morning."

"Would you mind introducing your team, Roger?" the admiral asked.

Roger took a sip of water and stood. "You've met Jim. This is Clint, John, Kathy, Lee, and Hayley. I told you about Hayley last night."

"Yes. She's the one who influenced my decision. Her talents

161

are intriguing." A wide smile crossed her face. "It will be an honor to work alongside each of you."

What did they say about me? Did they tell her I was possessed at the Del and that I couldn't protect myself from being influenced by the hotel's spirits? I wonder if the doctor knows my so-called "talents" are working only periodically.

"We're happy to have you on our team, Doctor," Roger said. "I'll go over some of the equipment with you and lead you through the investigation."

"Thank you. I'd like that."

"How about we belay this meeting and get down to breakfast?" Admiral Wayne said.

Jim raised his hand. "I second that."

Roger nodded. "Okay, meeting adjourned for now. I'll call the waiter."

* * *

After the waiter cleared the last of the dishes and left the room, Hayley decided to learn more about Dr. Song. After all, unknown to the rest of the team, Hayley knew the doctor would be with their group far longer than they anticipated. "What kind of research are you doing, Doctor?"

Dr. Song set her coffee cup down, giving Hayley her full attention. "Please call me Laura," she said. "There are a couple of things I've had the opportunity to be involved with. For instance, by using EEG, in order to develop telepathic technology, we're tapping into the human brain to analyze neural signals that exist before words are spoken."

"Telepathy between man and computer?" Lee asked.

"Yes. Between a jet pilot and his controls, for example. In some cases, a split second to react may be too long."

"What about telepathy between humans?" Hayley asked.

"That's also included in our EEG observations. We're

162

working with psychic volunteers and learning to pinpoint, then map, portions of the brain that produce abilities such as yours. It's really exciting. In the future, we'll be able to perform surgery with full knowledge of what damage has been done or will be done before we proceed."

"Are you psychic?" Hayley asked.

"No. I'm impressed by people who are, though. What I'm really looking for is a tangible answer to where cognitive sensing comes from."

"You're asking for the impossible, Laura," Lee said. "From our team's experience, we've found it's possible to communicate between dimensions, but there's no solid proof. Pictures and voice recordings don't hold up in court. They're still considered theory. 'Tangible' is the issue."

"I guess you're right. Theory is only a guess until there's proof, and proof is subjective." The doctor glanced at Hayley. "Isn't it possible that time has no boundaries, and a sensitive person can intercept residual energy from past, present, and future events?"

"There's more to it than that," Hayley said. "There are guidelines and rules. For example, I'm not allowed to foresee my own future."

"Rules? I had no idea. So your clairvoyance isn't sensing what we'll encounter on board the ghost ship?" Laura asked.

"I'm not sure yet. I'm hoping that's not the case — although I can offer some proof that clairvoyance exists," Hayley said. "How about a prediction? It won't be a controlled experiment, although, it should be interesting."

A smile crossed the doctor's face. "How fun! Let's try to make it as controlled as we can. Can you tell me what's going to happen a year from now? That will help eliminate the element of chance. The closer to the immediate future, the more complicated it is. I'd have to take under consideration the possibilities of TV, personal events, and anything else that could pollute the prediction."

"I understand. Something that will happen in a year—no problem."

"It also has to be specific. It can't be a prediction having any possibilities related to more than one event."

"I can do that. Clint, would you please go to the lobby and ask the clerk for paper and an envelope?" Hayley turned and winked at Lee, hoping he'd catch on.

He smiled and winked back.

Clint returned with a sheet of paper and an envelope with the hotel's logo and return address.

Admiral Wayne stood. "Hayley, come sit next to Laura so you can work out the details." He moved closer to the window, out of their way.

"Thank you, Admiral."

"I'll need the signatures of two witnesses," Laura Song said.

"How about Admiral Wayne and the manager of the hotel?" Hayley suggested.

"Perfect."

"Roger, would you be kind enough to ask the hotel manager to participate in our experiment?" Hayley asked.

"Certainly." Roger returned with the manager—a tall, thin man with dark, receding hair. "This is Mr. Denning," Roger told them.

The manager walked over to Laura and waited at her side. "I'd be happy to help."

"Thank you, Mr. Denning." Laura looked around at the others. "If you don't mind, I'd like for all of us to leave the room, except the two witnesses who are to stay and watch Hayley write the prediction."

"Would it be all right with you if I give the prediction to the admiral for safekeeping?" Hayley asked.

"Yes. It couldn't be safer," Laura said.

Laura and the rest of the team left the room, then Hayley wrote her prediction: Congratulations to Dr. Laura Song and Roger Hudson on their wedding day.

Hayley signed and dated the forecast.

The admiral's eyes widened. "You're not serious."

"Is this specific enough?"

"I would say so."

"Okay, would both of you sign, please." Once they signed, she folded the witnessed letterhead, slipped it into the envelope, and instructed the admiral, "Keep this until she sends you a wedding invitation. Let her open it on her wedding day."

The admiral smiled, nodding.

"Can I assist you with anything further?" the manager asked.

"No, Mr. Denning," Hayley said. "That's all we need. Thank you."

He bowed. "My pleasure. I'll tell the others you're ready for them." He turned and left.

Hayley handed it to the admiral. "Here you go."

He slid it into his shirt pocket. "Done."

When Hayley again sat next to Lee, the admiral reclaimed his chair, then stood after everyone had settled in their seats. "I guess we're ready to go on with our meeting." He glanced at Roger, who nodded. "Like I mentioned, Laura has assisted the military before and has security clearance. We invited her along on our ghost-ship investigation, but we didn't give her any details… until now."

He turned to Laura. "So, let me start from the beginning. My sister's son, Paul—of course, you know Paul—was conducting research on a remote island in Micronesia. Down a wide river in the jungle, he came across a World War II Japanese warship that had run aground, and after all these years, it's covered in vegetation. Out of curiosity, he cleared his way into the ship and found no signs of Japanese remains, only those of American military. Not knowing what to do next, he contacted me."

Hayley watched Roger. He listened to the admiral, but his gaze remained on Laura.

"Americans…how odd," Laura said. "Where are the remains now?"

"Odd indeed. JPAC transported the remains to CIL. After a long discussion with my superiors, it was agreed it would be in our best interest to keep this secret until we could investigate. We didn't want to take any chances telling the Japanese about the ship. They might seal the ship to pay honor to their heroes. We intend to tell them about the vessel when we're through."

"How did you hook up with this team?" the doctor asked, looking around the table.

Jim leaned forward. "I've known the admiral since elementary school. From the time Roger, Lee, and myself started this business, I told him lots of stories 'bout our cases."

"Because the island people believe the ship to be haunted," Admiral Wayne said, "the higher-ups decided to use the haunting as a cover to JPAC's involvement." He glanced at Hayley and the rest of the team. "They agreed to run a check on the team, and were impressed by their reputation. I was given clearance to hire them."

Hayley looked at Jim. *I wonder what Jim said about me.* He caught her gaze and smiled. She turned her attention to Laura again and noticed a spark of excitement in Laura's eyes while she spoke to Roger. "This sounds like a movie," she told him.

"It does," Roger agreed.

"We have to remember it's a military secret," Admiral Wayne said. "I've been keeping a low profile dressed as a civilian and traveling with the team. It's important to leave the connection between the military and the team hush-hush."

"I understand," she said.

"Now you've heard the details, are you still interested in joining us?" the admiral asked.

She beamed. "More than ever. I can't think of anything more exciting."

Lee leaned in and whispered to Hayley, "You were right again. She's joining us."

"I'm glad I told you. This will be enjoyable to watch."

"Great!" Admiral Wayne said. "Our trip to Guam will take seven-and-a-half hours," said the admiral. "We'll leave shortly."

"So we'll get to Guam around four this afternoon," Roger said, checking his watch.

"Actually, no. There's a twenty-hour difference between Guam and Hawaii. We're crossing the International Date Line. So we'll jump ahead and be there at noon tomorrow."

Roger counted on his fingers.

The math made Hayley's head spin. She didn't look forward to another time change. Just the thought of it made her want to take a nap.

"I think it'll be a good idea not to worry about time and days," the admiral said. "When we get there, we'll just set our watches. If we keep track of all these time changes, we'll be too confused." He shrugged. "We'll have lunch on the plane. Then, I guess, we'll have lunch again in the hotel restaurant when we land. After that, we'll meet to go over the investigation. Paul will be your guide. We'll meet him on Guam."

"We're all packed and ready to go," Roger said.

The admiral smiled. "Okay, let's get going."

CHAPTER 22

The long flight virtually in a straight line due west from Hawaii to Guam gave the team the opportunity to tell ghost stories. Since this was only the fifth day of Hayley's employment with PSA, the stories gave her the first good glimpse into the team's history.

While Clint and John sat far in the back playing video games, Hayley and Lee relaxed on a couch, and Jim turned the tales to their investigation at Lucy's restaurant.

Laura's eyes widened. "Is it normal to see ghosts during your investigation?"

Jim shook his head and shrugged his shoulders. "No. Seein' their antics — like things movin' or doors closin' — we see nearly all of the time. Seein' a full apparition is like winnin' the Super Bowl."

Roger nodded. "He's right."

Laura sat back in her seat and sighed. "So there's a good chance we won't see a ghost on board the ship?"

Regretting she couldn't give the doctor a definite answer, Hayley said, "I can't say for sure." Seeing the disappointment on Laura's face, she added, "I wouldn't narrow a sighting to just the ship, though. There's always a chance you'll experience activity in Guam."

"Do you think our hotel will be haunted?" Laura asked the admiral, seated next to her.

"I was assured it isn't," Admiral Wayne said, glancing briefly at Hayley. "But considering it was built in an area drenched in combat history, I wouldn't be surprised if it is."

The co-pilot approached Admiral Wayne. "Sir, we'll be landing in Guam in thirty minutes."

"Thank you." The admiral took a sip of his coffee, then handed his cup to Lee, who had stood and started gathering all plates and glasses to return to the galley.

"Can you tell us a little about Guam, Admiral?" Hayley asked.

"If I had to give you a visual description, I'd say the island is shaped like a Christmas stocking. The foot is on the south side and the toes point southeast. It's a beautiful island with jungles, mountains, and waterfalls. Tropical plants are everywhere. Palm trees hang over white sandy beaches, and the waters are turquoise." He looked over at Kathy, whose attention focused on a book. "Kathy, did you get a chance to research any of our layovers?"

"Yes, Admiral. Guam's a beautiful island." She placed a bookmark between the pages.

"Sounds like the perfect place to live," Hayley said.

"It would be if it didn't get hit by so many typhoons, and if the mosquitoes, ants, and bugs weren't so hideously huge," Kathy told her, setting her book on the side table.

"How heavy do you think the residual energy will be from World War II?" Hayley asked.

"Very," Admiral Wayne said. "The Japanese headed for the islands in the North Pacific after attacking Pearl Harbor. They bombed for two days before they landed on Guam. The small number of troops we had there, plus the island's people, weren't enough to fight them. The island was occupied from 1941 until 1944. We had to build up our forces again after Pearl Harbor, and weren't capable of getting to Guam to defend it. When we arrived, the fight lasted twenty days before we liberated Guam."

"Did the Japanese really think they'd win? Why didn't they just surrender?" Clint asked.

"They believed in no surrender—honor above all—taught to them since birth," the admiral said.

Jim shook his head and laughed. "Talkin' 'bout not surrenderin', did ya hear 'bout the Japanese soldier who hid in the mountains of Guam for over thirty years? Some farmer caught him raidin' his farm late one night in the seventies. Seems he was hidin' in a cave in the mountains all that time, and didn't know the war was over."

"That's incredible," Lee said, coming back from the galley and settling on the couch next to Hayley.

"I remember that," Laura said. "When he returned to Japan, they treated him like a hero."

"Exactly," the admiral said. "That's what made us wonder how they'd react to our finding their warship and why we didn't rush to tell them. We've built a lasting friendship with Japan, and this situation is not important enough to cause hard feelings."

Hayley turned to glance out of the window behind her. She got up and knelt on the couch to get a better look at the island below. "Are we there? Is that Guam?"

Admiral Wayne stood and looked out the window near him. "No. That's Saipan. When we confronted the Japanese in Saipan, those who didn't surrender jumped to their deaths from high cliffs into the ocean. Senseless. They only knew what they were told by their emperor, and blindly did his bidding."

"It's still that way in some parts of the world," Lee said.

"Sadly," Hayley said. She glanced out the window again. "How much farther to Guam?"

The admiral moved away from the window and took his seat. "Saipan's only one hundred miles north."

"How extreme was the warfare at the airport where we'll be landing?" Hayley asked. She was hoping the images wouldn't be as overwhelming as they had been on Oahu.

"You shouldn't have any visions of combat at Andersen Air Force Base," Admiral Wayne told her. "It wasn't built until we took the island back from the Japanese. We cleared the forest so we could build an airstrip big enough for our B-29s. We staged our air attacks on Japan from there and Saipan."

"That's good to know," she said, nestling into her seat again.

Hayley saw a hint of concern in the admiral's eyes.

"Are you having any more trouble protecting yourself from the residual energy?" he asked her.

"No," Hayley said, appreciating his thoughtfulness. She looked at her hands, hoping she was right, and shuddered to think what would happen if she were unable to shield herself.

Memories of her childhood flashed through her mind. Screaming at someone nobody else could see, shaking uncontrollably, and sometimes fainting in front of her schoolmates proved to everyone that the doctors' misdiagnosis of schizophrenia was correct. No wonder everyone shunned her and called her names. *They were right. I was weird. But things have changed.* She glanced around at the team. *These are my friends, and I'm in control of my gifts now.*

The admiral looked at his watch. "We'd better buckle up."

"You know, the hauntings at Pearl Harbor were residual," Roger said, tightening his seatbelt. "It wouldn't surprise me if that's what we'll find on the ship. There might only be leftover

171

memories playing over and over."

"I hope that's not the case," the admiral said. "We need information."

"If we find the spirits of our military men on board, won't we have a problem?" Lee asked. "Weren't they trained to give only their name, rank, and serial number? They don't know us. We're not military."

"We'll have to check it out. If they don't want to help, we might have to bring the admiral back to give them orders," Roger said.

Visualizing the circumstances put a smile on Hayley's face. "You might have to wear your dress whites again, Admiral."

"You're not serious!" He swiped his hand over his mouth. "Hell, I never thought I'd be giving orders to ghosts."

"We don't even know if they'll be American or Japanese," Roger said.

The admiral rubbed his brow. "I never thought of that."

Laura raised her hand. "I speak Japanese if you need a translator."

The admiral nodded. "You'd be perfect. Thanks for offering."

"Normally, we can't hear a spirit's conversation until we play back the voice recorder," Roger said. "But Hayley can hear them. If they speak to her in Japanese, she'll have to repeat what they say. It could get tricky."

Hayley tried to imagine how she'd pull that off. She could see herself trying to form the words. The thought made her laugh. "It would be hysterical," she said.

The admiral chuckled, glanced at her, and chuckled again. "It would certainly be worth the trip to see that."

The plane began its descent.

* * *

When their twinjet landed, two black vans awaited them on

the tarmac. The vans were loaded with luggage and the team boarded. Then the caravan drove away from Andersen Air Force Base toward the hotel.

Hayley began to have visions of the warplanes, exploding bombs, ground attacks, and bloody deaths. She closed her eyes and surrounded herself with white light to block the energy. *Breathe deep. Put your mind on something relaxing. How about the night Lee and I slow danced?* A smile crossed her face.

With closed eyes, she concentrated on how their slow dancing flowed into kisses…the softness of his lips and his warm breath in her ear that sent shivers through her body. She remembered how all her passions had churned inside her. Her body warmed at the thoughts.

She opened her eyes, took a deep breath, and reached over, lacing her fingers through Lee's. All traces of the battles on Guam disappeared from her mind. The gentle squeeze of his hand helped bring her back to the present. She noticed the questioning look on his face.

Should I tell him why I was smiling? No, let him wonder.

Their van stopped at a hotel on the beach near the base. After checking in, they stood in the lobby, making plans.

"I think thirty minutes should be long enough for a quick change," Admiral Wayne said. "We can meet in front of that restaurant over there, and I'll fill everyone in on the rest of the agenda while we eat."

* * *

The hotel restaurant overlooked the Philippine Sea. The sound of waves hitting the beach caught Hayley's attention. While the waitress poured water into her glass, Hayley looked out through open patio doors at the sun glistening off the turquoise water. From flying across the International Date Line, their day had been fast-forwarded.

She shook her head as she played with the fork by her plate. "This feels so weird. My body doesn't know what time it is anymore."

Lee covered his mouth and rocked back in his chair as he looked at Roger.

"Stop yawning, Lee," Roger said. "Before you know it, everyone will be doing it."

He took his hand down. "I can't help it. I've tried to fool myself, but my body's still on North Carolina time."

"I know," Roger said. "Everyone's feeling the changes. Not much longer."

The admiral folded his napkin and laid it across his lap while the waitress filled their coffee cups. "We'll be meeting my nephew in about an hour to go over your final instructions. From here, you'll fly to Yap International Airport, then catch a helicopter to your destination. Paul has a map of the island, and he'll be telling you more about the hike. I'll be going over the details about the ship and giving you an idea about what's been discovered." He picked up his menu and studied it.

"When are we leaving?" Roger asked.

Admiral Wayne lowered his menu and glanced around the table. "Tomorrow—oh-seven-hundred. That'll give you the rest of today to catch up on sleep."

"We'll be ready," Roger said.

CHAPTER 23

After eating, the team moved to a conference room brightened by a large window looking out on a tropical garden. It reminded Hayley of all the research she'd gathered for her flowerbeds at home. She recognized the colorful birds of paradise, bougainvillea—one orange and another yellow—the red hibiscus, a variety of colorful plumeria trees, and the red anthuriums. Tall and short palm trees mingled among large and small ferns. Winding walkways led to secluded benches tucked into intimate alcoves.

She looked around, enjoying the surroundings. *Something seems to be missing.* A double-tiered fountain adorned with a large cement pineapple stood among the tropical plants. She thought of the small birdbath in her front yard. Then she remembered… no inland birds on Guam. From information Hayley had gathered on the web, using Lee's computer on the plane, she was struck by the fact that brown tree snakes were brought as stowaways in cargo just after World War II. They multiplied in abundant numbers and fed on bird eggs until many species of indigenous inland birds became extinct on the island.

The sound of rolling chairs interrupted her thoughts as Kathy,

Jim, John, and Clint took their seats across from her and Lee.

Roger pulled out a chair for Dr. Song and sat between her and the admiral.

Once everyone was situated, a thin man with a confident stride hurried breathlessly through the door. He wore a Hawaiian shirt, blue jeans, and a wide-brimmed canvas hat.

"Sorry I'm late," he said.

The admiral stood and put his hand on the man's shoulder. "Team, this is my nephew, Paul."

Paul cleared his throat, took off his hat, and hooked it on the back of his chair. He had long blond hair tied in a ponytail. Without a word, he lifted the satchel's thick leather strap over his head and placed the case on the table.

Admiral Wayne told him the names of his soon-to-be hiking companions.

"Good to meet everyone." He smiled and rubbed his hands together. "Let's get to this, okay?" Paul unzipped his leather case and handed his uncle a stack of photos of the Japanese escort.

The admiral passed them to Roger.

"The ship we'll be boarding is approximately 250 feet long fore to aft, and has a 30-foot beam," the admiral said.

Roger looked at the photos showing the vessel's exterior. "It's really incredible you found this, Paul. The vegetation is so thick." After he finished studying the pictures one by one, he handed them to Hayley.

"It was pure coincidence," Paul said, sitting as the admiral took a seat. "I looked up to see a hawk-eagle with prey clenched in its talons, taking flight from the hillside. Two minutes later, another bird of prey swooped down and then another. Curiosity led me to the ship."

Hayley covered her mouth to stifle her remark, then looked up, catching Paul's inquisitive expression. "I'm sorry. I don't believe in coincidence," she said.

"You're the psychic, aren't you?"

"Well, yes, but there's more to my abilities than just sensing. I can visual the past, present, and future," Hayley said. "Oh, and I can see the dead."

"Yes, of course." He looked around the table at each of the investigators and chuckled. "This is some bunch you've got me involved with, Uncle."

The admiral raised his eyebrows, nodding. "We'll have to get together sometime so I can tell you about our trip here."

His nephew smiled and nodded. "Bet it was interesting."

Roger turned to Hayley. "Do you know anything we don't know? Pick up anything from the photos?"

She looked at Roger, then back at the pictures he had given her. "No, sorry. I've been meditating on this, but I'm just not getting anything." She wanted so badly to get a mental picture of what they'd be walking into. After Hayley finished with each photo, she passed it to Lee.

"Maybe you have to get closer to the island," Lee said.

She nodded, but didn't really think she'd succeed. "Yes. I'll keep trying."

"What can you tell us about the ship, Paul?" Roger asked.

"It looked to me like it was badly hit in battle. I don't know how they made it up the river."

Roger frowned. "How's the interior? I'd imagine it's extremely rusted from being in all that humidity." He glanced at the admiral. "What kind of lighting will we have?"

Hayley listened closely and tried to imagine the ship and its surroundings, but still nothing triggered her clairvoyance.

"The only energy is what the navy brought on board in our initial investigation," Admiral Wayne said. "There's a generator on the forecastle, and our guys strung floodlights throughout the interior."

Roger continued to study the other photos. "Looks bad. Paint's gone; metal's rusted and eaten away."

"Paul can take you through. The ship's in great shape considering its age and, like you said, the humidity. Anything that's dangerous has been clearly marked by our men and well lit."

"How clearly marked? Remember, we do our investigating with the lights out."

Paul's eyes widened. "Why? Are we going to be ghost hunting in the dark?"

Hayley remembered asking the same question at Lucy's. She'd never forget working in the dark, and the adrenaline rush when coming face-to-face with the lingerings. *I love this job.*

"Our instruments are sensitive," Roger told him. "Anything electric or putting out heat would give a false reading. We'll carry flashlights. Don't worry about anything. You'll be with professionals."

"I don't believe you'll find anything working on board," the admiral said. "All the ship's original electrical equipment has been damaged by time or rodents."

Roger cleared his throat. "When you're talking about rodents, are you by any chance talking about rats?" He looked at Kathy, who had a rodent phobia.

Her eyes were wide.

Hayley could relate. *I know that feeling. Nothing's worse than spiders.*

"How about bats or any other dangerous animals?" he asked.

Kathy put her head in her hands.

"There may be a rat or bat around, but as for other dangerous animals, no," Paul said. "Our reconnaissance unit went in and out of there a dozen times in the last week, making lots of noise and pulling vegetation off the ship. Nothing around there should be bothersome or we would've seen it by now."

Admiral Wayne reached for an object Paul had pulled from his case. "As for the mosquitoes…we have a device for each of you."

"What kind of device?" Roger asked.

"It's military equipment, a pocket-size repellent," the admiral said, handing one to Roger, then passing the other units to the rest of the team.

Hayley leaned toward Lee, watching him turn the device around in his hand. "How does it work?" he asked Paul.

"It heats a mat saturated with repellent made from a plant. It's odorless and repels within a fifteen-foot radius. When you turn it on a little green light should come on. Make sure you power it up ten minutes before you reach the island."

"It must be some powerful plant," Lee said. "Does it work on any other insects?"

"Yes, several, but not on spiders," Paul said.

Hayley cringed at the thought.

"Just remember, some of the spiders will bite, and all of them are venomous, some even deadly," Paul said, putting on a serious expression. "So don't be a hero. Brush them off as quickly as you can."

Roger looked around at his team. "No heroes in this bunch."

"Now, about snakes…." Paul looked around the table.

Hayley followed his gaze. She saw Kathy's face freeze while staring into space, and John's eyes widened, while Clint seemed to move nervously in his chair. To Hayley, no one looked relaxed.

Paul let out a deep belly laugh. "Sorry…I couldn't help it. If you could see your faces!" He leaned back in his chair and bit back a smile.

"I don't think this group likes your twisted sense of humor,

Paul," Admiral Wayne said. "Get on with it."

Paul nodded and sighed. "Okay, okay." He cleared his throat and glanced around. "I've been doing this job for a long time, and I know if you watch your step, you won't have a problem." He looked at Roger and grinned. "Don't worry; you'll be with a professional."

"Speakin' of damn snakes," Jim said. "Earlier, I went outside to get some fresh air and to take a look around. I was mindin' my business when one hell of a long snake dropped down from the tree beside me. I nearly had to change my drawers."

"Probably a brown tree snake. Guam has a problem with snakes," Paul said. "Currently, there's predicted to be roughly fourteen to fifteen hundred per square mile."

Hayley glanced at the others. She wasn't the only one squirming.

"Was the one that attacked me poisonous?" Jim asked.

"Only if he tried to eat you. Its venom is only strong enough to numb its prey, so its meal can't get away before being swallowed."

Jim folded his arms. "Maybe it was tryin' to eat me. Damn thing looked hungry."

Paul held up a finger. "That reminds me. Things in the wild aren't always what they appear to be. For instance, a frog might look like a leaf or a bug might resemble a twig. Don't pick up anything once we reach the island. That includes sticks. You might get a surprise."

Hayley saw Jim swear under his breath, and the others fidgeted.

Paul reached into his satchel and pulled out some papers. "I've got maps of our route." He passed them out. "You might notice I marked our trail in red. We'll be landing where you see the small red X, just south of the village where we first heard the islanders' fears about the haunting. We'll follow the shoreline until we reach a mass of rocks and debris along the beach. It'll be too difficult to cross, so from there, we'll cut into the forest. After we get to the river, we'll follow its bank. The ship's about a half mile upstream, where I've marked the big red X."

The admiral held up an eight-by-ten photo showing most of the ship. "Looking at this photo, you can see there's a brow—you might call it a gangplank—making it easy to get to the quarterdeck." He passed the photo to Roger. "Just aft of the gun, our men cleared the way along the starboard deck.

"As you can tell, the plants were thick. It took almost an entire week to remove as much as they did. The bow and forecastle were completely cleared, and when our men came to the innermost hatch, they made their way inside and removed the six bodies Paul had found previously in berthing."

Roger held his pencil up and cleared his throat to get the team's attention. "We'll split into three groups—one on the mess deck, one in medical, and Hayley, Jim, Dr. Song, and I will take berthing. After that, we'll make our way around the rest of the ship."

"You'll only have about ten hours of light by the time you get there," Admiral Wayne said. "There are camping supplies and food in a clearing not far from the ship if necessary."

"Sounds like everything's in order," Roger said.

Paul returned the photos to his satchel. He pulled out a stack of papers and handed them to his uncle.

"Before I forget," Admiral Wayne said, "I'm going to hand out a few pages of naval terminology and a diagram of the ship. The navy has a language of its own. For instance, a door is not a door; it's a hatch. A wall is not a wall; it's a bulkhead. What I'm giving you will help you communicate with the crew." He looked around to make sure everyone had copies. "I think that covers

181

everything. Have a nice day or night, whatever the case may be. I'll see you all in the morning. Be out front at oh-six-thirty."

Following the others, Lee and Hayley headed for the elevator.

"Maybe we can hold each other up until we get to our rooms," Lee said.

Hayley's eyelids felt heavy. Her excitement to see the ghost ship was suppressed by her need for sleep. "Just think...we'll be going through a ghost ship tomorrow." She tried to sound enthusiastic, but knew she'd failed.

He nodded. "My adrenaline wants to pump, but I'm too pooped to pump." He laughed. "I'm not even making sense anymore."

"We better get a lot of sleep," she said. "It sounds like tomorrow will be a long, exciting day."

CHAPTER 24

Hayley remembered from geography class that the ocean floor moved along faults, the earth's crust fracturing under the turquoise waters of Micronesia. She'd read there were thousands of big and small islands throughout this part of the world created by Earth's constant dynamic changes. For her science project, she had built a simulation of the Pacific plates and showed their involvement in the creation of volcanoes along the coastline and Pacific islands. She'd made the volcanoes out of clay and placed small red Christmas lights in each of their centers. Unfortunately, someone plugged in the lights and left them on, and the volcanoes melted.

Now she saw the area she'd written her report on firsthand when she looked down from the helicopter. As far as her eyes could see, a multitude of islands with sandy beaches and jutting limestone cliffs were scattered over the vast sea below.

Wow! This is amazing. It's hard to believe that in this day and age some islands have gone unexplored. She looked into the distance. *This is so cool.*

Trying to adjust the strap of her backpack, she turned and caught the pack on something behind her.

Lee reached forward to help her, shouting over the thunder of the helicopter, "Do you have bottled water? Paul said it'll be a hundred degrees in the jungle."

Hayley peered over her shoulder at him. She patted the bottle on her belt and nodded, then glanced around at the team. Each, with a pack filled with paranormal tech equipment, looked the way she felt—eager and unable to keep excitement from their faces.

"It's time to power up your mosquito protection," Lee shouted. "It needs to warm up so it'll be effective by the time we land."

She reached into her pocket and pulled out the device. Turning it on, she checked for the green light, then gave him a thumbs-up.

When they flew over the blue waters, she watched local fishermen pull in their nets, while seagulls helped themselves to an easy catch. She saw the life as carefree, without the stress of high-rises or tourism, just the slow life of the island people.

Soon their helicopter swooped over rolling mountains covered with a lush green canopy. Hayley now knew the meaning of "breathtaking" as she watched waterfalls cascading from cliffs and into hidden valleys.

"Doesn't this remind you of the movie *Jurassic Park?*" Clint said, raising his voice above the helicopter's roaring blades.

"You're right. I wouldn't be surprised to see a dino bird flying toward us," John yelled.

This is the island time forgot.

The Sea Knight circled to the southeast, finding a clearing. Waves of grass blew when the helicopter descended. Flocks of cranes took flight from the surrounding trees.

The rotor blades slowed, then a crewman opened the door, letting the team exit with their equipment and move away.

Nearly a dozen villagers stood on the beach, women's sarongs fluttering in the breeze, and children running, pointing, and laughing. A shirtless, barefoot man wearing short pants approached Paul, who walked toward the beach.

Paul spoke to him, then joined the team. "The islanders won't be of any help. That side of the island is taboo. They've seen ghosts walking the beach and heard strange noises coming from the jungle. I thought we'd have an escort, but I guess we're on our own."

"You know the way, right?" Roger asked.

"You're forgetting I found the ship," Paul said. "Protocol. In my line of work, it's helpful to talk to the locals. I don't like walking blindly into uncharted areas, although I have plenty of times. When I first arrived here, I studied the cause and effect typhoons had on mangrove trees. After that, the villagers knew me fairly well and showed me some undocumented fungi and local medicinal flora and herbs in the jungles north of the village.

"But they refused to guide me west. They said the entire area is haunted. I told them I'd bring wise ones who'd drive the spirits away. They were very appreciative. Now I'm back, I just wanted to see if they'd changed their minds and wanted to join us. It is their island, after all."

"Understandable," Roger said.

Paul led them to the wet sands of the beach. "The helicopter will fuel up on a carrier off shore. The crew will return when we contact them," he explained. He began their hike at a moderate, steady pace.

Hayley looked back, watching the helicopter ascend. Turning in a circle, she took in the beauty of the island. Palm trees, a variety of tropical plants, red leaf and silver, big leaf and small, grew among giant lacy ferns following the shoreline. She walked behind the team with Lee at her side, marching west along the damp sands. She shielded herself and opened her mind, allowing her senses to feel, hear, touch, breathe, and see what normally wouldn't be sensed.

A vision came to her. The sound of waves hitting the beach seemed louder. The blue sky disappeared, becoming a sunrise. Her friends, who walked along the beach ahead of her, and Lee, standing at her side, were gone. In her mind, Hayley was transported to another time. She lost herself, becoming the young naval officer she'd seen in her nightmare on Tuesday.

This time, the entanglement of her essence with his was overwhelmingly skewed, Hayley's being nearly diminished. Only a sliver of her awareness remained, like a thought pushed to the back of the lieutenant's mind. She had to focus and hold on tightly to herself while she became the lieutenant in mind, body, and spirit.

While he lay on the sand, she felt the sting in his tired eyes, heard the thundering thoughts in his mind, the visions of his dying crew he was trying desperately to save. She cringed at his pain shooting through his aching bones.

Like a whisper in the wind, the sliver of Hayley heard a voice call her name, but she didn't have the strength to respond. Her awareness of herself was a blink from disappearing, leaving her actual body on the beach with Lee and the others, while her essence entirely merged with Lieutenant Sanders. She waited, knowing the outcome she'd seen in Tuesday's nightmare.

While the sun rose, she vaguely heard the waves in the distance. She shivered, feeling the sweat drenching his face, the pain arching his back and darting through his stiffened legs. In his dry, cracking voice, she heard herself plead to God.

"Please, God, don't let this happen. I have to bring help. Please, God." She felt the malaria consume the last of his body. He drifted in and out of consciousness.

"Please, God, please, God," he/she moaned.

Just as he took his last dying breath, Hayley pulled herself away from the vision, escaping death.

Lee's anxious voice called, "Hayley? Hayley."

When she opened her eyes, she saw him kneeling beside her.

"Is she all right?" Roger asked Lee. "I'm worried. She's been out way too long."

"Give her another minute," Lee answered. "Pass me her backpack."

Lee took the pack from Roger and placed it under Hayley's head.

As she tried to ground herself again in her own time and reality, she extended her hand. Her voice trembled. "Get me away from here, Lee."

The remainder of the team approached.

"I'll let them know she's okay," Roger said. He left them to meet with the others.

Lee stood and quickly scooped her into his arms. The farther up the shore he carried her, the less she felt influenced by the residual energy. "I'm okay now. You can put me down."

He bent to place her feet on the sand, but kept his arm around her shoulders while she straightened.

She wiped her hands across her forehead and breathed deeply. Every detail and emotion of her dream six days ago played in front of her while she compared its details with the vision she'd barely escaped. Hayley groaned, not wanting to see any more.

"Are you sure you're okay?" Lee asked. He dropped his hands from her shoulders when she stepped forward.

She gazed at him, nodded, and looked back to where she'd fallen. "Do you remember me telling you about the dream I had? The one about a lieutenant who died from malaria?"

"Yes."

"It was true." Hayley pointed. "That's where he died. I became him, Lee. I knew his thoughts, felt his pain. I almost died when he died. Before my vision, when I opened my senses to the energy around me, I protected myself. I made sure I did, but it didn't work. I was only supposed to be an observer. Damn! What's happening to my abilities?"

His hand touched her shoulder, and she turned. His brows narrowed. "This is serious. I had no idea your visions could be so dangerous. Did you ever tell Roger about your dream?"

When she started to speak, the words stuck in her throat and she coughed. He handed her his water bottle. She took a couple of swallows to clear her throat, then handed the bottle back to him.

"No. I never connected it to this case. I guess they should know." Hayley glanced at Roger, Jim, Laura, John, Clint, Kathy, and Paul, who had gathered around her. Turning in a circle, she met all of their concerned gazes. "Okay, well…. I had a dream Tuesday night. It was about a lieutenant named Sanders and his crew marooned on a tropical island. Malaria was killing his men, and the lieutenant was ordered by his captain to bring help for the crew." Hayley pointed to the spot. "That's where he died. He never completed his mission."

"Malaria. That makes sense," Laura said. "It could be fatal without quinine."

"Crew? How many men?" Paul asked. "I only know about the remains of six."

"No," Hayley said. "He remembered fifty-five that never made it to the island. Eighty-nine survivors, including him, made it to shore and discovered the Japanese ship. After they boarded, malaria began killing the lieutenant's men."

"Strange," Paul said. "I wonder what happened to the rest of the bodies?"

"Are you able to walk?" Roger asked.

"I'm fine."

Lee studied her, his eyes filled with worry. He glanced at Roger. "I'm not leaving her side."

She grimaced. *This is getting crazy. Why am I always getting into these situations? Not that I mind Lee's concern, which comes with a few enjoyable extras, but by the time this case is over, he's going to think I need a keeper. I can handle this.* "It was only a vision. I should be fine."

Paul cleared his throat. "I think we should get going."

Lee walked back, picked up her backpack, brought it to her, and helped her put it on.

"Thanks, Lee, but you don't have to worry about me. I'm tougher than I look."

His adjusted her backpack and said firmly, "Like I said, I'm not leaving your side."

They joined the others as they continued the journey.

The team picked up their pace, heading down the beach. While they hiked by the place where Seaman Palmer had succumbed to malaria, Hayley said nothing.

The shoreline curved toward the north along the west side of the island. A gust of wind whipped at Paul's blond locks and threatened to remove his hat. He reached up, held on to it with one hand, and motioned toward the jungle with his other. "We're close to completing our first leg. Just before we get to the rocks, we'll cut in through the forest. Then we'll shadow the river."

They followed Paul along a path he made through the low growth and stopped at the edge of the jungle. A wooden crate sat under a large-leafed plant blooming with orange buds. He brushed flowers aside and pulled the crate lid open. The lining was insulated and the crate held ice. Bottles of water stood crammed inside.

"The military set us up with water," Paul said. "The jungle's hot. It's one hundred degrees, if not hotter. When we get through to the river, there'll be another supply along with whatever camping gear we'll need for tonight if we choose to stay."

"It's easy to get dehydrated," Dr. Song said. "It's essential we drink lots of water in such heat." She had pulled her hair into a ponytail. She brushed back her sweaty bangs and wiped her forehead. Then she tugged her pack from her shoulder, opened it, removed a medicine bottle, and handed it to Paul. "Salt pills. Everyone will need a few. Take one every three hours."

Hayley leaned toward Lee and whispered, "Keep your eyes on Roger and Laura. Remember what I said about links?"

Roger reached inside the crate, pulled out a bottle of water, and handed it to the doctor. "Here you go, Laura."

Laura brushed a drip of sweat from her temple and took his offering. "Thanks." She closed her eyes and held the cold bottle to her forehead.

Hayley and Lee watched Roger's face while Laura cooled herself, rubbing the cold bottle against her neck, then running its icy cold surface down her chest.

Lee whispered to Hayley, "Is that the link?"

"It's a link for Roger. This is the moment he realizes he's attracted to her. Laura's awareness of him is next. When that happens, you'll almost be able to hear their links clink together."

Lee nodded. "Clue me in before it happens. I want to get the full effect."

The team members removed their backpacks, unzipped them, and placed bottles of water inside.

Paul raised his voice. "I spoke to the chief in charge of our needs and told him to give us a clearly marked trail." He pointed to a ribbon strung on a bush a few feet from them. "And he came up with fluorescent yellow glow-in-the-dark streamers. You'd have to be blind to get lost." He chuckled. "Well, let's get going."

As they made their way through the jungle, they brushed back foliage and hanging moss. Large ferns grew under filtered light shining through the canopy. Climbing vines and parasitic plants covered tree trunks. Moist ground, packed with dead leaves, muffled their footsteps. Those who didn't watch their step soon regretted it, tripping over nature's debris.

Several birds resembling small parrots about six inches long, green overall with yellowish under-parts and pale blue faces, flew so low Hayley could almost touch them. Caught up in their beauty, she reached up, taking her eyes off the trail. She tripped over a tree root and fell forward, knees hitting the ground. Instantly Lee's arms were around her, saving her from landing on her face.

"Got ya." He lifted her.

She brushed the dirt from her hands, reached down, and rubbed her leg. "Thanks."

"No sweat." He wiped his brow. "Well, maybe a little."

Hayley sat on the trunk of a fallen tree and rolled up her mud-soaked pant leg to inspect the damage. She slipped the backpack straps from her shoulder, letting the pack drop to the ground.

Lee took a white handkerchief from his pocket, wet it with his bottled water, and washed the sticky mud from her knee. When he finished, he handed her the cloth to clean her hands.

"Well, it's not skinned anyway," she said, looking at her knee. "Can we rest a minute?"

He watched the others walk out of sight, then glanced around at the yellow ties along their pathway. He nodded. "I'm sure they'll notice we're not with them and stop up ahead."

Hayley looked over her shoulder. "Is something crawling on my back, Lee?" She thought about Paul's lecture on things that crawled and slithered. "Is it a spider?" Her heart raced. *If I can feel it, it has to be huge.* In her mind, she contrived a tarantula with eight twelve-inch, hairy legs, a four-inch body, and two ghastly fangs. Her fear soared.

Lee peeked behind her. "And if it is?"

"Do something!" She mashed her teeth together, clamped her eyes shut, and held her breath to stifle a scream.

Lee slowly stood, stepped to her side, then backed away, hesitating.

"What are you waiting for?" Her voice rose two octaves.

"I need a strategy."

"I have a strategy." She reached up and unfastened the top button of her blouse. "I'm going to rip this blouse off and go screaming through the jungle."

"No!" he said, raising both palms. "Can you imagine what the others would think?" He calmly placed his hand on his chin. "Anyway, you don't have to. It's just a tree lizard. It won't bite."

The hairs on her neck stood on end. "I don't believe you."

"Would I lie? Stay still. Don't move. I have a plan. I'll try to get him to walk up a leaf." From a plant at his side, Lee ripped off a leaf as wide as her back and as long as his arm. While clenching the end of its stem, he held the leaf against her back and waited.

She looked down, cringing.

"He's green and yellow with orange spots around his head," Lee said, holding his hand steady. "He has big black eyes. It looks like he's smiling."

"No lizard on earth looks like that," she said, grimacing. "So, why don't you just pick him up?"

"I don't think that's a good idea. It might be more dangerous than it looks." He jumped back, but kept hold of the leaf's stem. "Damn thing's a little aggressive."

"The spi…spider?" she stuttered.

"No. The lizard."

"Sure." She clenched the handkerchief and glanced around.

Orange mushrooms resembling small fans grew at the base of the moss-covered tree trunk. Ferns draped their leaves over red flowering bromeliad. Squinting, she strained to see behind leaves and into creepy dark places. *I hope that spider doesn't have any close relatives.*

"I got it!" He lifted the leaf away from her back.

She jumped up, body shaking, heart racing.

Before Hayley could see her attacker, Lee flung the leaf into the shrubs. "I think we should catch up with the others," he said. He bent down and picked up her backpack, grabbing her hand. Giving Hayley a tug, he stepped down the trail.

"If it was a lizard, why are you shaking?" she asked, following behind him, her hand in his.

"I have a really big lizard phobia," Lee said, looking straight ahead.

"Spider."

He peered over his shoulder. "Lizard."

Hayley glance back at tree trunk where she'd rested. The leaf Lee had thrown rocked. She swallowed hard and turned away.

Lee helped her put on her backpack.

"Thanks, Lee," she said, still trembling.

CHAPTER 25

"Be careful," Lee said, moving a prickly vine aside, allowing Hayley to pass.

Foliage grew densely along their path. Hayley slowed her pace to take pleasure in the blooming forest around her. Blossoms perfumed the moist air. She stepped over a thick tree root covered with yellowish-green velvety moss. Mushrooms sprouted in the crevices of its marinated wood. She glanced up. A vine with purple flowers spiraled up a nearby tree toward rays of sunlight streaming through the canopy.

"We need to keep moving," Lee said. "I'm sure the others are wondering what happened to us."

A drop of perspiration pooled on Hayley's brow. With the back of her hand, she wiped it away, turned to Lee, and nodded.

By following fluorescent yellow ribbons tied to bushes, they reached the bank of a stream.

Hayley opened her senses to the energies around her. "They're just ahead," she told Lee, staring at his sweaty body.

While moisture beaded on his forehead and trickled down his temples, her gaze followed the curve of his granite jaw to his strong chin and up to his sensuous lips. *He looks "hot" sweaty.*

Hot. Ha, that's funny. I think this heat is damaging my brain. The sight of his shirt clinging to his biceps and sculptured abs filled her veins with a surge of longing, a yearning quickly turning to lust. Alarmed by her thoughts, she turned away, reined in her heightened senses, and shielded herself.

What in the hell just happened? Her vision of the lieutenant on the beach was the most overwhelming experience she'd ever encountered. Whatever crawled on her had triggered a fear stronger than any she'd ever felt. And her lust for Lee — her modest daydreams had turned to sexual fantasies. *What's amplifying my reactions? Is it the island? Am I the only one being affected?*

"Hayley, come on."

She saw Lee standing on the other side of the stream. How would she ask him if his libido was being kindled? *From one to ten, how aroused do you get when you look at me, Lee?* She stepped on a smooth rock and leaped to the next.

Lee extended his hand and grabbed hers, helping her across. She peered back across the stream.

He followed her gaze. "What's wrong?"

"There's something strange about this island."

"Are you sensing danger?"

Not knowing what more to expect, she shut her eyes and let her senses probe. "Not danger. There's a massive energy flux coming from somewhere up ahead. I'm sensitive to its vibrations." When she thought about its erotic side effects, she blushed.

"From the ship?"

Hayley looked off to the east. "How could a ship create so much energy? And anyway, there's no power on board. Did Paul say anything about a volcano?"

"Hell, I hope not," Lee said. "But you said it wasn't dangerous."

She shrugged. "I can't tell where it's coming from."

"Should we tell the others?" Lee asked.

"No. I don't sense danger. It's probably some kind of an anomaly of nature."

"I hate keeping secrets from Roger."

"It might not have anything to do with our investigation."

"That's true. I guess we'll find out." He turned, and they continued to walk.

When they hiked farther into the jungle, the canopy thickened, depriving the forest floor of sunlight. The tropical garden thinned. Their pathway became drier, easier to walk.

Without the dense plant life barring her view, Hayley could see Paul ahead in the clearing. "I see them."

"Wow, I can't believe it," Paul said, looking up. "A great hornbill." He pointed to the treetops. "They shouldn't be anywhere around here, and it looks like there might be an entire family of them up there."

Looking up, Hayley saw a bird about four feet long with a white tail, tipped with a black strip, and with black under wings. Its black-and-yellow head had a U-shaped horn on top of its massive yellow bill. She hesitated before entering the clearing and blocked Lee's way. "Watch."

From a branch high above, one of the hornbills dropped a gift, targeting John's bald head.

John froze. "What the...?" Reaching up, he touched the pile of droppings, then brought his hand down covered with a milky white substance. His lips twisted into a distorted grimace. A groan escaped through his clenched teeth. He leaned forward and shook his head, trying to remove the bird's runny excrement, making matters worse. The foul matter dripped down the side of his head. His groan turned to a roar.

Above, the birds flew from branch to branch. Hayley sensed they watched the team.

Clint doubled over in hysterics. Kathy and Laura stood horrified, staring up into the canopy.

While tears welled in Roger's eyes, his laughter took his breath away. "Jim, help him out," he managed to say, gesturing toward his nephew.

Jim's eyes widened. "Don't look at me."

"Hold on. I'll get it," Paul told him. He bent to pick up a leaf, went over to John, scooped the splattered feces from the young man's head, and tossed the leaf away. "Makes you think twice about looking up, doesn't it?" Chuckling, he untied the bandana around his neck, grabbed his water bottle from a loop on his belt, dampened the cloth, then wiped off the remaining substance. Paul glanced upward. "Incoming," he yelled.

After running zigzag across the clearing, John stopped, leaned forward, and put his hands on his knees to catch his breath. Standing, looking pleased with his strategic moves, he was bombarded again. "Damn it!"

Roger's laughter overwhelmed him. Bent over and barely able to stand, he braced himself against a tree. Abruptly, his amusement stopped. He jerked his hand back and slapped himself feverishly. "Ouch! Ouch! Ant! Ouch! Ants biting me!"

Standing at the edge of the clearing, Hayley watched the drama unfold, then glanced over her shoulder at Lee. "Heads up," she told him.

He gazed upward.

"No, a link," she said.

"Oh." Lee raked his fingers though his mussed hair and studied the situation in front of them. "So, we're looking for Laura's link?"

Hayley nodded. "Yes. Remember, Roger's already linked to her. When she realizes she's attracted to him, their lives will be bound together."

197

Lee silently watched while Laura wrestled the backpack off Roger and tossed it to Jim.

Cringing, Roger tore at the buttons of his ant-infested shirt.

Laura took his hand. "Let me help." She unfastened his shirt buttons, grabbed the back of his collar, yanked his shirt off, and flung it toward Jim.

Together, she and Roger brushed the ants from his sweaty body. With that taken care of, Laura loosened the straps on her backpack and lowered it to the ground. Bending down, she unzipped the casing and pulled out a medical supplies bag a little more substantial than a first aid kit. "I've got something to stop the pain." She took out a tube of clear gel.

Starting on his right arm, Laura spread the gel on his moist skin. Her hand gently rubbed across his arm muscles, then up to his broad shoulders and down his sculpted chest. "This will numb the inflamed tissue and stun any ants that come in contact with your skin." She covered his front and back torso, her hands never leaving his skin until she stood face-to-face with him again.

"Now," Hayley whispered to Lee.

"Your perspiration will eventually remove the gel," Laura told Roger. "I'll have to do this a few times before we get back to the hotel."

Roger's boyish eyes met hers. The sheepish smile on his lips turned sensuous, then into a playful grin. "I'm looking forward to it."

While mumbling under his breath, Jim shook the aggressive attackers from Roger's shirt. "Ouch! That ant's got piranha teeth."

Laura blinked shyly away from Roger's gaze and looked at Jim. "Are you okay?" she asked.

"Just peachy! I'm standin' in the middle of a damn outhouse, duckin' bird turds and pluckin' piranha ants." Jim shook his stinging hand and put his finger to his lips. "And gettin' eaten alive." He slapped the remaining ants off Roger's backpack. "I think I got 'em all," he said, tossing Roger his shirt.

Hayley didn't want to share Lee with the others so soon. Seldom during this trip did she have the chance to be alone with him. She took his hand and led him around the distracted team. Brushing by Kathy, Hayley told her, "We'll meet you guys up the trail."

Fifty feet down the path, as the foliage thickened again, Lee stopped and slipped the backpack from his shoulders. "I need water. Want some?"

"Sounds great."

He removed a water bottle from his pack and tossed it to her.

Unable to get a grip, Hayley's hands slid around the bottle's cap. She reached into her pocket and pulled out the handkerchief Lee had given her when she fell, then wiped her sweaty palm. "Did you see the life-link? The gift on John's head led to the ant attack. Then, as Laura helped Roger, their links were joined." She twisted the cap off.

Lee laughed. "So the birds are in on it?"

"And the ants. Everything's connected in life." Hayley gazed upward. Treetops swayed in the breeze. Blue sky peeked through the thinning canopy. "I think we're just about to the river. It seems to be getting cooler, don't you think?"

Lee nodded. "I think you're right. The rest of the hike to the ship should be a little more bearable."

While she rested, Hayley looked down at Lee's handkerchief in her hand. Running her thumb across the soft linen, she felt a raised pattern. She studied it, her eyes following the uplifted threads. White on white letters scrolled out Lee's initials. *Who owns monogrammed handkerchiefs?* Her eyes pored over him — long khaki pants, a finely striped, blue, long-sleeved shirt, and tennis shoes. Nothing about him shouted monogrammed handkerchiefs.

"Ah, Lee, don't you think this is a little fancy for me to be wiping my sweaty hands with?" She ran her finger along the lettering again.

His brows narrowed. "It was a gift. Nothing special. Don't worry about it." He lifted his pack and strapped it on. Her mouth opened to ask something more, but he interrupted her thoughts. "Can you see a person's complete life-link?" he asked.

"Sometimes," she said. "There's always a chance of links breaking and not leading to anything." She drank from her water bottle and hiked slowly along the trail toward the river.

Lee walked at her side. "Do you think Laura's link started the night she met Roger?"

Hayley shook her head. "No. I'd guess it started the moment she became interested in the paranormal."

Lee hesitated, looking at her with one brow raised. "That could've been as far back as childhood."

She nodded. "Yes. I think this is probably one of her longer links."

"One of? How many links can a person have?"

"Maybe thousands. Lots of times there's only one." She took another sip.

"If it's one link, what does it link to?"

Hayley stopped and turned to him. "I'll tell you a story I read in a magazine about a woman who submitted a letter. I'll call her Sally. When she was in high school, she was bullied unbearably and couldn't take it anymore. So, one morning before school, after her parents went to work, she made plans to commit suicide by hanging herself from the beams in the garage."

"What made her change her mind?"

"You'll see. She was going to wait until after school before her parents came home from work, afraid the school would notify them if she didn't show up for class. During her last class, her teacher gently placed her hand on Sally's shoulder while complimenting her on her work. That simple touch was a link that stopped her from killing herself. It placed the thought in her mind that at least one person cared about her."

"Did she ever tell the teacher?"

"The magazine had a follow-up and asked her about that. No. It happened years ago. This was the only time she'd ever mentioned it."

They followed the path slowly.

"So just a simple link could save a person's life," Lee said.

"Yes. It could be as simple as a smile or the lending of a pen."

"Wouldn't that make each person just as important as the next?" He moved a branch out of their path.

Hayley smiled. "Think of that." She stepped over a root and brushed back a fern. "It's not a new concept. All cultures throughout time had words for life-links."

"I understand. It's kind of like destiny, fate, kismet, or karma."

"Exactly."

They reached the edge of the river. A breeze swirled around them. Hayley reached out, rubbing her hand across Lee's chest. Her urge to be intimate with him was strong.

He pulled her close, brushed the damp hair from her face, leaned, and caressed her ear with his lips.

Shivers danced across Hayley's skin. When his kiss found the hollow of her neck, she tilted her head in offering. Her eyes closed as pleasure surged through her.

His kisses ceased once they reached her chin. She opened her eyes to see his brown eyes filled with purpose. Then his lips found hers and they moved together in a passionate rhythm.

When Lee pulled away, he gave her a small grin, then pointed to his neck. "Ouch! Ant!" he said.

Her brows narrowed, and she looked concerned. "Let me help you." She leaned up, kissed his salty neck, and tasted the lobe of his ear.

Lee swallowed hard, raising his finger to his chest. "Ouch! Ant!"

Hayley unbuttoned his shirt and kissed his sweaty skin.

He moaned.

Voices came from the jungle behind them.

"They're coming." She sighed and drew her hands away from him.

Lee looked up at the heavens, glanced back at her, and reluctantly buttoned his shirt, his eyes still caressing her. "Wish we were home right now."

While the others approached, she and Lee moved apart. The energy between them pulsated.

Hayley sighed. *Wish we were home, too.*

CHAPTER 26

Across the river, nearly five hundred feet from where they stood, the rainforest ran to the north. Above the canopy, white cranes with five-foot wingspans flew inland. East, in the distance, the tropical blanket spread upward covering majestic mountains, with foggy mist shrouding their peaks.

Paul pointed upstream and raised his voice above the roar of the river. "See those green mounds up ahead?"

"You mean hills?" Roger said sarcastically.

"They aren't hills," Paul told him. "Well, one isn't anyway. It's the ship."

Hayley gazed to the east at the river's bend where the mound extended outward at the water's edge.

"Are you joking?" Roger asked. "That's the ship?"

"You're looking at the stern. Not much was cleared aft," Paul said. "The portside and superstructure are still covered with vegetation. When we're closer, you'll be able to make out the ship, or at least a third of it."

Stern, aft, portside, superstructure. Hayley was glad she'd studied the ship's terminology the admiral had given them. She'd forced herself to study before she slept last night, knowing she would be the one communicating with the phantom crew. *Good thing I have a good memory. Forecastle…who knew? I would've called it the forward deck.*

Clint, John, and Kathy hurried to the riverbank and leaned out, trying to get a better look at the alleged ghost ship. Lee, Jim, and Laura studied the pictures of the rusted war vessel, while Hayley listened to plans.

Roger glanced to the east, then at the river. "Why's the current so strong?"

"The river's fed by a waterfall coming off the mountains just a ways past the ship," Paul said.

"What does it sound like on board? Will the noise interfere with our voice recorders?"

"No, not at all. Can't even hear the river once you're inside."

"Good," Roger said. "How much longer before we get there?"

"Fifteen minutes. The trail's not as bad as it looks."

Ahead, the jungle appeared to spill into the water. A few feet from where Hayley stood, she saw a trail had been carved out.

"Before we go," Paul said, "I suggest you check your repellent devices. It's a good idea to keep an eye on them every so often. If the strip needs replacing, replace it or you'll be in deep trouble. The mosquitoes around here are as big as birds."

Jim mumbled as he unhooked the device from his shirt pocket. "Damn remote island…now jumbo jet mosquitoes. What's next?"

Lee moved to Hayley's side. "Trying to get a feel for what's ahead?"

"I was just about to."

He reached out. "Want me to check your repellent?"

She unhooked it from a loop on her pants and passed it to him. While he inspected it, she cleared her mind and allowed her senses to search for insight. As she looked toward their destination, a familiarity of the area washed over her like a tidal wave. She tried to remember a dream, a vision or anything that could explain the sensation. *Is this feeling even real or is something still playing with my mind?*

Hayley pushed the confusion aside, closed her eyes, and tried to examine the anomaly she had noticed earlier. It wasn't coming from a volcano or the island. She opened her eyes. "That energy flux is coming from the ship, Lee."

"What flux?" He looked toward the vessel. "So, what are we walking into?"

"Could be just a portal. Maybe that's what the island people are mistaking for a haunting."

Roger asked. "What do you mean by portal?"

"A portal's a connection between two dimensions. Grams told me all about them. She said the flux is caused by the other dimension's stronger energy feeding into ours."

"Is it natural or are we facing a paranormal nightmare?" Roger asked.

"It's natural. It happens all over the world. Such places are considered spiritual or sacred, like Stonehenge. Grams took me to Sedona, Arizona once and I saw a portal in the mountains there. It was small, hardly noticeable, but the energy coming through it is legendary and felt by almost everyone." Hayley gazed up. "But this one's enormous, stronger than any I've heard about." She turned to Paul as Laura joined them. "Did you have any unusual experiences while you were on board?"

"No, nothing," Paul told her.

"There's a chance the ship's not even haunted," Hayley said.

Paul nodded. "The military has considered that. When they hired you, they were grasping for straws. If they could learn anything at all, it would be worth the expense. They're desperate for answers."

"Hopefully, I'll be able to get a clue about what happened to the crew from the fragmented memories still trapped inside the ship," Hayley said. She looked toward the ship, then at Roger. "I feel like I'm missing something. Could be just the side effects from the energy flux."

"What kind of side effects?" Roger asked.

"The hairs on my neck feel like they're standing on end the closer I get to the ship. I'm surprised that I don't hear some kind of buzz, crackle, or something coming from it. Plus, my emotional perception has somehow been manipulated a few times since we've landed. And now, I feel as if I've actually been here before."

"Like the feeling you had at the Del?" Lee asked.

"Not exactly," she said. "At the Del, I was receiving someone else's memories. Here, they seem to be my own."

"High energy fields are known to affect the mind," Laura said. "They can cause hallucinations."

"It's not a hallucination," Hayley said, "but it's weird. In most places where there's a dimensional rift, it causes feelings of inner peace. I'm not insinuating the energy's negative. It's just exaggerating my emotions. Maybe because of its strength. Hopefully I'll know what's going on when we get closer."

"So, it's just energy coming through? Not demons from hell?" Paul asked.

"You've seen too many movies," Lee said.

Roger glanced to the east. "Interesting as a portal would be, it's not what we're looking for. We need to get answers. We need a ghost." He looked at Hayley. "Keep your psychic antenna up. If you find the spike relative to our case, let me know."

"I think we should get moving," Paul said. He looked at Roger. "What do you think?"

"Yeah, okay." Roger turned to the others. "This is our last leg, guys. Let's head out and get this investigation over with."

When Hayley neared the vessel, the sight stunned her. The

mountain of smothering vines struck her as a work of art, a 3-D sculpture of a ship breaking free from its captor. She stared, recognizing portions of the superstructure and three-fourths of the ship emerging from the vegetation.

"It looks so eerie," Lee said. "Like something out of a movie."

Paul did a double take, then walked toward the ship. He came back blinking nervously. "Look at the photos, then look at the ship!"

Everyone stared up at the vessel as Roger grabbed the photos from Jim.

Hayley walked closer to the ship, unable to take her eyes off it. She remembered the photo. The vessel's corroded skin, now smooth and gray, appeared newly painted. The gaping holes blasted open by gunfire were impossible to imagine without having seen the photos. After a long moment of staring in awe, she forced herself to walk away and join the others.

"The ship healed itself!" Paul said, visibly shaking. "It's damn spooky."

Jim scratched his head. "Now doesn't this just beat all?" He turned to Paul. "Ya doctored the photos, didn't ya? Guess the laugh's on us."

"No. I swear I didn't touch the photos."

"So you're trying to convince us that some damn fairy flew through that dimensional portal and sprinkled pixy dust on the damn ship?" Jim asked.

"Believe what you want. The photos weren't faked."

"Hayley, what's happening here?" Roger asked.

"Paul's not lying. The photos haven't been touched."

"Thank you for that," Paul said.

"I think it has to do with the portal," Hayley told them.

"Some kind of time warp maybe?" Lee asked. "Can you get any kind of impression or clues to this phenomenon if you touched the ship?"

"I can try." Hayley walked to the brow and placed her hand on the railing. She cleared her mind and waited for any sensings, visions, or knowings. She pulled her hand away. "Sorry. I'm getting nothing."

"Lee, any ideas?" Roger asked.

"I've got to go with Hayley. If she thinks it has something to do with the portal, I'm leaning toward that."

"Clint, what do you think?" Roger asked.

"I'm going with the fairy and the pixy dust."

"I second that," John said.

"Kathy, what's your take on this?" Roger asked.

"I think Laura was right—we're all hallucinating."

"I guess we won't know anything until we go aboard," Roger said. "We need to take a moment and figure out where we'll start. Let's break open the crate and grab something to eat while we go over the plans."

After everyone gathered around him, Roger opened his backpack, pulled out the ship's deck plan, and laid it on the ground for all to see.

Roger studied the layout. "We'll have to spread out as far away from each other as we can to avoid echo. Let's make the mess our hub. We'll go from there." He picked up the map, folded it, and slipped it into his shirt pocket. "Get your gear out, guys."

The team spread out their equipment.

Roger surveyed the gear. "EMF, digital cameras, EVP, DV cameras, and Lee with the thermal imaging camera," he said. "All right, we're ready. Hayley, I'd like you to take the lead." He slipped on his backpack. "Okay. Let's get going."

When they approached the ship, Hayley saw each of them stare up at the vessel and assumed they searched for apparitions hidden among the vines and steel.

Roger glanced over his shoulder. "Clint, get a temperature reading before we board."

Clint peered at the digital thermometer. "It's ninety degrees."

Hayley led the others up the ladder to the brow. Cool air flowed from the deck.

"Feel that?" Roger asked. He looked back at Clint. "What's the reading?"

Clint slowly moved the meter, scanning the air in front of him. "Eighty-two degrees and falling."

"That's strange." Paul shivered. "I was here while the military investigated the ship and JPAC recovered the bodies. They were on and off the ship all afternoon. This never happened. It's damn uncanny. It heals itself and has its own climate."

They stepped on board.

"Temperature's still dropping," Clint said.

CHAPTER 27

Vegetation smothered the quarterdeck, giving the investigative team only a small portion of deck to stand on. John carried a voice recorder, catching everyone's conversation for evidence. Kathy also carried a recorder, hoping to catch a disembodied voice. The team followed Clint, who held a digital thermometer to take the air temperature.

While Roger waited for everyone to gather, he ran his hand along the side of the ship. "It's eerie," he said, lifting vines and examining the ship's surface.

"It's impossible," Lee said. "This can't be the same ship."

Hayley reached out and touched the ship's exterior also, trying to perceive the memories entombed in its walls. "I'm not detecting any residual energy. It's as if the ship has no history. All I'm sensing is an enormous amount of energy that the ship's probably absorbing from the portal."

"Interesting," Roger said. "No history, but by the looks of all this vegetation engulfing it, it's pretty obvious the ship's been here for a number of years. One more mystery."

Paul looked at the sky, then back at Roger. "When I found this place, like I said, I was drawn by the number of birds of prey. I watched a hawk-eagle and about four other species of carnivorous birds swoop down to catch rats darting in and out of the vines. The birds' beaks and claws cut through the foliage and into the rodents' nests. Huge areas of vegetation were ripped away, exposing the ship's skin."

Roger jerked his hand away from the plants. "So you had to fight off rats and hungry birds to get inside the ship?"

Paul stood tall. "Indiana Jones is my hero." He grinned. "And anyway, I was carrying one hell of a machete. Sliced right through the vines and everything else that got in my way."

Jim scratched his chin. "Let me get this straight. We're standin' in a ship load of rats, interruptin' a smorgasbord for flesh-eatin' birds. Have I got that right?"

Hayley nervously glanced around and noticed Lee had moved closer to her. A feeling of security washed over her.

"Not really. Ever since the military came in to clear the path for your team, not one rat has been seen," Paul said.

Jim glanced around. "Maybe they're just hidin'."

Roger looked at Kathy. Her gaze darted everywhere. "Clint, watch her. You know how she gets around rats."

A leaf rustled on an encroaching vine and Kathy flinched, almost dropping her voice recorder.

"I've got her back, boss." Clint stepped to her side.

Laura stood behind Roger. He turned to her. "Got any rodent phobias?"

"Do you think I can walk between you and Paul?" she asked.

He chuckled. "What, so if anything jumps out, we'll be the ones to get it?"

Laura smiled nervously. "Exactly."

Hayley sensed Lee's trepidation. She met his gaze.

"Rats…I've always hated the little pests. How about you?" he asked.

"I'm not really fond of rats either, but I'm sure Paul's right. The rats have abandoned ship."

Roger stepped aside to let Laura get between Paul and him, then glanced around. "Anyone else feeling squeamish?" With no one responding, he looked at Paul. "So if it weren't for the birds, you probably wouldn't have noticed the ship under all this."

"Not likely," Paul said.

"And the ship was rusted?" Roger asked.

Paul's face hardened. "I have witnesses. It was still corroded when the military came in to clear the vegetation."

"I'm not calling you a liar, Paul. It's nothing against you. It's just so damn unbelievable." Roger glanced around. "It's crazy. Not a trace of rust anywhere. There's no possible way this ship can look like this." He turned to the others. "Okay, team, let's get ready to go. Clint, what's your reading?"

Clint held out his digital thermometer and scanned the area. "In the few minutes we've been standing here, it's dropped another ten degrees." He gave the meter a closer look. "It's acting strange, boss."

"How so?"

Clint shook the meter. "I can't read it. The digits are changing too fast."

"John, check yours," Roger said.

John held a voice recorder in one hand, a digital thermometer in the other. He scanned the area with the thermometer. "Mine's doing the same thing."

"Another mystery," Roger said. "Keep an eye on them; maybe they'll start working again." He looked forward. "We seem to be wasting a lot of time. I think we should head for the bow. How's the forecastle look, Paul?"

"Cleared of foliage from port to starboard," Paul replied.

The investigators, moving along the hull, brushed aside

tentacles of vines cluttering their pathway. As they made their way along the starboard side, the air grew even colder. By the time they reached the forecastle, the temperature had plummeted, and a freezing fog rolled over the bow.

Hayley hugged herself, trying to keep warm, and noticed everyone else had done the same.

Roger shone his flashlight into the thick mist. "Paul?" he asked.

Paul rubbed his arms. "Never seen this before." His breath turned to vapor.

"What's causing the fog?" Laura hugged herself. "And why so cold?"

"I'm guessing we've got company," Roger told her, rubbing his hands together.

"I don't understand," Laura said. "So you're saying it's not fog, but a ghost?"

"Right," Roger said. "And by the looks of things, a hell of a lot more than one." He glanced at her confused face. "They're pulling energy from the air in order to materialize. That's why it's cold. As they gather energy, they look like fog."

Laura's eyes widened and her teeth chattered. "So, we have company."

Roger shivered. "It feels as if the whole crew's on deck." He peered into the mist, then turned to Hayley. "Am I right?"

"Yes. I feel their presence. I'll try to get some answers." Hayley surrounded herself with white light to shield herself from experiencing the pain of their deaths. With her shield in place, she moved around the gun battery, planning to cross the bow.

"Lee, go with her. Take a digital video camera, scan the fog," Roger said. "We'll get her voice on tape and have hard evidence to give to the military."

Lee traded his thermal-imaging camera for Jim's DV camera.

213

"Clint, what's your reading?" Roger asked.

"Forty degrees and dropping."

Lee walked behind Hayley, scanning the fog with the camera. He watched her closely, aiming the lens where she looked.

Hayley hesitated, peering at the sailor in front of her. His misty face became pronounced. His cloudy white skin turned to an olive complexion. Gradually, she could see his thick black brows, brown eyes, Roman nose, and his ruddy cheeks. He didn't meet her gaze, but looked straight ahead, eyes fixed. He wore dress whites, as did all the other men standing at attention.

While she inspected the crew, each of their names became a knowing…names she knew as well as her own. Tears welled in her eyes. A lump formed in her throat. She knew without question that not one was aware he had died. They were stuck in a dimension where time didn't exist, where they would live for eternity without knowing they were dead, and where they would never see their families again. Deep depression filled her. She realized her shield had been broken, and the depth of her sadness was an overreaction. Side effects.

"I see them as clear as life," she told Roger.

"Nothing has changed here. We're still seeing fog."

Hayley turned to the olive-skinned sailor. As if recalling a memory, a vision of the young man played in her mind. He was one of the first on the ship who had died from malaria. "I'm Hayley Johnson, Seaman Rizzo. Can I ask you some questions?"

He met her gaze. "We have orders not to speak to you or your friends, miss."

"But you're speaking to me now," Hayley said.

"We were told not to be rude, miss."

"To whom can I speak?"

"Our CO, miss."

"Can you tell me where to find him?"

"I'm not at liberty to say." He fixed his eyes straight ahead.

She turned to Roger. "I've got nothing, Roger. They've been ordered not to speak to us."

"I was afraid of that," Roger said. "Damn shame if we have to bring the admiral into this. Let's finish gathering evidence while we hope for some answers."

Disappointed, she gazed away from the men.

"It's okay, Hayley. I've got them on camera," Lee said.

She and Lee returned to the others.

Paul peeked over Jim's shoulder, watching the temperature fluctuate on the thermal-imaging camera. "Fascinating!" he said. White, blue, yellow, orange, and red showed temperature variations. Paul looked at the mist and then back at the camera. "It clearly shows the forms of human energy."

"Another damn mystery," Jim said. "Thermal imaging doesn't record mist. That's why Lee and I traded cameras."

Hayley glanced at the men as their forms dissolved into fog. Her eyes widened when the vapor streamed toward her, weaving between her and the others.

Laura held out her hand, gently touching the mist as it passed. She pulled her hand back, then held out her palm to Roger. "It looks like white crystals," she said.

"Snow," Roger said.

The fog dissipated along the bow after it moved eerily past them, then flowed through an outer hatch, as if the ship had sucked it in.

"Creepy as hell," Lee said.

"It's getting warmer," Hayley said. "Feel it?"

He nodded.

"Damn remote island," Jim mumbled. "Head-seeking bird turds, piranha ants, jumbo jet mosquitoes, pixy dust fairies, flesh-eattin' bird buffets, and now specter inspection. What in the world were they standin' there for if there ain't a CO to inspect 'em?" He shook his head. "Knowin' the navy like I do, gettin' answers is gonna be harder than pullin' ghost teeth."

Roger looked down at the trail of electrical wiring leading into the ship. "What's all this, Paul?"

"The military brought in a generator and floodlights when JPAC went in to retrieve the skeletal remains from berthing."

"Perfect," Roger said.

"I'll start it up." Paul walked over and turned on the unit. The noise from the generator echoed off the forest. Bright light emanated from the opened forward hatch.

Hayley closed her eyes and searched for danger.

"Anything we should know about?" Lee asked.

"No. It's safe. The crew went back to their duty stations as if it were a normal day aboard the ship." Melancholy swept over her. "They don't know they're dead, Lee."

"I know. That's the sad part of this job. It leaves a hole in your heart to know there's nothing you can do to change things."

"Maybe I can," Hayley said. "I've helped spirits cross over a number of times, but never on a scale this size. Are we able to go below, Roger?"

"Good question," Roger said. "Paul, how much of the ship is lit?"

"Nearly everywhere below," Paul told him. "Nowhere in the superstructure."

"Great. I'd like to take a look at the interior before we start the investigation so, when we turn out the lights, we'll know our way around. Mind leading us to the mess deck?"

"Yeah, sure." Paul led the way through the forward hatch. He placed his hand on the metal frame surrounding the entrance. "When the hatch closes, it seals against the coaming." He pointed toward the deck. "This lip is called a knee knocker. You'll be

216

going over a few of these, so watch your step."

Roger stepped through, then reached back to Laura, giving her a gentlemanly hand. Lee lent a hand to Hayley as well. After they turned to follow Paul, one by one the others entered the ship behind them.

A few feet inside, Paul halted. He glanced down at the companionway, then at the investigators. "These ladders are steep and narrow," he said, loudly enough for everyone to hear. "Stay alert and hold on to the chain railing." He began descending the ladder.

Hayley didn't have to be told twice. The steps were uncomfortably narrow in length and in width. *Just going down these steps would be classified as hazardous duty.*

Once below, Paul led them through hatch after hatch until they came to a small dining area. He spread his arms. "Here you have it. The ship's mess."

"This is too freaky," Roger said. "The ship's too clean."

"You should've been with me when I found it," Paul said. "Where we're standing, parts of the ship were corroded away, gaping holes everywhere. This seems like a hallucination, but I know damn well it's not."

Hayley glanced around. The sense of knowing every inch of the ship as if it were etched into her memory sent shivers up her spine. She surrounded herself with white light. *What's manipulating me? It's not just energy. Something or someone came through the portal.* She closed her eyes, trying to sense the intelligence that not only affected her mind, but manipulated molecules and atoms. The paramnesia grew stronger. She swore under her breath, then opened her eyes.

"Lee, take pictures of everything," Roger said. "The military isn't going to believe this." He looked at Hayley. "What's happening? What's going on?"

217

"I think something came through the portal," Hayley said. "Whatever it is, it isn't letting me sense it, but I'll keep trying. If there's a crack in its armor, I'll find it." She took a deep breath, pushing her frustration aside, and cleared her mind to scan the ship with her senses. The only presences she perceived were the spirits of the crew.

"The answer's here somewhere," Roger said. He glanced toward the galley. "Jim, what do you know about this part of the ship?"

Jim peered up and around. "The Japanese probably used this area same as we did. It wasn't just for eatin'. Medics would've used it for the wounded and the dead. And weapons would've been stored here. They'd bring 'em up from below through that hatch over yonder."

When the others turned to look where Jim pointed, the hatch door swung on its hinges, then slammed closed. Thunder erupted inside the ship.

BOOM, BOOM, BOOM.

Hatches were closing all around them. The lights went out, but came back on seconds later.

Hayley jumped. Lee moved to her side. The group gathered together.

"What the hell?" Paul ran toward the hatch to his right, the one they had just come through. The three-inch-thick hatch door slammed shut before he could reach it. He skidded to a halt and backed away.

The hatch's locking mechanism, covering its entire outer skin, began to move on its own. The wheel in the center turned and the metal spider arms moved the dogs into place one by one.

Paul glanced back at the others. "They locked us in!" He stepped forward, his jaw set, eyes fixed on the door.

"Stop, Paul," Hayley warned. "There's a guard."

He froze, stared at empty space in front of him, then, with a frustrated look on his face, turned and rejoined the team.

Roger looked sharply at Jim. "What the hell just happened?"

"They battened down the hatches," Jim told him. "Looks like they don't want us to go anywhere."

"So, we're prisoners?" Roger asked.

"Looks that way," Jim said.

"Hayley?" Roger asked.

"I'll find out." She started toward the guard.

In front of the hatch, the sailor stood at ease, staring straight ahead with his legs apart, hands behind him. He wore denim straight-leg dungarees with a lighter blue, short-sleeved chambray shirt topped by a white swabbie hat.

Across the room, the hatch slowly opened when she began to speak. They all turned.

"Looks like they're takin' over our investigation," Jim said. "Only allowin' us to go where they want. Just like the navy."

"They're ghosts, Jim," Roger replied. "They have no control. We can walk right through them."

"Well, they're doing a damn good job so far," Jim said.

Roger's eyes searched the room. "We'll see about that."

CHAPTER 28

Roger's voice bounced off the overhead strung with pipes, cables, and vents as he discussed his plans to collect evidence of the haunting. "Okay, I'll take Laura, Jim, and Hayley with me, and we'll go where they obviously want us to go," he told everyone. "If any more hatches open, Paul, you know the ship, so take Kathy and John. Investigate all you can. Lee, you and Clint take the mess, galley, and scullery."

Their equipment was spread on the table in front of them.

"Grab what you need," Roger said.

Roger, Laura, Jim, and Hayley left the mess. Their footsteps echoed as they moved through the narrow metal passageways. Floodlights, strung earlier by the military, lit their way. As they approached another major compartment, the dogs on its hatch released and the barrier swung open.

"There's a guard at the hatch," Hayley said.

Roger turned to the doctor. "Follow Hayley. We don't want to walk through him."

Laura hesitated. "Have you before?"

"Yes, and it's painful," Roger said. "It disrupts every cell in your body, not to mention the energy he's able to pull from you.

It takes a while just to recover from the numbness."

She smiled faintly. "Interesting."

He grinned. "Want to try?"

Laura shook her head. "I think I'll take your word."

Hayley carefully edged Roger, Laura, and Jim around the ghost, then followed.

Jim peeked into an adjoining compartment. "Looks like we're in berthing," he said. "This is where the enlisted sleep." He glanced into another area. "More racks."

They followed the passageway to a compartment lined with racks. Six delirious navy personnel lay shaking, sweating, their mumbles turning to moans.

"What's going on?" Roger asked in a low tone.

Hayley glanced at him and the others. "Can you see them?"

"As clear as day," Jim said. "Who are they?"

"Captain Jordan, Doc Wagner, Cook Davis, Seamen Price, Andrews, and Holden," Hayley said in a soft voice. It stunned her that their names came so easily to her.

"This can't be real," Laura said.

"It's not," Hayley said. "It's a memory."

Roger looked closer at the sick men. "I think they're the crewmen whose bodies the military took off the ship."

"Doesn't make sense," Jim said. "What're officers doin' in the enlisted men's quarters?"

"Easy," Hayley said. "They knew they were dying and wanted their remains to be found together. Their humanity outweighed their ranks."

Laura raised a brow. "So they're ghosts, or lingerings as Hayley calls them?"

"No," Roger said. "This is what we refer to as a residual haunting—a memory of the past. We're seeing their deaths."

"Oh, like a video." Laura gingerly moved closer to examine

the symptoms. "Hayley was right. It appears to be malaria."

Roger glanced at Jim. "You getting this?"

While looking at the camera's view screen, Jim double-checked to make sure he was filming. "Got it, Roger."

"Keep recording until it plays out. They're trying to show us what happened to the crew."

One by one, the men died. As their bodies lay still, the visual time capsule played out rapidly. Hours, days, and weeks flashed by. The corpses decayed and the flesh dissolved.

Hayley swayed, feeling dizzy as each man's face swept across her mind.

"Jim, get her out of here," Roger said.

Being careful not to lose the shot, Jim handed the DV camera to Roger, then helped Hayley out of the room and to a small compartment off the passageway.

She rubbed her temples while she sat on a chair in the corner. Then the vision of the dying crew filled her sight. Whatever had been manipulating her before was forcing her to continue seeing the bodies decomposing as if she'd never left the room. Hayley saw the time capsule slow its motion, then pause. The skeletal remains of the six crewmen rested on the bunks, dog tags lying on their sternums.

In her mind's eye, she witnessed Laura move closer to the racks and reach toward one of the IDs. The residual haunting evaporated, and Laura jumped back.

"This is the stuff nightmares are made of," Roger said.

Laura's voice trembled. "I'm beginning to think we're in one."

Roger glanced toward the passageway. "Jim?"

Hayley's vision stopped. She blinked and looked up at Jim standing in front her, his brows narrowed with concern.

"We're in here," Jim called out. He studied Hayley's face.

222

"You okay, darlin'? Ya look pale."

"Just great," she grumbled. "Apparently, that whatever-it-is thinks it can control me anytime it wants." She glanced at Roger when he entered the room. "That thing invaded my mind," she told him, her voice raised. "After I left you and came in here, I was forced to have visions. I saw it all as if I'd never left that room."

Laura stepped around Roger, went to Hayley, and checked her pulse. "How do you feel?"

"Violated," Hayley said.

Laura lowered her hand, then looked into Hayley's eyes. "Any headaches?"

"I'm fine."

"So, now it's attacking my team," Roger said.

Hayley took a deep, calming breath and tried to look at things objectively. "I wouldn't call it attacking. I don't feel it's a negative entity. It's just controlling."

"Can you stand?" Laura asked.

Hayley nodded and stood.

"Still dizzy?" Laura asked.

"No."

"How close to the ship were you when you first felt influenced?" Roger asked.

"Not long after we landed. On the beach. During the vision I had, I lost myself and became the lieutenant."

"I remember," Roger said. "I wonder if you're the only one it's controlling." He looked at Jim. "Notice anything different?"

"Nope," Jim said. "No changes in me. I'm just as lovable as always."

Roger glanced toward the ceiling and shook his head, then looked at Laura. "How about you?"

"No," she said.

"I've mastered protecting myself from outside influences," Hayley said, her anger stirring. "This shouldn't be happening."

"There's a hell of a lot that shouldn't be happenin'," Jim added. He counted on his fingers. "Mind manipulation, ship resurrection, and climate control. Did I miss anythin'?"

Roger scanned the room. "Why is this room lit? There're no floodlights in here, and the ship doesn't have power."

Jim rubbed his chin and glanced around. "It was lit when we came in." He reached into his pocket and pulled out an electromagnetic field detector. While holding it in front of him, he walked around the compartment, then held it up to the lit bulb encased in a wire cover overhead. "There's power comin' from somewhere."

"Hell, who knows what else it creates?" Roger said. He stepped to the entrance and glanced down the passageway. "The hatch is still open. We should get back to the others."

Hayley led the way, searching every alcove with her senses. The ship was eerily quiet. She looked over her shoulder at Roger. "No signs of the crew so far."

After the four of them stepped through the first open hatch on their way back to the mess, Jim called out. Hayley, Roger, and Laura turned around. A few feet back, Jim straddled the knee knocker, gazing upward. They waited for his explanation.

"Lookie here," he said. "The wires are severed." He pointed to the lines feeding the floodlights. "Remember when the hatches closed and the lights went out? It was just for a second. Then they came back on." He held up the EMF, checking the electromagnetic field around the wires. "When the hatch slammed shut, it sliced the wirin'. These floodlights are lit, but there's no power comin' through these lines. There ain't any way these lights should be lit. That control freak is a damn Houdini."

He's got that right. Hayley turned to Roger. "Have you ever encountered anything like this before?"

"Never." Roger reached up, grabbed the floodlight, and studied the electrical connection. "Amazing. Get pictures of this, Jim. Nobody in their right mind is going to believe any of this."

Jim grabbed the digital camera from around his neck and started to take pictures. "Damn island, damn ship, damn Houdini," he mumbled.

* * *

Hayley noticed the aroma of coffee permeated the passageway when she and the others approached the mess.

Jim raised his chin and sniffed. "What's cookin' now?"

One by one they entered the dining area and glanced around, looking for the rest of the team.

Lee, appearing excited, came out of the galley with Clint close behind. "While you were gone, I got some fantastic stuff," Lee said, holding up the thermal-imaging camera. "Must be close to chow time, because the kitchen's buzzing with activity. Smell the coffee? It's damn weird. The coffee pot's empty, but my camera picked up heat radiating from it."

Roger sniffed. "So you two have been experiencing a few things yourselves. We have to have a meeting. Where's Paul?"

Lee pointed across the compartment. "When that hatch over there opened up, he took Kathy and John with him to investigate the ship." He glanced at Hayley, his brows narrowed, and he moved to her side. "What happened?"

She nodded. "Things keep getting stranger and stranger."

He gazed at the kitchen. "You're telling me."

Footsteps echoed in the passageway across the mess. Paul, Kathy, and John entered through the hatch.

Roger turned toward them. "Glad you're back. We have to have—"

"Holy moley," Jim interrupted. "Turn around, Roger.

Slowly."

CHAPTER 29

Roger turned and his eyes widened. He stepped back and stared, mouth agape.

The seaman standing before him wore a light blue shirt, denim pants, and a white Dixie Cup-hat on his head. With his round face, he looked to Hayley no older than nineteen.

Roger glanced at Hayley, then at the seaman. "Is he real?" He looked the sailor directly in the face. Floodlights strung along the bulkhead reflected in the young man's eyes.

"He's as real as the sailor we met at the memorial," she told him.

"The CO requests the presence of you and your team," the sailor said. "Follow me, sir."

"Incredible," Roger whispered. He looked around at the others' expressions. They stood with mouths open, unable to speak or move—frozen in the moment. "Okay, team, you heard the man," Roger said.

Hayley smiled inwardly. *Now I'm going to get some answers.*

The sailor led them up a ladder and waited while the team followed. From there, he brought them to a compartment one flight above the mess deck. The seaman knocked twice and removed his hat. Someone said, "Enter."

When the hatch opened, their guide stepped aside, allowing the team access. They filed into a small dining area and were met by a second crewman dressed in khaki.

"This is the officers' mess. It's called the wardroom," Jim whispered to Roger.

"There're no floodlights in here either," Roger said in a low voice. "This room's lit by the ship." He looked around the room. "Nothing's aged. Everything looks as it did when the ship was first commissioned. Unbelievable."

In front of them, chairs surrounded a long narrow table. "Please have a seat," the crewman said. "Hayley." He pointed to her seat.

He knows my name. How freaky is that? She sat, realizing the seat next to her at the head of the table was reserved for the person in charge, the person who could move molecules and atoms. *Time to meet the man behind the curtain.*

"Get your equipment ready," Roger said.

Across the table, Paul laughed nervously. "This ghost-hunting stuff is way cool. I'll—"

The room grew cold.

"He's here," Hayley said, aware the others followed her gaze.

"We can't see him," Roger told her.

"Okay. He's at the door," she replied, then remembered the terminology she'd studied. "Oh, I mean, he's coming through the hatch."

All but Laura and Paul had voice recorders resting on the table in front of them, while their other tech equipment lay within reach. They sat on the edge of their seats, not speaking, waiting for Hayley to communicate with the apparition.

She was ready to confront the captain, to ask why he had singled her out. Was it because she was the most susceptible, the

228

only one in the team he could control? But as she watched him approach the conference table, her irritation vanished for reasons she didn't understand, and was replaced by admiration. *He's manipulating me again.*

Hayley felt he looked at her as if he had read her mind. His brows narrowed.

She studied him while he stood at the head of the table. He appeared stately and confident. His khaki long-sleeved shirt displayed combat ribbons on the breast pocket. Silver eagles were pinned on his collar.

"We want to know your intentions," Hayley said, forcefully. "You've been manipulating me since I stepped off the helicopter. How dare you invade my mind and take control of my emotions? I want to know why."

He met her gaze. "You'll know in due time."

"We didn't come here to play games," she said.

"What did he say?" Roger asked.

Hayley turned to the others, having forgotten they only heard a one-sided conversation. Her patience felt nearly at its end, but she had to remember the investigation wasn't about her. "Sorry, Roger. He said I'd know in due time." She gazed at their host. "I'm sensing you need our help as much as we need yours."

"Yes. You're right. You of all people should know that things aren't always what they appear to be. I suggest we cooperate with each other and let the story unfold."

She knew he wasn't a lingering because his vibrating frequency was that of a visiting spirit. So, what knowledge of her did he possess allowing him to make such an accusation?

"I'd like to address you and your friends, but I'll need your help, Hayley."

She realized the only way the team would get answers would be to do as he suggested.

Roger stared at the empty space beside Hayley. "Is he still here?"

"Yes, he's standing at the head of the table. He wants me to talk for him."

"I've started your EVP for you, Hayley," the captain said, "so you can record this discussion."

Hayley looked down at the recorder, then glanced at the captain, keeping her disapproving comments about his manipulation to herself.

"So let us begin. I'm Captain Thomas Elliott Jordan, United States Navy."

"What's going on, Hayley?"

"Oh, sorry, Roger. This is Captain Thomas Elliott Jordan, United States Navy. I don't know how, but he started my EVP."

Roger glared. "So he imprisons my team and now he takes over my investigative equipment. I think the captain is too damn controlling. Ask why he doesn't show himself like the sailor he sent to bring us here?"

"He hears everything you're saying. I don't need to speak for you. You can ask him anything you like, and I'll tell you his response," Hayley told him.

"Yes, I admit I'm controlling. I'm the captain. It's my duty." He chuckled. "But you have no idea how controlling I am."

She repeated his comment.

Roger looked at Hayley. "What's that supposed to mean?"

"If you've noticed, the condition of this ship defies logic. I'm using an infinite amount of control to hold this vessel together. For that reason, I choose to remain in my present form."

Hayley again relayed his message.

"Sounds like an excuse," Roger said.

"I'll give you an example. You'll need your DV cameras." The captain smiled briefly. "I'll let you start it yourself."

Hayley repeated after him and watched the team react.

Lee and Clint each grabbed a digital video camera. Then Clint moved to the right of the table and Lee to the left. Roger, with his DV camera, stayed where he was, directly across from the captain. They aimed their equipment at the head of the table.

"He's standing to the right of his chair," Hayley told them, allowing them to pinpoint their coverage.

The rest of the team gathered their digital and thermal-imaging cameras and moved to their selected positions, poised like paparazzi waiting for a close-up. Voice recorders lay on the table, continuing to capture the audio.

"Focus on the bulkhead behind me."

Hayley told the others.

The team adjusted equipment as Lee, Clint, and Roger zoomed in on the bulkhead.

Captain Jordan hesitated, then glanced over his shoulder. Suddenly, the polished surface of the bulkhead melted. Rust spread across the tarnished metal. Nuts and bolts dropped from their anchored positions as corrosion disintegrated the ship's bulkhead. Jagged holes exposed the frayed electrical cables dangling inside.

The lights in the room flickered, then stabilized.

"Does that make it a little clearer about how much control I'm using?" He closed his eyes briefly. The decay reversed until the skin of the bulkhead became unblemished. "You can stop recording now."

Hayley relayed his message.

"We already know you're controlling the ship," Roger said. "So your demonstration wasn't necessary." He gently set the video camera on the table and leaned back in his chair. "But I have to admit your show was impressive. So if you're controlling the condition of this ship as you say you are, why was it found

231

rusted?"

"If this ship had been found unnaturally intact, attention would have gone to the condition of the ship. If seaworthy, it would have been moved. There's a reason for everything. Some things have to happen in order to have the desired outcome."

Hayley repeated his explanation. *Hhmm, this is getting interesting. Where is he going with this?*

"Links," Lee said.

The captain nodded. "Exactly."

"He said 'Exactly.'"

Lee, standing to Hayley's side, looked at her, then at the head of the table. "So our being here was the desired outcome?"

"Yes."

"He said 'Yes,'" Hayley relayed.

"How long have you known we'd be coming?" Lee asked.

"The moment I passed over."

"Wow, that's amazing." She repeated his reply.

The team looked at one another.

"That was during World War II," Lee said.

"Yes, that would be correct in your view. But time is relevant only in your plane."

Hayley told the team.

"Why did you come back?" Lee asked.

"There are many levels of existence. This is obvious, since I'm here in front of you. When I died, I passed over—the crew did not. I chose to come back for a number of reasons. One reason, clearly, was to be with my men."

Hayley explained.

Lee looked confused. "Don't your men know they're dead?"

"No. They were ravaged by fever; their conscious minds were no longer aware of their condition. But more than that, death is as simple as walking into another room. The transition isn't as obvious to the departed as it is to you, the bereaved. They still see themselves as they were before their illness, as if nothing had changed. This is one of the reasons for your arrival."

Hayley parroted, anxious to hear more.

"So, you're telling us that plans were made for this investigation since before our birth?" Roger's voice rose. "Is this our purpose for living? Are we just puppets?"

"I can't tell you about purpose."

Hayley echoed.

Roger leaned forward. "Can't or won't?"

"Both."

"Both," Hayley told Roger.

"You're lying," Roger said. "If you were telling us the truth, you'd have the answers. We didn't come halfway around the world to be lied to. Did you expect us to believe what you're saying just because you showed us a few tricks?"

"I can't tell you because you can't understand, and I won't tell you because I wasn't sent here to be a teacher. I'm here as a catalyst."

Hayley gave his answer. *A catalyst?*

Roger huffed. "Why don't you try to make some sense? I think we deserve it."

"You're not puppets. You had just as much choice as Hayley."

She repeated his words. *I had a choice? To do what?* She let his comment pass, hoping his remark would become clear.

With crossed arms in front of his chest, Roger stared at the space where the captain stood. "That's like saying, 'This blade of grass is green because that blade of grass is green.' You're talking in circles."

"You're right about grass, but your analogy is wrong." He caught Roger's confused expression. "Okay, Roger, let me try to explain."

233

Hayley repeated his answer.

"I wish you would."

"Laura, how many strands of DNA are in the human body?"

Hayley turned to Laura and asked his question.

Laura's green eyes widened. The mention of her name, Hayley noted, clearly had caught her off guard. She blinked. "That's impossible to know," she said nervously.

"Would you say DNA makes a person unique?"

Hayley translated.

Laura nodded. "Yes, without a doubt."

"What does this have to do with anything?" Roger asked.

"Just follow where I'm going with this, Roger. Now, Laura, taking the complexity of creating the design and function of Roger's DNA, not to mention the other miraculous matter comprising his being, do you think Roger's creation took more knowledge than can be comprehended by the human mind?"

Hayley told Laura what he'd asked.

"Yes, definitely."

"So, Roger, if the complexity of creating you as an individual is beyond comprehension, why would you think purpose would be something you'd be able to grasp?"

Hayley giggled, then repeated his words.

Roger took a deep breath, "So what you're saying is I'm unique and too stupid to understand?"

"That's it exactly." Captain Jordan laughed. "Like I said, I'm not here as a teacher. Let's stay away from things like purpose and life's secrets and stick to your investigation."

Hayley laughed to herself and told Roger.

Roger rubbed his forehead and softened his tone. "Can you tell us why we're here?"

"The most obvious reason you're here is to take care of my men. The military always likes to have facts, and you can provide the evidence. The footage and recordings will dispel any doubt of our existence. That will explain the drama you've experienced so far."

Hayley echoed his words. *That explains most of it, but not all.*

"How can we take care of your men? Isn't it a bit too late?" Roger asked.

"You are the links to taking my crew's remains back to their families. Without your action, I never would have returned, their remains would lie unfound, and my men would walk this ship for eternity."

A chill went up Hayley's back as she realized hers and the team's mission. Hayley repeated his explanation.

"You're right—the navy will need proof. A different reality isn't easy for some to believe," Roger said.

"That's about to change. This investigation is going to ignite interest in alternate realities. With the government's backing, science is going to be the vehicle to open minds. It's time for some 'seeing is believing.'" The captain smiled broadly. "Now, about your investigation…."

Hayley told them.

"I thought it was over," Roger said.

"Your investigation is divided into four parts. You've already experienced the first, gathering evidence, and the second, this meeting. The third will be returning to Guam to pick up the admiral and bring him here. The fourth will be a trip to the caves, which I'll explain when you return." He faced Hayley. "Thank you for all your help. I'll take it from here. Get your tech equipment ready. I'm going to materialize."

"You're welcome. I'll tell the others."

CHAPTER 30

Hayley glanced around the table at her friends. When she was a child, her day was spent with what her parents called her imaginary playmates. By the end of first grade, because classmates and neighbors teased her for talking to imaginary friends, she learned to remain quiet, guard secrets, and keep to herself. After her parents died in the car accident, as she grew older and found balance in her life, while she lived with Grams, she continued to be detached from others. She'd never had a close living friend until she took this job and got to know her co-workers. And now they were about to see an apparition solidify and become a person, as real as the rest of them, something she had seen happen all of her life.

She turned her attention away from Captain Jordan, who stood waiting while the team prepared to watch him materialize. Instead, she chose to watch her friends' reactions.

Excitement lit Roger's face as he gave orders to his team. "Grab your cameras and spread out, team. The more angles we get of the captain materializing, the better chance we'll have of convincing skeptics that this is real. If you need to stand on furniture to get your shot, go for it."

He turned to Laura at the end of the table. "Laura, I'll give you an EVP. Just check it now and then to make sure it's still recording the captain's voice." He set the recorder on the table in front of her.

Her ponytail bobbed up and down when she nodded. "Okay. Simple enough."

Roger walked to their hiking guide sitting across from the doctor. A playful smile crossed his face. "Paul, are you able to do two things at once?"

"I've been known to," Paul said.

Roger gave him a digital video camera and a small device that monitored fluctuations in energy levels. "Hold the camera on this EMF. Keep it pointed at the meter. I know it can't be used as scientific proof. It's more of a curiosity. I want to see the electromagnetic distortions caused by materialization."

Paul examined the equipment and nodded. "Got it."

Glancing around the room, Roger turned to find Kathy standing beside him. "Kathy, use the video camera. I want shots of the team as they record evidence, as well as the shots of the captain. So stand back and get a wide shot."

"Okay, Roger." She pushed a chair into the far corner, stood on it, then looked through the lens and adjusted her camera.

Hayley could sense Lee and Roger's elated anticipation.

"Lee?" he asked.

Lee stood behind Hayley with his video camera ready to capture the captain's profile. "All set, Roger."

"Clint and John, I want each of you to take a thermal-imaging camera."

The cousins grabbed their equipment and took strategic positions. They adjusted their equipment and stood alert.

"And Jim, you know what you're doing," Roger said.

Jim nodded. "Ain't my first time fryin' chicken."

Roger surveyed his crew. "We're ready when you are, Captain."

The captain slid his chair to the corner and moved back, stepping away from the table.

In sight of all, a transparent veil oscillated two feet above the floor. The wavering mist streamed to the ground. The fog took the vague shape of legs. As the mist moved up, the captain's torso gradually appeared. Then his beclouded arms and head slowly formed. His legs solidified, giving detail to his shoes and pants. The materialization fortified itself, continuing upward until everything about him became crisply defined.

Silence filled the room as the World War II naval captain stood before them. Hayley thought he appeared to be in his mid-forties, his age when he passed, and looked distinguished in his uniform.

She gazed at his face. The flash of cameras reflected in his green eyes.

Seeing Hayley's interest, he smiled. "How am I doing so far?"

"You're putting on quite a show, sir."

"Can you hear me?" Captain Jordan asked.

"Perfectly," Roger said.

"Exactly my intention. Is there anything you wish me to do that might help your investigation?"

Roger smiled at "your investigation." He nodded. "How about putting your hand through the table? Would that be possible?"

The captain nodded. "Yes, of course."

Captain Jordan extended his hand, resting his fingertips on the tabletop. He hesitated, making sure everyone was ready.

Lee bent over Hayley's shoulder to get a close-up. The team positioned its cameras.

Slowly, the captain slid his hand downward through the

238

table, stopping at the wrist. Then he withdrew the hand. The captain stepped forward. His body appeared to be cut in two by the table. He revolved in a circle until he returned to face the camera.

"Amazing!" Roger said.

The captain looked up. "Thank you."

"So what's next?" Roger asked.

"I'm remaining in this form only for a short time. I need to make a visual plea to Admiral Wayne."

Hayley blinked. *He knows the admiral's name. I can't wait to see Admiral Wayne's face when he sees this video.*

While standing at the other end of the table, Roger adjusted his video camera for a direct shot. "Okay. Look this way."

The captain squared his shoulders. "Admiral Wayne, I'm Captain Thomas Elliott Jordan, United States Navy. Thank you for sending your investigators. I understand the events shown on this video appear unbelievable. I assure you that not one piece of evidence has been tampered with. Since I crossed over and then returned to my crew, I've been tethered to Heaven and am able to tap into a copious amount of energy. I'm using a vast amount to reconstitute this vessel. Unfortunately, this dimension leaves my spirit with limitations, so I'm only able to materialize for a short time. There are plenty of unanswered questions. Some I'll go over now, starting with our arrival on this island."

Memories of Captain Jordan and his crew coming ashore flashed through Hayley mind. *Telepathy? These aren't my memories. I haven't been able to do this before.*

"The Japanese, after Pearl Harbor and Midway, turned their attention to Australia, planning to release a lethal strain of malaria. They had used biological weapons before in China with gruesome effects. This very ship was stocked with the deadly parasites.

"The United States stopped them, and the Japanese ship was damaged. The Japanese command had secret orders and found this hiding place, but their cargo was compromised. The wounded crewmen, scrambling to save their deadly weapon, were infected. Mosquitoes carried the malaria to the rest of their crew.

"When our ship was bombed, it was obvious it would not stay afloat, and our loss of personnel was heavy," Captain Jordan went on. "Out of a crew of one hundred forty-four, only eighty-nine made it to shore."

The faces of the crewmen lost at sea crossed her mind, one-by-one. *It must've been hellish.* She felt the chill of the ocean water against her skin and glanced around, trying to make sense of the sensation. The officers' quarters and everyone in the room had vanished. With the sound of aircraft above and the smell of smoke almost gagging her, she felt herself treading water. Hayley panicked, quickly closed her eyes, and surrounded herself with white light, returning to the present. *That was damn scary!* She fixed her gaze on the captain and suppressed her clairvoyance. *Focus, focus.*

"When I sent scouts to search the island, my men came across this ship. They watched the surviving Japanese take their crew's bodies to a cave and followed them to bring me a full report. We killed ten and captured two. By the time we saw their symptoms it was too late. Those damn mosquitoes fed on our prisoners, then carried the deadly malaria to my men.

"We took our dead to the same caves, all except the six bodies your personnel recently recovered from the ship. They were the last to succumb...I was one of those men."

Hayley felt nauseous as she remembered the residual haunting remaining after the bodies were removed from berthing, showing the captain's death, his flesh decaying. Lee put his hand on her shoulder as she fought against the memory.

With his eyes on the camera, Captain Jordan continued his message. "It is my request, Admiral, that you come aboard so I can give you the details the military needs. Also, we need your help to take my crew's remains from the cave and home for burial, giving closure to them and their families." He glanced at the hatch while a chief materialized, standing patiently waiting for orders.

The captain nodded. "Chief."

He stepped into the room. His chief's uniform looked identical to the captain's, although the pins on his collar were anchors and the stripes of his chief's rank were high on his sleeve, not near the cuffs like the captain's.

Captain Jordan looked back at the camera. "Admiral, this is Command Master Chief Langford. I wouldn't have been able to hold this ship together, so to speak, without this man. I would like to suggest that our chiefs sit down together and discuss procedures. Nothing gets done right without a chief."

Master Chief Langford took a step back.

The captain closed the discussion. "Thank you all. I'll end this now and see you when you return."

CHAPTER 31

Roger sat with Hayley, Lee, Jim, and the admiral in a small conference room at their hotel on Guam. He stopped the video of Captain Jordan's message. "Well, Admiral, what do you think?"

After sitting a few moments, Admiral Wayne stood. Hayley saw his hands shaking.

"I've never seen ya so shook up before, Larry," Jim said, grinning. "Ya look a little green."

The admiral gave him a piercing stare. "This isn't funny. My reputation is at stake. I can't be shaking like a Chihuahua in front of my men. I'd never live it down." He looked at Hayley. "You say things happen for a reason. Maybe that typhoon southwest of here has stalled for a purpose."

"It's stalled?" Hayley asked. "Is it going to delay our trip back to the island?"

"I believe so. JTWC says it's moving slower than anticipated. It looks as if I'll have another day to control my nerves. The question is, how? What do you suggest, Hayley?"

"It might help if you didn't think of him as being a ghost," Hayley said.

"But he is."

"No. He's a spirit."

"And that shouldn't make me nervous?" He studied her calm face. "Well, yes, of course it shouldn't." He looked down and rubbed his neck. "How am I going to pull this off without looking like a fool?" He took the seat across from her at the table. "Tell me more about him."

"Once a person dies and crosses over," Hayley said, "no matter where he goes, if he returns to this plane, he never loses his connection to the other side, Heaven. We're still connected, too, since that's where our energy originated before birth. But because we're limited in our understanding, we feel disconnected. Not completely, though, because we sense enough to want to create religions or have beliefs of one kind or another."

Hayley caught herself going off in another direction. She hesitated. "Okay, so, the captain is using his connection to draw energy, giving him the control to manipulate his environment. And he has access to unlimited knowledge of our past, present, and future. He knew our names and that we were coming. He knew all about our equipment, and I'm sure he knows the outcome of this investigation."

"So, there's nothing to be uneasy about," Admiral Wayne said.

"No, sir." She wished she could help him believe that. "If you're still worried about how you'll react around him, I know a woman who can help." She glanced at Lee.

He coughed, disguising a laugh.

"Living or dead?" Admiral Wayne asked.

"She seems quite alive," Hayley said, twisting the facts.

"Why is she in Guam? Have you revealed our mission?"

"No, sir. I only see her once in a while. She's kind of a free spirit. Seeing her on Guam doesn't surprise me." Hayley tried to phrase it so she wouldn't be lying.

243

"Is she an expert in the paranormal?"

"Most definitely. She knows a lot more than I do. I'll introduce you to her later. Maybe you two can take a walk along the beach. She'd like that."

"And her name?"

"Julia. But you can call her Grams."

"I suggest we get down to business." He reached across the table for a notebook and pen. "I have to set things up for our return. JPAC will make the recovery. We'll accompany them to the cave. With that many bodies, it will take them weeks to retrieve and detail the recovery. Everything should be set up before we head to the island."

"Will we be hiking through the forest again?" Lee asked.

"No. We'll be taking a RIB—it's a small boat—from the carrier off the island's coast."

Hayley let out a sigh of relief. No hours of humidity, sweaty clothing, and no sore body the next morning. Glancing around, she noticed she wasn't the only one relieved.

"That's good," Roger said. "None of us were looking forward to that hike."

"After we fly to Yap, we'll take the helicopter to the carrier," the admiral continued while writing a list. "I have to pick up Chief Hospital Corpsman Drexler there. It's been awhile since I've seen him. He's stationed at CIL, working to identify the remains taken off the ship." He stopped writing and looked up, smiling. "You know, a chief can't be a chief without knowing how to deal with the unexpected. Since this will be his first time aboard the vessel, and I doubt he's seen pictures of the ship, he won't know the ship's previous condition or that it's haunted. I don't think I'll tell him he's going to meet with a ghost."

Hayley smiled. *This ought to be interesting.*

Roger frowned. "Nothing personal, Admiral, but in the midst

of retrieving bodies, is a joke appropriate?"

"Good point," Admiral Wayne said. "But because our men are put in high-stress situations, pranks are a priority, not only in the navy, but in all the branches of our military. It's expected."

"Strange, but understandable," Roger said.

"I've known this man since I was an ensign on my first tour," the admiral said. "He was my third-class petty officer twenty years ago. This will be payback for some pretty good pranks he pulled on me over the years. Bring your video camera — the other chiefs will love this." He handed Roger the schedule for the day of their departure. "It's going to be one hell of a day. I can't wait to see Chief Drexler's face."

"I'll be taking Hayley and Lee with us when we return to the island," Roger said. "The rest of my team will stay and continue working on the evidence we brought from the ship. If they start right now, by the time we return, they should have all the data examined."

"Yes. Keep your team here. I can't wait to see and hear what they find," Admiral Wayne said.

* * *

At the end of the day, Hayley and Lee sat on the patio by the pool. Looking toward the ocean, they could see Admiral Wayne and Grams walking along the beach.

"After the admiral spends some time with Grams, he won't have any trouble being around the captain," Hayley said.

"Thanks for introducing me to her. I've wanted to meet her," Lee said.

"You're welcome. I'm glad you had the chance." With the stem of the glass between her fingers, she swirled her wine. "I wonder if she's told him yet that she's, as he would put it, dead?"

* * *

Hayley stirred in her sleep. In her vivid dream, she stood at the edge of the forest not far from the ship. Above the mountaintops lightning lit the sky, its thunder barely audible over the roar of the wind. Rain pounded the island, causing the waterfall to swell and surge. She watched the riverbanks overflow, the Japanese warship breaking free of its silt mooring, its rusted hull filling with water. Her heart sank, knowing no one would board the ship again. She gazed toward the cave of the dead and saw a vision of the cave flooding, human remains scattered. Panic rousted her awake.

While Kathy slept comfortably, Hayley picked up the phone and dialed Lee's room.

Kathy sat up in bed. "What's wrong?"

"Everything," Hayley told her. She heard him pick up. "Lee, you have to wake the admiral. The typhoon is turning. It's going to hit the island and destroy the ship."

"I'll call him right away. Get dressed. I'll wake the others, then come for you."

"Hurry, Lee. Tell Admiral Wayne we have to leave this morning or it'll be too late." By the time she cradled the phone, Kathy had grabbed a few clothes from the closet and started to dress. Hayley followed her lead, and they were ready when Lee came to their door.

"We're meeting in Roger's room," he said, as Hayley stepped into the hallway and Kathy shut the door behind them.

At the end of the hall, Jim and John hurried out of their room.

* * *

Hayley paced the floor of Roger's room while everyone waited for the admiral. She glanced at the door as the officer walked in.

"Sorry I took so long," he said. His thinning hair looked slightly disheveled, as if he'd combed it with his fingers, and his Hawaiian shirt was left unbuttoned over a white T-shirt. At the hem of his khaki pants, he still wore his brown bed slippers. "I called JTWC. They told me the typhoon had gathered speed and assured me that it's on its rightful course."

"Not so, Admiral," Hayley said. "It's going to turn. I'm positive."

"JTWC says by the time I set things in motion and fly out of here, we'll run directly into the storm."

Hayley met the admiral's gaze and said softly, "It's time, Admiral. Either you believe in me or you don't."

A smile crossed his face. "Exactly. That's why we'll be leaving at oh-eight hundred."

Hayley swallowed hard, holding back emotions that made her want to kiss the admiral. She beamed. "Thank you, Admiral Wayne."

He nodded. "I believe in you, young lady, and nothing is going to convince me otherwise." He turned to Roger. "Will you have time to get your gear ready and grab a bite to eat before we go?"

"Gear's ready, sir. We'll be ready to leave at seven thirty."

"Great. I still have a few calls to make," Admiral Wayne said. "I'll meet you in the restaurant."

* * *

After taking the Sea Knight to the carrier and picking up Chief Drexler, the admiral, in full uniform, with Hayley, Lee, and Roger, rode in a rigid-hull inflatable boat to the island and into the river.

The forest cast shadows while they motored up current against the silt-darkened water. Humidity lay over them like a blanket the farther inland they sailed.

Ahead, to their right, rose two lush green hills, one deceptively the ship. They docked the RIB along the shore and walked to the brow.

Admiral Wayne, Chief Drexler, and the three paranormal investigators ascended to the ship's deck. They were met by a seaman, appearing as alive as each of them. He led them to the forecastle. While they walked along the starboard side, stubborn vines reclaiming their territory muffled their footsteps. Only jungle noises broke the silence.

Hayley glanced around for signs of apparitions during their progress, but she did not see or sense anything pertinent.

"This is a damn spooky place to be having a meeting, Admiral," the chief said.

"You're right about that, Doc."

"You know, some remains removed from this ship were those of a Captain Jordan," Chief Drexler commented. "I wonder if this Captain Jordan we'll be meeting is related to him."

"Maybe it's the same Captain Jordan whose remains were removed and he's haunting this ship," Admiral Wayne said, his voice deep and low.

"Oh yeah, right. There're no such thing as ghosts," Doc said. "They're all Hollywood make-believe."

If Doc only knew the admiral's telling the truth and that he saw the footage of the residual haunting of their deaths; but that would ruin the chief's surprise. This should be good.

The admiral glanced at Hayley and winked.

Things looked different when they reached the forecastle. The floodlights that had been strung throughout the ship were in neat piles next to the generator.

Captain Jordan's crew must've done this. Hayley suppressed her thoughts, not wanting to mention the fact. She watched the admiral scan the area. He had seen footage of the bow along with the rest of the evidence. She sensed he noticed the equipment had been dismantled and kept his cool not to let on to the chief.

The forward hatch stood open. Lights were on, awaiting their arrival. The admiral and Roger exchanged glances, both knowing the ship was being lit by the uncanny abilities of their host.

"This way if you will, sir," the seaman said, entering the forward hatch.

As they descended the ladders and walked through the ship's passageways, their footsteps echoed. After reaching the mess deck, the seaman led them to the wardroom one flight above. The seaman knocked, and the hatch swung open.

Inside, Captain Jordan stood at attention, saluting Admiral Wayne.

Hayley watched the admiral. He kept his dignity and returned the salute.

"I'm honored to meet you," the admiral said.

Chief Drexler's brows pulled together, apparently confused by the remark.

"The honor is mine, sir." Captain Jordan turned to the others. "Glad to see you again, Hayley. Roger, Lee. Thanks for delivering my message."

"Our pleasure," Roger said.

"Would you join me in my stateroom?" the captain asked the admiral. "I'd like to tell you my recommendations for procedure."

"His stateroom? I thought this ship was…." Chief Drexler said under his breath. "Um, Admiral?"

"Not now, Doc. If you have any questions, ask me later." He turned to his host. "Of course, Captain. Lead the way."

"We won't be long," Captain Jordan told the others. "Please make yourselves comfortable."

After they left the wardroom, Doc turned to Roger. "So, you're with Search and Analysis? What type of analysis?"

"We work with the dead to find out their cause of death," Roger said.

"Oh, forensics," Hayley heard Doc say.

While she strolled around the wardroom, Hayley's interest pulled toward the World War II memorabilia. She traced her finger over the Japanese writing under a display of nautical flags hanging on the bulkhead. It was easy to forget this was a Japanese ship. From what she had seen so far, the American sailors had removed all traces of their enemy. This was the only room where she'd seen the graceful lines that slanted and curved to form a word or a complete thought. They seemed more of an art to her than text. It was chilling to think such a word as "kill" or "annihilate" could be written with such beauty.

Across the room from the others, Hayley wandered to the passageway leading to the captain's stateroom.

When the admiral and captain stepped back through the hatchway, Admiral Wayne leaned close and whispered to her, "Master Chief Langford will be making his appearance shortly. Tell Roger and Lee to get their cameras ready."

She peered over her shoulder at Doc, then nodded to the admiral. Not wanting to arouse Doc's curiosity, she kept the smile off her face when she approached Roger. "Admiral Wayne wants videos taken of the meeting."

"I understand," Roger said. He nudged Lee. "Showtime."

Hayley laughed to herself.

"Doc," the admiral called.

"Yes, sir."

Admiral Wayne sat next to the head of the table. He pointed to a chair across from his. "If you don't mind, Doc, I'd like you to take a seat."

Chief Drexler went around the end of the table and pulled out the chair.

"Over one more, Doc, so you'll be sitting across from Master Chief Langford when he joins us."

Doc stepped to the next chair and took his seat. He placed

his palms flat on the table. While he glanced at the chair across from him, a ball of mist the size of a dinner plate appeared, then hovered, wavering. It oscillated, fluctuating in size and shape. Gradually, it elongated from the floor to three feet above the height of the chair.

"What the hell!" Doc stared wide-eyed, then jumped out of his seat and stood with his back pressed against the bulkhead.

The vapor morphed into a cloudy human shape.

While standing with Lee as he filmed the meeting on video, Hayley watched Doc's reactions, trying to keep a straight face.

Doc darted a look at Admiral Wayne, then gazed at the ghostly image.

The apparition solidified. Detailed arms, neck, and head were followed by a torso wearing a naval uniform. The phenomenon continued until the entire persona of Master Chief Langford stood before Doc. "Surprise," the apparition said, broadening a smile.

Doc slowly returned the smile, then glanced around and under the table. "I don't know how you pulled this off, Admiral, but that was one hell of a trick."

"It's as real as it gets," Captain Jordan said.

Admiral Wayne grinned. "No such things as ghosts, huh?"

As his skepticism lost its validity, Doc's mouth gaped.

Master Chief Langford pulled out a chair and sat. "Nothing like a good first impression, huh, Doc?"

"This is priceless," Hayley whispered to Lee.

Lee held his camera steady, not taking his eyes from the shot. "Can't get any better than this."

With a sweep of his hand, Admiral Wayne introduced them. "Chief Hospital Corpsman Drexler, Command Master Chief Langford."

Chief Drexler nodded, forcing a smile, then turned and studied the captain. "Are...are you...the remains.... Are you *that*

251

Captain Jordan?"

"Afraid so, Doc."

Doc glared at Admiral Wayne, then looked at Roger, Lee, and Hayley standing at the end of the table recording audio and video. "You're not planning on showing this to anyone are you, sir?"

"Payback," Admiral Wayne said.

"And a damn good one," Doc said. He reached for his chair, steadying himself as he pulled it out, never taking his eyes off the solidified chief. "I have to admit, this is your best yet, Admiral." He sat hesitantly.

"Should we call it even, Doc?"

"No way, sir. I'm afraid I owe you big time for this one."

"All kidding aside," Captain Jordan said, "we have serious matters to discuss and little time. Master Chief, would you mind filling the doc in on the cave?"

While Chief Langford spoke about the ship and its crew, Hayley noticed Doc's interest seemed to replace his fear. He listened intently as the chief explained how he had died.

"As our lives were taken by malaria, our bodies were removed from the ship and taken into a cavern in the mountain not far upriver," Chief Langford told him.

Captain Jordan turned to Admiral Wayne. "I suggest Master Chief Langford take you and your party to the cave. Once you're inside, you'll need lighting to guide you. You may wish to contact the carrier and request a crew to transport the generator and the lights we removed from the ship."

"Good idea," Admiral Wayne said. He looked at Doc.

"I'll get right on it, sir," Chief Drexler said.

CHAPTER 32

Admiral Wayne, Chief Drexler, Roger, Lee, and Hayley followed their guide off the ship, hiking a third of a mile to the edge of the mountains. The crew transporting the floodlights and generator by boat were to meet them at the river's edge a few yards from the cave.

The river began its journey at the foot of an immense waterfall, flowing down from the high cliffs between long-leafed green plants and moss-covered rocks. Stone and rainforest blanketed the mountainside. While they waited for the boat to arrive, Hayley strained to see if she could spot the birds she had read about. The megapodes were strong fliers and known to visit islands in the vicinity. Their species fascinated her. The adults over time had given up incubation. Instead, they piled slow-decomposing vegetation over the eggs. Once the chicks hatched, there were no adults to protect them or teach them how to find food, leaving the chicks to fend for themselves. Therefore, she recalled, the newborns had to be advanced enough to survive as soon as they hatched.

So, is it a coincidence they hatch fully feathered and immediately take flight into the forest? No. I don't believe in coincidence. Their

253

survival had to be planned before the eggs were laid. She suddenly realized that not a single bird, megapode or any other, was anywhere in sight. *The storm. They've all left the island.*

When they rounded an outcrop of boulders, a gap appeared in the mountainside. At the entry, five of the carrier's crew began to set up the generator taken from the Japanese warship. They strung lights as they followed Master Chief and Doc through the cave. When they finished, Doc told the admiral, Roger, Lee, and Hayley they could enter.

The mouth of the cave led to another entryway not more than ten feet wide. Loose gravel covered the floor where jagged rock walls formed a tunnel. Farther ahead, the passage widened. Compacted sediment made the trail easier as they moved forward. Piles of gray fallen rock cluttered small offshoot chambers, giving no signs of a larger cave.

Roger wiped his face with the back of his hand. "It's stuffy." He called back to his team, "Is everyone okay back there?"

"Right behind you," Lee said.

They moved single-file. A cool breeze hit them when the tunnel curved to the right. When the tunnel widened in front of them, they came to a sudden halt.

Hayley gasped at a breathtaking grotto. It loomed upward, from forty feet in places to one hundred feet in others, she estimated. The back wall varied from nearly eighty feet away to distances unseen in the blackness beyond the reaches of the floodlights.

To her right, drops of clear water falling from an array of stalactites fed crescent-shaped pools. White minerals formed a thick crust lining each pond of liquid crystal. The largest of the three pools hugged the south wall. Water lapped over its edge. The overflow trickled down into terracing pools.

Hayley stared in awe. "This is the most beautiful place I've ever seen."

Lee turned his camera toward the ceiling's dripping formations. "I've never seen anything like it either."

She stepped forward and leaned, gazing into the smallest pond. The water's clarity magnified mounds of rocks covered with white minerals. It gave the illusion the bottom was only inches away. Above her head, a stalactite gathered moisture at its tip, forming a tear. As it dripped into the pool, Hayley watched it silently splash and cause a ripple, its gentle sound stilled by the echoing roar of a waterfall flowing down the north corner of the cave. The thundering white waters glowed under the beams of the floodlights, its rushing water forming a river, flowing out of the cave's opening behind the mountain's cascading falls outside.

Mist cooled the cavern. Moisture on the weeping walls intensified the colors of the limestone. The tone and texture reminded Hayley of red and yellow candle wax melting down the walls, streaming into various shapes and mounds puddling on the cave's floor.

"I've never seen this cave lit so brightly," the master chief said. "When we brought the bodies of our crew in, all except the victims your navy personnel found aboard ship, our flashlights dimly lit our path. This is, no doubt, the first time in the cave's history that its beauty has been seen." He turned and started up the trail.

Memories of the residual haunting replaying the deaths of those six men whose bodies were found on board surfaced in Hayley's thoughts. She shook them away and followed the others.

Their guide led them along a path lined with columns of stalagmites and stalactites fused together as though kissing. The path turned sharply to the right toward a smaller cave in the south wall. Doc handed each a mask for nose and mouth to help them avoid breathing anything noxious that might linger inside.

Then they entered the chamber of the dead.

With the mask placed snug against her mouth and nose, Hayley walked into a chamber much larger than the grotto. Before her, a path forked.

"That trail leads to the chamber containing the remains of the Japanese crew," Master Chief Langford said, pointing to the left. He turned, then led the five of them up an incline to their right.

Hayley glanced up at floodlights that glowed through a wall of stalactites and stalagmites rooted along the edge of a huge terrace. Below, shadows fell on a valley of mineral formations.

"It's magnificent," Hayley said to Lee, "like the golden pillars of Olympus."

He removed the camera from his pocket and took pictures. "I think that's where we're headed. It's the tomb."

Before the group went any farther, the master chief halted. "This is where I leave you. I'll see you back on the ship."

"Thanks for everything," Admiral Wayne said.

"This shouldn't take long," Doc told him. "I just need to get an idea of how to proceed with the recovery. I'll see you later. We still have a lot to talk about."

Master Chief Langford smiled, nodded, and walked back toward the grotto, his image fading with each step.

"I almost forgot he's a ghost," Doc said.

When they entered the cloister, the floor leveled across an extensive hall. About sixty feet inside, they stopped. Along a wall covered with white knobs of crystalline calcite were two rows of remains, each row consisting of forty or more skeletons.

Hayley stood with Lee, Roger, and Admiral Wayne a few feet from the bones, and Doc walked forward carrying a rolled canvas tool kit cinched by a brown leather strap. He pulled latex gloves from his pants pocket, put them on, knelt, and unfastened the straps, rolling the kit onto the limestone floor. Inside, fifteen pockets held small tools ranging in size from long-nosed pliers to a metal toothpick.

Doc painstakingly lifted away the debris covering one set of bones. Taking a small brush, he swept the dust away. Carefully, with tweezers, he lifted the dog tags and chain from the sternum. Before he inspected the metal tags, Doc took a cloth from his tool kit and wiped away a film of gypsum covering the embossed words. He studied the ID.

"Ronald J. Preston," he read.

Before Doc finished saying the crewman's name, Hayley envisioned the man's face. Thick black brows arched above his deep-set brown eyes. Below his long hawk nose, thin lips pulled back into a smile showing his buckteeth. He snorted a laugh after hearing a joke told to him by Seaman Morris. When the vision left her, she glanced around at the other remains spread across the floor. A tsunami of faces and memories hit her. She watched many of their deaths unfold. As bits of dialogue and laughter switched to moans and screams, bile rose in her throat. She gagged. Instinctively, she raised her hand to her mask-covered mouth.

Overwhelmed by the haunting deaths, she vaguely became aware of Lee's arm around her shoulders. When he led her back to the grotto, she began to feel the ground beneath her feet.

He walked her down the path beyond the kissing stalactites and stalagmites to a rock formation near the peaceful crystal pond. They were alone.

"Better?" He sat on a rock, took her by the waist, and gently lowered her into his lap, removed her mask, reached up, and pulled off his own.

She nodded and frowned. "You'd think I'd never seen the dead before. It was just a lot all at once." She folded her hands in her lap and looked down. "I was wrong about the captain. I thought he was placing thoughts in my head, but now I know it wasn't him."

"Then who or what?" Lee asked.

"It might be me," she said, meeting his concerned gaze.

"What do you mean?"

"What just happened to me is a lot like what I'd experienced before I was fourteen, when I had no control over my abilities." She took a deep breath. "Things overwhelmed me then, kind of like they've overwhelmed me on this island. I need to keep my mind on the here and now. Somehow I have to focus on something else and push away the visions of the past."

"Let me see if I can help." Lee pushed strands of hair from her brow and kissed her forehead, then feathered kisses down her temple to the soft sensitive skin by her ear. His lips followed the line of her jaw, then kissed the corner of her mouth.

"Well?" he asked.

"I think you're onto something, but I need a little more therapy before I'm sure."

He streamed kisses down her neck.

She leaned her head back.

He pulled back the collar of her blouse, and his lips tenderly caressed the curve of her shoulder.

Her heart raced. She forgot how to breathe.

"What are you thinking about now?" he asked.

"Don't stop. It's definitely working."

Slowly, he brushed the soft skin of her neck with his tongue. Then, pushing her hair back, he breathed into her ear. "Like this?"

Her body came alive with desire. Goosebumps shot across her skin. "Mm," she managed to say. With every inch of her wanting his kiss, she put her arms around his neck and unwittingly glanced over his shoulder. "They're coming." She sighed, then reluctantly stood.

Lee rose and whispered, "I think we should finish your therapy tonight. Don't forget where we left off." He winked.

She raised a brow. "Left off? I don't think so. I'm sure I'll need the entire session from the beginning. With wine."

As Roger, Admiral Wayne, and Doc walked toward them along the path, Hayley noticed their hastened stride. She glanced at Lee when they approached. *Soon, we'll be home.*

"Doc's finished for now," Roger said.

"Let's get going then," Lee suggested.

The five followed the floodlights out of the cave.

Once outside, Hayley sensed a loud rumbling beyond the thunder of the waterfall. She glanced up, saw the clouds moving quickly to the southwest, and realized the noise came from the rustling of leaves throughout the forest. Sadness pierced her heart. *No! Not yet! We're not finished here. The crew's remains.*

One of the crewman from the carrier stood at the entrance and shut down the generator. The cave went dark. He turned and saluted the admiral.

Admiral Wayne returned the salute.

"Need a ride to the Japanese ship, sir?" The sailor pointed towards the RIB.

"Yes, thanks, Seaman," the admiral told him.

They all climbed on board.

"Well, our case is almost over," Roger said as they rode downstream.

"Not soon enough, by the looks of it," Lee said. "We need to finish up here before the typhoon hits."

Hayley yelled back to Doc, "What's the prognosis for recovery?" She didn't need to ask. She'd seen it in her dream.

"I'll have to contact JPAC. Looks like we'll have to wait out the storm."

Her heart sank. A lump formed in her throat, and she held

back her tears, remembering the premonition of the human remains floating in the storm's waters. But she knew it was a race against time and no one, not even the captain, could stop a typhoon.

Once they made it to the ship, Hayley and Lee followed the admiral to the quarterdeck, with Roger and Doc close behind them.

"Well, our case is almost over," Admiral Wayne said.

A peek at what they would soon see crossed Hayley's mind. She smiled.

"All that's left is your talk with the captain and the grand finale," Hayley said.

"Grand finale?" the admiral asked.

"You'll see."

CHAPTER 33

The increasing flutter of the tree leaves high on the rainforest canopy caught her attention. She gazed up at the overcast sky. Darker clouds blew toward the southwest.

Hayley felt Lee's hand on her shoulder, and she turned to him.

He studied her face. "You look worried."

She shook her head. "We need to hurry."

When Roger stepped onto the quarterdeck next to her, a large raindrop wet his cheek. He wiped the moisture away and ran his fingers through his dampened hair.

"Have you noticed anything strange?" Lee asked Roger.

"This whole trip has been strange. I think you need to be a little more specific."

"On our first trip, two days ago, when we came on board, the captain somehow had formed a bubble around the ship and created his own atmosphere. Today, the temperature's the same as the rest of the island."

"And look," Roger said, pointing at the deck. "Rust. Know what's going on, Hayley?"

"Captain Jordan's taking his attention away from the ship's

261

atmosphere and focusing on his men," Hayley told him. "It has to do with the farewell I mentioned earlier." She sensed their surroundings and the stillness of the ship. "I'm getting a strong feeling of urgency to get away from this vessel."

"Hell, I'm not a psychic and I feel it, too," Admiral Wayne said. "Listen. There's not a sound coming from the jungle. We're not the only ones who know a storm's coming."

"That urgency you spoke about?" Lee asked Hayley. "How much time do you think we have?"

"I don't think we need to run for it yet. I'm sure the captain knows more about the weather than we do." *But should I tell him that I foresaw his crew's remains being destroyed by the flood? Or maybe I should tell him how sorry I am. No. What am I thinking? He's already aware of it.*

"You're right," Admiral Wayne said. "He'd warn us if we were in danger. So, let's get a move on. Captain Jordan and I have things to discuss."

They continued toward the bow, where Captain Jordan stood with his master chief. Once the chief noticed their approach, he left the captain's side and joined Doc. They talked baseball, politics, current events, and strolled the deck.

"Master Chief Langford's been dying to catch up on news of home since our ship went down," the captain said. "He wants to start with the 1945 World Series."

"You're joking, right?" Roger asked. "You knew about us before we were even born and everything that's happened since World War II. Why haven't you told him?"

"No need. He'll know as much as I do soon enough."

"So you'll be crossing over again?" Admiral Wayne asked.

"Yes. All of our loved ones have passed over. When we cross, it will be as if our ship has finally reached home." Captain Jordan turned to the others. "Thanks to all of you." Meeting Hayley's gaze, he said, "Thanks for being my spokeswoman. You were more help than you know."

"Not more than anyone else, I'm sure," she said.

"You'll be surprised. Your mission is complete. Give the rest of the team my thanks." He turned to Langford. "It's time to get started, Master Chief."

"It was nice talking to you, Doc," the chief said.

"Unforgettable," Doc replied.

"Would you mind coming with me, Admiral?" Captain Jordan asked. "The rest of you can stand by the gun, if you don't mind."

Master Chief Langford followed the captain and the admiral to portside, while Hayley and the others moved to middeck by the gun. Moments later, a fog, unscathed by the wind, streamed from the open forward hatch, and the temperature on the deck dropped.

"Here we go again," Roger said. He pulled out his digital video camera.

Lee prepared his camera as well.

The stream of fog divided, half sweeping across the port bow, and the other half across the starboard bow. Movement stirred in the mist, and vague shadows started to emerge. Gradually, the clouded silhouettes became clear. Forty-three men portside and forty-four starboard stood at attention wearing dress whites.

"Can you see them?" Hayley asked the others.

"Yes," Roger replied.

As Captain Jordan and Admiral Wayne stepped forward, the men saluted.

Roger and Lee followed the admiral's movements, staying out of the way while they videoed the inspection.

Captain Jordan and Master Chief Langford walked at the admiral's side.

"Thank you for this, Captain," Admiral Wayne said.

"It's our honor, sir."

It seemed to Hayley that time stood still while Admiral Wayne walked the deck, inspecting the crew. The admiral gazed at each crew member, as if trying to remember each face. He returned their salutes and told them to stand at ease.

"Master Chief," the captain said, "there's not much time. While I finish my briefing with Admiral Wayne, would you escort our guests off the ship, then report back to me?"

"Yes, sir."

Captain Jordan turned to Roger. "Mind if we use your video camera? Oh, and a new memory card."

Roger reached into his shirt pocket, pulled out a new SD card, and changed the camera's digital memory. "I still can't believe you know so much about today's technology." He passed Admiral Wayne his digital video camera.

"In my state, I can honestly say I'm a know-it-all," Captain Jordan said, with a chuckle.

After leading them ashore, the chief turned to Doc.

"Guess this is goodbye then," Doc said.

"Not from what Captain Jordan tells me. Don't be surprised if I drop by and see you sometime."

"Yeah, wow, that would be great," Doc told him. "But try not to scare the wits out of me next time."

The master chief turned and left.

The wind picked up. More threatening clouds darkened the sky while Hayley and the others waited for the admiral.

Twenty minutes later, Admiral Wayne joined them on shore. He handed Roger his camera. "Need to put your memory card back in. I'm keeping this one."

While they peered up at the ship, watching to see what Captain Jordan was up to, the space above the bow shimmered.

In the darkness of the approaching storm, a tiny sphere of bright light appeared. It expanded in width.

Hayley realized the glow radiated from a doorway — a portal.

Roger aimed his video camera at the phenomenon, while Lee, camera in hand, moved down the shore to get a different angle.

Doc and Admiral Wayne stood at Hayley's side.

Doc stared, wide-eyed. "What do you think is going on?" he asked Hayley.

"Drama. God knows how to put on a show."

"What?"

"Captain Jordan's helping his crew cross over. They're going home, Doc. It's a dimensional portal."

"A dimensional portal?"

"A gateway to Heaven," she told him.

On deck, Captain Jordan stood to the side of the gateway, calling each man's name. One by one they crossed over the threshold and into the light. Captain Jordan followed the last man into the light, crossing over once again.

The portal diminished into a speck of light, hovered above the ship's bow, then blinked out, the doorway vanishing.

In the storm's gathering darkness, Hayley and the others stood on the shore, staring up at the ship.

"I've got it all on video," Roger said.

A deafening whine came from the ship.

Lee and Roger steadied themselves in the wind and raised their cameras to catch the vessel's transformation.

Loud creaking and grinding, sounding to Hayley like a giant's fingernails clawing across a chalkboard, sent chills down her spine. The unblemished ship's skin turned to rust, then gaping holes widened in the hull, revealing the decomposing interior. While the ship died in front of her eyes, becoming a corroded skeleton, Hayley silently stared at the dramatic end of their investigation.

Like a whispered warning, a raindrop fell on Hayley's face. "I suggest we leave quickly, Admiral, before we're unable to make it downriver."

The admiral nodded and cleared his throat. "I want to make it back to Guam tonight. I hope we can outrun this storm."

She visualized their return. "We will. It'll be fine."

"Let's get out of here," the admiral said.

They boarded the RIB.

The admiral faced the cave of the dead, then gazed back at the Japanese warship's rusted carcass. "Chief Drexler, take us out of here."

* * *

Once aboard the carrier, off the south coast of the island, everyone waited out the storm. The typhoon had veered to the west, just skimming the island. While below, Hayley had hardly felt its effects.

Close to nine o'clock in the evening, their plane landed at Andersen Air Force Base in Guam. A black car waited on the tarmac. Hayley, her tired joints aching, slid into the back seat between Roger and Lee, while the admiral climbed in next to the driver.

"We'll go over the evidence in the morning, if that's okay with you, Admiral," Roger said.

Admiral Wayne nodded. "All I want is a hot shower and a soft bed."

Hayley could hardly keep her eyes open during the short drive to the hotel. After arriving, she leaned against Lee while they rode the elevator upstairs.

While they stood in front of Hayley's room, Lee kissed her goodnight. "Just one more day and we'll be done with all this."

Hayley raised a brow. "I don't think so. Something's telling me it's not over yet."

He looked at her in disbelief. "What more can happen?"

CHAPTER 34

On the seven-and-a-half-hour flight from Guam to Oahu, Hayley felt exhausted. The time differences over the days had finally devoured her energy. All she wanted to do was sleep.

When the plane landed in Honolulu, they were driven straight to the hotel they had stayed in previously. While she and Lee took the elevator to their rooms, Hayley looked forward to a much-needed nap. She wasn't about to let sleep deprivation ruin her romantic evening with Lee.

Lee walked her to her door. "Get some rest. I'll see you tonight."

"Can't wait." She opened her hotel room door and turned toward him.

He gave her a passionate kiss that she felt to the tip of her toes, then stepped away. "I'll see you later."

"Later." She closed the door just as Kathy came out of the bathroom.

"So you've got a date tonight?" Kathy asked.

"Yes. We're having dinner on the balcony."

"Well, you'll have the room to yourself," Kathy said. "I'm spending the day with Clint and John, then hanging out with them to watch the ballgame tonight. Clint said it doesn't start until seven because of the time change. So have fun."

"Thanks. Right now, I'm in desperate need of a nap." Hayley pointed to the beds. "Which one is yours?"

"I'll take the one closest to the bathroom, if it's OK with you."

"Sure." Hayley sat on the edge of the bed and removed her shoes.

"See you," Kathy said, and headed to the door.

When the door closed, Hayley already had her head on the pillow. "'Bye," she said, as her eyes shut.

Hayley woke and realized she'd slept most of the day. She shook off the remnants of her dreams and remembered her date. "Lee." She hurried to take a shower and get ready. Just as she put the last touches on her makeup, she heard the knock on the door. She glanced at the clock. He was a few minutes early.

Just as she opened her hotel room door, the phone rang on her nightstand. "Hi, Lee. Come in." She turned toward the phone and sensed tension, anxiety, and deep sadness coming from the caller. Her mind raced, trying to visualize the cause of the urgency. "Lee, it's for you. It's Roger."

Lee hurried inside and answered the phone.

Hayley sat on the bed next to him. While he and Roger spoke, the drama they discussed played out in her mind.

It was the major link she'd been waiting for between John and Clint. She knew what was being said. She'd dreamt about it while she napped. John had lost another bet, but he found out at the hotel desk in the afternoon that Clint had picked up a video of yesterday's ballgame. When Clint invited him to his room and acted as if the game had just started, then made the bet, John was furious. Jim stepped in and pulled them apart before someone got hurt. He took them to the hotel barbershop, and they settled it by Clint getting his head shaved. The barber used a razor to give him the same shiny bald look as John's, but as he worked he noticed a lump on Clint's head. They went to Laura. She looked and believed it was a tumor.

Before Lee hung up the phone, she closed her eyes and, as she had once before in a vision, followed Clint's past betting links, connecting them one by one until they came to the present circumstance. While her precognitive abilities showed her the future, she put the shocking news into perspective. In Oahu, she'd foreseen only pieces of Clint's trauma. Now all of the details linked together. Clint's condition was still serious, but this time her vision showed that it wasn't life threatening. She opened her eyes.

Hayley decided to go out to the balcony and let Lee finish his conversation. On her way, she grabbed the bottle of wine and a couple of glasses off the entertainment unit in front of the bed. She took them outside, set them on the table for two, and returned for the cheese, crackers, and knife. She watched Lee's body language.

His face was pale. He hung up the phone then sat silently with his head down. She went back outside with the snacks, giving Lee a moment to compose himself.

When he reached the balcony, the solemn look on his face cautioned her against speaking.

He walked to the railing, standing with his back to her. "It's about Clint."

"I'm sorry," she said.

He turned. "So you know."

"Yes."

"Is it true?"

"Yes, I'm sure Laura's right."

Lee's eyes welled. "My grandfather died from a brain tumor. The entire family watched him suffer." He was silent for a moment and then cleared his throat. "That same year, my parents died in a plane crash."

Hayley swallowed hard. She remembered Kathy telling her that Lee had lost his family. Her parents died when she was fourteen. She sympathized with him. "I'm sorry."

"Reality bites sometimes. Clint's as much family to me as he is to Roger. I know his condition is different from my grandfather's…Clint's tumor is on his skull. But from all that I've read, the prognosis is the same — fatal."

"It's not. Clint's going to be all right. It's serious, but not as bad as it looks right now. When the tests come back, you'll see."

His brows narrowed briefly, and he walked to the table. He pulled the wine bottle to him, peeled off the seal, and picked up the corkscrew. As he placed the screw into the cork, he asked, while keeping his eyes on his task, "How long have you known?"

"Since the last time we were in Oahu. But I didn't know everything."

"Why didn't you tell me?" He poured wine into the glasses, then handed her one.

She took it. The lack of emotion in his voice and on his face sent shivers up her spine. "What I foresaw scared me. I had a vision of Clint on the operating table. His family was crying. I thought he might die." She looked up at him and met his pensive gaze. "You told me once that you hated to keep anything from Roger. If I had told you what I saw, you would've had difficulty keeping it from him."

"You should've told me."

"But if you had told…. All the links weren't connected yet. We hadn't met Laura. She needs to be the one to operate. She's a major link. If you'd slipped, I felt Clint could die. I might've been wrong, but I can't be sure. If Laura doesn't do the operation, who knows, there might be serious complications. So, it was better I

271

didn't tell you." She saw a dark cloud of emotions cross his face. "What are you thinking?"

"You don't trust me."

Her eyes widened. "I do, Lee. But if I'd told you, the link would've been severed. I didn't want to be responsible for Clint's possible death."

His eyes held a depth of seriousness she had never seen.

"Trust seems to be a major issue," he said. He glanced at the door, then back at her. "But we can't discuss this now. You have to pack. You're joining the others and flying back home in the morning. I'm staying in Oahu with Roger and Clint. We'll talk about this when I get home."

She wanted to make sure he understood. *Maybe I should've told him what I'd seen. No, we would've gone back to North Carolina. Everything would've changed. Laura was a link. We had to meet her first. I was right to keep it from him. Now's not the time and place to discuss this. He made that perfectly clear.* She raised her chin. *I was right.*

He turned and left.

She looked at the floor. *Things happen for a reason. Will this be the end of us?* She heard the hotel room door close behind him. Tears filled her eyes.

* * *

The flight from Hawaii to North Carolina took ten hours, not counting a fuel stop in San Diego and dropping the admiral off in Florida. During that time, Hayley sat with the others, only vaguely hearing anyone speak to her or anything being discussed.

Kathy had told her that Lee had his share of dates, but he'd never had a girlfriend any longer than a month.

What did I expect? Why should I be any different than the rest?

* * *

After their plane touched down in Greensboro, the team was

driven to the office. All gathered their luggage and left.

Once home, Hayley turned the key in the lock and opened her front door, picked up her bags, carried them inside, and dropped them at the foot of the stairs. Exhausted, she went into the living room, not bothering to open the curtains, and curled up on the couch by the fireplace. Over and over, she visualized Lee's solemn face and wondered what was going through his mind.

What'll I do if this doesn't work out? I could quit my job, move to another town – no, state – well, maybe an outhouse on the moon. Damn it, Lee, I'd be miserable no matter where I went without you.

When the clock on the mantle struck ten, Hayley forced herself to stop thinking. It was Wednesday night, only a week since they had left on the case. The office was closed until Monday morning. She needed that time to reset her inner clock and her life.

* * *

Hayley opened the front door to get the Thursday morning newspaper while thinking only of Lee. *Why doesn't he call?* She paid no attention to her garden or the shades of red blushing across the apples on the old apple tree. The garden's beauty hazed across her mind as she shut the front door and headed back to the kitchen.

When the phone rang, Hayley threw the morning paper onto the breakfast table. She knew it was Lee.

CHAPTER 35

Before she answered the phone, Hayley tried to sense Lee's emotions. *Is he still upset with me?* She perceived nothing and answered the phone.

"Hayley, it's me, Lee."

His voice was gentle. Relief washed over her. "Hi. How's Clint?" she asked.

"His tests have proved negative for cancer so far. He still has a few more tests to go today. Roger and Laura are flying home with him Monday morning, and I guess Laura's staying with him to do the surgery." He yawned. "Sorry, I haven't been able to get to sleep."

"What time is it there?"

"Midnight."

"It's six in the morning here."

"I know. I wasn't sure if you'd be up yet. I couldn't sleep. It's been bothering me about the way we left things on the balcony. I thought about what you said, and you were right. You shouldn't have told me about your vision. I don't think it was a matter of trust. It was a matter of not knowing each other well enough. How would you know if I would or wouldn't sever the link? At the time, you'd only known me for a couple of days."

"So, there are no trust issues?"

"No. You didn't lie to me, Hayley. You just delayed telling me. Sometimes there's a good reason. And you were right." He chuckled. "I think I said that already. I'm really tired."

A big smile crossed her face. She wouldn't have to argue her case. They wouldn't have to split up over something so trivial. "I don't mind hearing it again. So, when are you coming home?"

"Tomorrow. I should be in North Carolina early in the morning. I'll call you when I get in. I know I'm going to be a wreck getting over the time changes. Give me Friday to catch up on some sleep, and we can get together on Saturday."

"I know what you mean. Saturday sounds good."

"Oh, and after Laura and Roger take Clint home on Monday, they're coming to my house for dinner. I'd like you to come."

"I'd like that, too."

* * *

Hayley filled the long hours of Thursday and Friday with housework, shopping, and yard work. On Saturday morning, Lee called, asked her to dinner, and said he'd pick her up at five.

By four o'clock, she peered into the full-length mirror in her bedroom and was pleased with what she saw. The black dress Kathy had insisted she buy in Coronado fit her perfectly. When she had tried it on she'd felt sexy, though too self-conscious. But Kathy wouldn't let her leave the store without it. "I guarantee Lee will love it," she'd said.

The dress hugged her curves. The hemline was short but not outrageous. The heart-shaped neckline caressed the rounds of her breasts, and dipped at her cleavage enough to make her blush.

When Lee arrived, Hayley couldn't help smiling as he stood at the door stumbling over adjectives. On their way to his car, she noticed he couldn't take his eyes off her. *Guess Kathy was right.*

275

Once she passed through the front gate, Hayley stopped and stared in disbelief. Parked against the curb was a steel-gray Aston Martin. She looked at Lee, then at the car. "We're going in this?" She was impressed, but confused. *It's a little much. We're just going to dinner, not a world premiere.*

"You don't think I'd take the company van, do you?"

"No, but I never thought...."

He held the door. "Get in. We're going to Greensboro."

They dined by candlelight and danced under the stars. It was as if the night in Hawaii had never happened. By the time they returned to Hayley's house, the hour was late.

Lee stood inside the door while Hayley put on the foyer light and turned to face him. He pulled her close, and his lips met hers. Their kiss goodnight left her breathless. As they parted, she sighed. *It can't go on like this.* She stepped away. "I had a great time tonight, Lee."

"Me, too."

She reached out and steadied herself on his shoulder as she slipped off her heels. "I guess I should head up to bed. It's late." She saw the disappointment of her calling it a night wash over his face. "Before I go, will you do me a big favor?"

He looked down at the floor, then up at her, and his gaze was soft. "Sure, what is it?"

"Do you think you could help me fix my stairs tomorrow? I'll show you which one." She walked over to the staircase and ascended to the fifth step from the landing. The tread creaked and moaned when she stood on it.

"I can see how that would drive you crazy. Sure, I can do that."

"Would you do me another favor, so I don't have to come back down? Can you lock the door for me, please?"

He nodded. "Well, I guess this is goodnight then. I'll come by

276

in the morning."

She watched while he opened the door. His head and shoulders slumped as he felt for the lock. While his back was turned toward her, she moved up to the next step. "Ouch!"

Lee stopped. He swung around, his eyes fixed on her face.

She bit her lower lip and held her hand to her neck. "Ant!" she said, continuing the game they had started in the jungle.

Lee shut the door, locked it, and dashed to the bottom of the staircase. He watched her intently with his left foot on the bottom step, waiting for her next move.

Hayley took three side steps to the top landing, then held her hand to the other side of her neck. "Ouch! Ant!"

He flew up the stairs, taking three at a time. When they met on the landing, his warm lips caressed her neck. "Is that better?" he whispered. Before she could answer, he continued their game, kissing her next imaginary ant bite.

She pointed to her soft white skin on the curve of her breast. "Ouch! Ant!"

His eyes widened. "Let me help you," he said on a breath.

She held her heels limply in her hand as he scooped her up. "Ouch! Lee, you better hurry." She pointed toward her bedroom.

With a playful grin, he broke into a trot.

CHAPTER 36

The creak from the staircase startled Hayley awake. Rain tapped at her window. The room was dimly lit. She glanced at the clock—six-thirty—rolled over, and stroked the pillow next to her, thinking of last night's pleasures. It wasn't a dream.

I remember Lee kissed me this morning, and I heard the front door close when he left. So, who's downstairs?

She got out of bed and snatched her robe from the back of the rocking chair. Then she grabbed the baseball bat she always kept next to the nightstand. Barefoot, with bat in hand, she sneaked across the hardwood floor and into the upstairs hallway.

Trying to stay out of view, she pressed her back against the wall, then sidestepped to the staircase. Hayley pushed her hair behind her ear and peeked around the corner. She didn't see anyone on the stairs or in the hall. The sound of kitchen drawers opening and closing echoed down the dimly lit hallway. She ducked back, pressing her shoulders against the wall, heart racing, and recalled Lucy's restaurant. *A ghost?*

"Who's there?" Hayley asked with a shaky voice.

Silence.

Slowly descending the stairs, Hayley held the railing and

stepped over the noisy fifth step. Hesitating midway on the staircase, she listened. Footsteps came from the kitchen. Her heart jumped into her throat. She clenched the bat in both hands. "Who's there?"

Lee walked out of the shadows. "You're scaring the hell out of me!"

"I'm scaring you? I heard you leave this morning. You shouldn't be here." She raised a brow. "Why should you be scared?"

"Think about it, Hayley. You're planning to confront an intruder with a bat. What if he had a gun?" He looked at the floor, then up at her, shaking his head. "What are you thinking?"

"That damn stair step startled me awake." Hayley looked at the bat and swallowed. "You're right. This is stupid." She lowered her weapon. "Why were you going through my kitchen drawers?"

"I was looking for tools."

"Why?" she asked.

"I thought I'd surprise you and start working on that step."

"Wait a minute. You weren't wearing blue jeans last night. Did you leave and come back?"

"I didn't leave," Lee said. "I just went to my car to get a change of clothes. I thought the clothes I wore to dinner last night were a little formal for doing repairs."

"That's strange, keeping a change of clothes in the car."

"I always keep a change of clothes in the car in case of emergencies. Habit, I guess." He raked his fingers through his hair. "Are you always full of questions so early in the morning?"

"Sorry." Hayley descended the rest of the way, set the bat next to the front door, and wrapped her arms around him.

He tilted her chin up and kissed her. "So…have some tools?"

"You know you don't have to do this, Lee."

"It won't take me a minute. I'd hate to scare you again. You might kill me with that bat, and I'd have to haunt your house."

She smiled. "There are tools in that closet behind you. Why don't I fix you some breakfast while you get started? Don't take the step apart without me. With all the suffering I've gone through these past months, I want to see what's making that noise."

Lee went to the closet for the toolbox. She heard him rummaging through it as she headed to the kitchen.

"Will bacon and eggs be okay?" she asked.

"Sounds great!"

"Call me before you pull the step apart," Hayley said.

* * *

After breakfast, Hayley went upstairs to change before they started to work. She noticed the rain had stopped. The morning was unusually cool for July. Hayley put on blue jeans and a scoop-neck T-shirt, then joined him on the staircase. She sat on the step above him and handed him tools, trying to keep her mind on work and off last night.

Lee removed the remaining nails, pried up the tread, and peeked inside. "It's hinged together like the lid to a box. I think we found the reason for the noise. The hinges are loose and rubbing against this nail." He pushed aside a yellowed newspaper, noticing its date. "Look at this," Lee said, pulling out the front page of the *Sutterville Daily News*. "It's dated 1943." From beneath a few more crumpled pages, he pulled out a brown, twelve-inch circular Hershey's Cocoa tin. He studied the small print. "Trademark, 1940. It looks vintage." He handed the box to Hayley and turned back to the alcove, pulling out baby clothes, a brown, one-eyed stuffed bear, and a handful of photos.

A mixture of emotions emanated from the tin—love, sadness, pride. A vision came to her of a man in his fifties placing the candy tin inside the step. A woman Hayley felt was his wife stood at the foot of the staircase. "Are you sure you want to do this?" the man asked his wife.

"Yes, I'm sure," she said. "I can't look at these things any longer, and I won't throw them out. Best just to tuck them away with our other memories."

Their sadness washed over Hayley. "It's a memory box," she told Lee. "The people who lived here had a son who died." She handed it back to him. "Why don't I get us some coffee? We can go through this in the living room."

"I'll finish repairing the step."

* * *

Hayley carried cups of coffee into the living room. She glanced out the window and saw the sun breaking through the clouds. Last night's storm had been a surprise, like their evening of passion. She smiled, thinking of their lovemaking—his hands exploring her body, his gentleness, knowing it was her first time. Thinking about the soaring pleasures she'd felt over and over again, heat flushed her cheeks. She cleared her throat, set their cups on the coffee table, and nestled with Lee on the couch.

He handed her the box.

She pulled on the lid until her knuckles turned white. It wouldn't budge. She passed the box to Lee.

Making it look easy, he forced it open, set the lid down, and gave her the tin.

From inside the box, she lifted out a news clipping depicting downtown Sutterville in 1943. A black-and-white photo showed young men boarding a bus, while a stern-looking man in a uniform, holding a clipboard, stood on the sidewalk.

"Recruitment, maybe. World War II."

He studied the picture. "Looks like it. What else is in there?"

Hayley pulled out a folded sheet of fragile yellowed paper resembling parchment, carefully lifted the edges, and spread

281

it open. "A notice for a prayer meeting dated September of the same year, 1943." She looked at the name. "Richard. He's the son of the people who lived here." Looking closer she read, "Missing in action."

She picked up an envelope, brown with age, the flap folded in. She opened it gently, trying not to tear it, slid out a letter and a photo, and read silently. She felt the hair on her neck stand up. "This can't be!"

"What?" Lee leaned closer to read the letter, then looked at the picture. "Isn't this the letter you dreamt about on the plane?" He took the snapshot from her hand. "And this is the photo Richard had someone take of him in front of the Del. The one he'd mentioned in your dream."

The strange events at the Del seemed clearer to her now. "The familiar feeling from the bar, the roast lamb, and the memories of living there."

"His ghost must've followed you to the hotel. This might explain who possessed you," Lee said.

"It's not the same room number," Hayley pointed out.

"It still might've been him. He seemed to be influencing you to do everything else. What's his last name? Kathy can do some research on his family."

She looked at the prayer notice. Her hand went up to cover her open mouth. "This is crazy." Speechless and confused, Hayley looked at Lee and swallowed hard. "It's Sanders. Lee, he's the lieutenant I dreamt of who died from malaria—one of the crew from the ghost ship. This is creepy."

"Are you serious?" Lee asked. "Wait a minute. He wasn't on board with the rest of the crew. You never mentioned seeing him."

Hayley stared at the photo. "No. Because his spirit wasn't there." She looked at Lee. "He's here." She glanced around the room.

"He's haunting your house?"

"What other explanation is there?"

"But how could he be here without you knowing?" Lee asked.

"Spirits can hide. Maybe he never wanted to be noticed."

Lee stood. "I've got some equipment in my car. I'll bring it in, and if he's hiding, we'll see if we can find him."

While she waited, she turned the box in her hand trying to sense some kind of clue, but she perceived nothing. She looked up to see Lee return to the room.

He passed her one of the handheld meters he'd brought from the car. "I'll scan for any electromagnetic fields while you take the voice recorder and ask questions."

They walked through the house for an hour, searching for anything unusual, but didn't find any sign of Richard.

Hayley pulled down the stairs to the attic. "Let's check up here."

"Is there a light?" he asked.

"No." She went to the closet across from her bedroom door, opened it, and took down a flashlight from the top shelf. When Lee started up the ladder, she handed him the light.

While she stayed below, he climbed until he could see over the top rung, shone the light into the darkness, stepped up into the attic, and disappeared from view.

A few minutes later, Lee started down. "Nothing," he said. "I give up. He's not here."

He took the voice recorder from Hayley and headed downstairs. She followed him to the kitchen.

Lee set the equipment onto the breakfast table. "Guess he's still at the Del."

"I don't sense his presence either. You're probably right."

"So we're calling off the search?"

Her glance followed the curve of his neck and continued down his biceps. "I think we should search my room."

"We did."

Hayley put her arms around his neck and lightly bit his earlobe, then whispered in his ear. "I think we should do it some more." She felt his heartbeat quicken.

He brushed her hair back and kissed her neck, then wrapped his arms around her waist and guided her out of the kitchen and toward the staircase. "More. Since you put it that way, how can I resist?"

* * *

The fifth step no longer creaked as Lee and Hayley came downstairs.

He ran his finger across her cheek and kissed her as they stood by the front door. "Why don't I pick you up in the morning for work since you'll be coming for dinner?"

"Sounds good to me."

"I'll leave the equipment with you in case you feel his presence later. And if you do, see if he'll answer some questions. I'm real curious about why he took control of you at the Del."

She remembered how she had felt—violated, used. "I'd like to know, too."

Lee hesitated, studying her face as if he didn't want to leave. He took her hand and squeezed it softly. "I'll be here at eight-thirty. Oh, and you might want to bring a change of clothes, just in case you spend the night and we further explore the definition of 'more.'"

Their lips met.

She kissed him passionately, showing him she looked forward to his heated lovemaking.

He cleared his throat. "You might want to pack a suitcase."

CHAPTER 37

The lid of the green tin set closed loosely and the box rested on the conference table next to Hayley's journal. Eager to show them the box's contents, she sat patiently waiting for the investigative team to gather for their morning meeting.

She lifted the lid, pulled out the picture taken during World War II, and studied it again. The grand Victorian hotel with its immense red roof and numerous dormers looked much the same as it had during their one-night stay almost two weeks ago. In the old photo, Richard stood in his officer's uniform near the curved driveway leading to the hotel entrance.

Something triggered Hayley's memory. During the vision she'd had on the plane, when she saw Richard in the mirror behind the hotel bar as he took a seat, his movements had felt so intimate, as if they were her own. When he sat, Hayley could feel the soft leather of the seat. When he picked up his drink, she could feel the smooth cool surface of the glass. And while he remembered his family, she'd heard his thoughts in her mind. *So strange.*

Lee sat next to her, and Jim, John, and Kathy sat across from them. They looked up when Laura, Clint, and Roger arrived.

285

"It's about time ya guys made it home," Jim said. "Clint, how are ya?"

"Fine. I feel the same as I normally do." Clint removed his backpack and set it against the reception desk, then walked over to the conference table.

"Good to hear, son. You're in good hands. Nothin' to worry 'bout," Jim said. He turned to Laura as she approached the conference table. "What did the tests show?"

"Very unusual to say the least," Laura said. "The lump I discovered turned out to be a benign bone tumor. But as I researched my findings, I found no similar matrix mineralization patterns or biological…. Well, anyway, his tumor is unique as far as I can see. There's no clinical or histological information available. I'm licensed to practice medicine in North Carolina since assisting the military at Camp Lejeune in 2001. I'll be staying here to perform the necessary surgery. And I'll also do further studies."

"Are you okay?" John asked, as Clint took the seat next to him.

Clint raised his eyebrows, the only hair left on his head. "Sure. I can't even feel it." He touched the lump on his head. "If the barber hadn't seen this, I wouldn't have known."

Roger pulled out a chair for Laura. "You can stay at my home. I have plenty of room."

She looked up at him, studying his face, and smiled. "I don't want to inconvenience you, Roger."

"I'd love your company."

"The guy's got an estate," Jim said. "I'd go for it if I were you, sweet pea. You'd have a choice of ten bedrooms. I think he even has a room Lincoln slept in."

"If it's no trouble, I think I'll take you up on that," Laura said, meeting his gaze.

A smile lit Roger's face. He stammered his reply. "T-t-trouble? No…no trouble. You can have an entire wing to yourself if you'd like."

She laughed lightly. "I'm sure one room will do."

Lee turned to Hayley. "I know that look on Roger's face. It's the same one I had on mine every time I looked at you."

She wished she had caught him looking at her that way, so it wouldn't have been such a shock to learn how he felt about her. "I never saw that look on your face."

"You weren't supposed to know how I felt, remember?" Lee said.

Hayley smiled. "Maybe we can talk 'more' about that later."

He whispered, "Key word is more, right?"

She replied with the same look she had given him the other night.

"Stop it," he said. "I won't be able to think about anything else."

"So, did we miss anything?" Roger asked. He sat at the head of the table.

"No, you're just in time." Lee touched the lid of the tin. "We might have the answer to who possessed Hayley at the Hotel del Coronado."

Roger looked puzzled. "I thought we already decided it was Kate Morgan or her maid."

"We might have another answer. A naval officer named Richard," Lee said. "I was repairing a step on Hayley's staircase and came across a secret compartment. We found this tin filled with keepsakes from 1943."

"So what's the connection?" Roger asked.

Hayley reached for her journal and flipped to a marked page. "I wrote everything down that happened while we were in Coronado. My first entry concerning the hotel detailed when we drove up the curved driveway toward the hotel entrance. That's when I first felt as if I'd visited the Del before." She gave Roger the photo.

Roger studied the picture. "This photo's old. So, who is this standing in front of the Del?"

"Richard," Hayley said. "See where he's standing? As we drove by that exact spot, that's when I sensed déjà vu. I bet Richard was in the car with us and remembered where he stood for that photo." She took the letter from the tin. "Okay, the next entry was about my recommendation for roast lamb." She passed the letter to Roger. "I believe Richard was also to blame for that. If you notice, in this letter, he mentioned it was his favorite dish."

"Maybe this is all a coincidence," Roger said, reading the letter.

"On our flight to Hawaii," Lee said, "Hayley dreamed about a naval officer. He went to his room and wrote a letter to his family." He pointed to the paper in Roger's hand. "That's the very same letter Hayley wrote about in her journal, and it's signed by Richard."

Hayley handed Roger her journal, opened to the page describing her dream.

"Okay, so Richard followed you from where?" Roger asked "This office? Somewhere in town? Your house?"

"My house. His family owned it before I did." She reached into the tin and pulled out another photo showing Richard and his family standing in front of her house, their home.

Roger compared her entry to the original letter. "So you're telling me that you're living in Richard's house? And by the looks of it, he followed you to the hotel."

"I believe my documented dream and the contents of this tin confirm that." Her thoughts turned to the Del, Room 3326, the room she repeatedly tried to enter. "The only thing I'm not sure of is who possessed me, Kate Morgan, her maid, or Richard."

"What was Richard's room number?" Kathy asked.

"Room 301," Hayley said.

Kathy got up and headed to the back room. In a few minutes she returned and set a laptop computer on the conference table next to Hayley. She sat and connected to the Internet.

"Do you think Richard is still living in your house?" Roger picked up the black-and-white photo. "Have you seen him or felt his presence?"

"No. Lee and I searched my house from top to bottom. No sign or sense of him."

"Well, just because you didn't find him doesn't mean he wasn't there," Roger said.

Hayley glanced with interest as Kathy brought up an article written about the haunting of the Del. "I think I found it. The hotel's been remodeled a few times, and each time they changed the numbers of the rooms. Room 301 was eventually changed to room 3326. That's the same room you were trying to get into, Hayley."

"That's it!" Roger said.

"The memories and the impulse to go into that room were so strong. I can't believe I didn't sense his presence, but it had to be him."

"That's not all," Lee said. "Read the first entry in her journal,"

Roger flipped to the first page and read. "You're not serious. His name is Richard Sanders? The lieutenant from the ghost ship?"

"That's damn eerie, if you ask me," Jim said. "Maybe he followed ya all the way to the ship."

"I don't think so," Hayley said. "I would've seen him with the rest of the crew."

"Damn eerie," Jim mumbled again.

"Speaking of the captain," Laura said, picking up her briefcase. She flipped back her hair and laid the case on the table. She unlocked it and withdrew a disk. "Admiral Wayne sent you a message from Captain Jordan." She handed it to Hayley. "He recommends that you watch it with the team."

"Why me?" Hayley asked.

"We'll need a big screen so everyone can watch. John, pull the TV over here," Roger said. He stood and moved his chair out of the way.

John rushed across the room and wheeled the TV on its stand to the head of the table, then ran the cord to the wall and plugged it in.

Roger put the disk into the DVD player. Hayley watched intently, wondering what the captain forgot to tell her. She noticed curiosity on the others' faces.

Captain Jordan appeared on the DVD as Hayley remembered him, sitting in the wardroom on board ship in his khaki shirt with silver eagles on the collar. "By now, I know you have lots of questions, so I'm going to try to sort things out for you, Hayley. Ruth and Frank Sanders lived in the home you own, with their son, Richard."

The photo of Richard and his parents standing in front of her house lay in front of Hayley. *So, he knows all about this. Why am I not surprised?*

"Their son joined the navy and eventually became a lieutenant. Richard stayed at the Hotel del Coronado in Room 301 while he waited to board ship."

"Yes, I saw him in my dream," Hayley said to the DVD.

"After each renovation, they renumbered room 301," Captain Jordan said. "Now it's 3326. I'm sure you remember that room."

"How can I forget?" Hayley mumbled.

Roger laughed. "He's too late. We've already solved the

mystery."

"Think back to the dream you had about the lieutenant who died on the island. It was Richard. He was my lieutenant. Lieutenant Richard James Sanders."

"Pause it a minute, Roger," Hayley said. "I'm going to take notes. He would've known that we'd figured this out. There has to be more to it." She took a deep breath as she opened her journal, flipped to the back page, started a list, and glanced around at the others. "These are called life-links, when one event leads to another. Just like each bet between Clint and John was linked to Laura's discovery."

"So, are life-links preordained or something?" Roger asked.

"It's better not knowing about links, Roger. They're supposed to happen naturally. Once you see the patterns, it's hard to keep it to yourself. You'd never know if something you've said or done changed destiny in some way." She looked over the list and shook her head. "Something's missing. There's normally a purpose for the chain. They usually lead to a major event, unless they're interrupted by someone ignoring an impulse and going off in another direction."

"Don't ya think the event we just went through on that damn island is big enough?" Jim asked.

"Yes, but why was this message given to me? And why didn't we ever meet the lieutenant on the ship?"

"Let's see if there's more." Roger started the DVD again.

"It's not just your house that's linked to my lieutenant. Think back to the dream you had of the lieutenant's death. Before he died, he asked God to let him find a way off the island and bring help to his men. His request was granted. He was able to gather a few of his friends, nine to be exact, who had shared previous lifetimes with him, and they chose to join him again in this life. One by one, they were born."

Holy – We're the reincarnated. She turned to Roger. "Stop the video."

He did as she asked.

Hayley said, "Remember the captain saying, 'You're not a puppet, Roger. You had just as much choice as Hayley'? This is what he was talking about."

"Seriously?" Roger asked. "You think he's talking about us? We're the lieutenant's friends from past lives?"

Laura stared at her with a questioning look on her face. Kathy's hand covered her mouth.

John pounded the table with his fist. "So, if our lives don't have a purpose anymore, what happens now? Are we going to die?" He glanced at Clint and back at Hayley.

She felt the blood drain from her face.

Lee shoved his chair back and stood, holding his hands up, calming the group. "Wait. Let's not jump to conclusions." He looked at Hayley. "So, what's your take on this?"

Hayley took a deep breath. The feeling of uncertainty made her stomach turn. *Grams, is that the reason I haven't been able to see their futures? Is John right?*

Grams replied in Hayley's mind. *Don't be foolish. Now give the captain a chance to explain.*

"We need to finish listening to Captain Jordan," Hayley said.

Roger restarted the video.

Without taking his eyes off the camera, Captain Jordan stood. "Everyone, I would like you to meet Lieutenant Richard James Sanders, otherwise known in this life as Hayley Elizabeth Johnson."

Gasps spread through the group, including Hayley.

She blinked repeatedly, and put her hand to her mouth. "Me? That can't be."

"In each incarnation, we are what and who we must be to

fulfill our purpose. You're born to learn from all aspects. There are no mistakes. As spirit, the spectrum of gender doesn't exist. It's irrelevant. While you evolve, each of your lives will become a part of your soul. Understand?"

She nodded. This was more than a shock. Her whole self-image had to change. Her feelings of being a weird freak of nature shifted to purpose. Tons of negative baggage slid from her shoulders.

"Without your unselfish plea in your life as Richard Sanders, the crew would still be walking the ship. Time would become eternity, and they would still be yearning to be with their loved ones."

She remembered the final words Captain Jordan had spoken on the island. "You were more help than you know," and "You'll be surprised." *What an understatement!*

"Before I go on, let me ease your mind. In the dream you had foreseeing the cave's flood, the remains you witnessed being roused by the waters were not bones but stalagmites that had been broken by the flood's strong current. Not to worry, Hayley. Without you, the crew's remains would still be in the cave, the question of each man's fate in the war would be unanswered, and their families would never have closure."

Tears filled Hayley's eyes. Thank God, they were recovered.

"Thanks, Hayley, and all of your friends from the bottom of our hearts — Roger, Lee, Jim, Admiral Wayne, John, Clint, Kathy, Laura, and Paul.

"And, Hayley, your gifts were never at risk. They were blocked under an agreement by you and your reincarnated friends, not allowing your gifts to show you their past lives or your own. The experience at the Del when you came face-to-face with your own previous life should explain the necessity of that decision. The repercussions would have severed your life-links. As for Lee, he's been your love throughout lifetimes, and couldn't pass up the chance to go through this with you. Thank you, Hayley. I will see you all again."

Roger turned off the video player. "I think we need time to absorb this. Wow! Unbelievable."

Grams spoke softly in Hayley's mind. *I'm sorry, dear, but you know I couldn't tell you. It would've broken the link.*

I know, Grams. I love you.

All the pieces of her life fit together in her mind one by one. The pain of the lieutenant on the beach, and the feeling she'd had in the cave when she saw the skeletons of the crew all made sense now. She knew them all...every ghost on board the Japanese warship. The statement, "Your mission is complete," echoed in her thoughts.

Blinking back tears, Hayley looked into Lee's eyes. She wasn't just another woman he would tire of. It explained the overwhelming attraction she'd had for him as soon as their eyes met. She and Lee were soul mates. They were truly made for each other. Linked together through eternity.

The End

Not quite yet, dear. You and your friends are now The Saviors of Souls.

About the Author

Shirley lives in Northeast Ohio. She turned to writing after taking an early retirement to care for her mother who had been stricken with Alzheimer's. While writing first started as a pleasant form of stress relief for Shirley, it soon became her creative passion. She thanks God for her family and her close friends, who have given her support and inspiration.